"The flourishing memory of the o........... ...... of French history and identity. . . . It is one of the contemporary paradoxes, moreover, that this book brilliantly brings to light: those who are nostalgic for the empire on which the sun never set are the quickest to refuse the best things to come from the overseas territories. *Mémoires d'Outre-Mer* is undoubtedly, resplendently, one of them."
—Bertrand Leclair, *Le Monde*

"A very beautiful piece of French prose. A writer who transcends banality, with a purity of writing."
—Sébastien Lapaque, *Le Figaro*

"*Mémoires d'Outre-Mer* is one of the most beautiful novels of this season, with all that you would want from a novel. . . . Add to that the cleverness of the novel's form (a hint of a detective investigation into the occupant of a nameless grave), which closes where you had opened it, and especially the beautiful language of Michaël Ferrier, who makes literature from many different written sources."
—Jean-Baptiste Harang, *Le Magazine littéraire*

"With his remarkable *Mémoires d'Outre-Mer*, Michaël Ferrier explodes all boundaries, all borders, geographical and mental. . . . With this novel, and its superb style, he enriches and renews the image that we might have of this country (Madagascar), which is much more than its lemurs and deforestation. The author also reflects on the notion of identity. 'To understand what France is, you have to go and look elsewhere,' he writes. It is the object of the book to show that France is not a small hexagonal space but a limitless territory, steeped in its history here and elsewhere, nourished by the experiences of all those it has welcomed. This very topical book is essential reading."
—Muriel Mingaud, *Le Populaire*

"What is the only thing that can fight against death? Memory. That's it. Ferrier has written an adventure novel on memory, a singularly intelligent novel."
—Vincent Roy, *Art Press*

"This rich novel (the term does not do the work justice) lives up to its title [and is] driven by a conviction to record the reality of a world made from diversity."
—Valérie Marin la Meslée, *Le Point*

"Great novels are like cyclones. They announce themselves in shudders, rustling, little shakes, and through narrative workings, these currents of hot air grow in strength and vigor; they rise like waves, breaking and multiplying in flashes and splinters, and become the very movement of the novel. *Mémoires d'Outre-Mer* is a literary cyclone, an art of the wind, the story of a man of the wind, a man who flies free, over an island and a time, and who grapples with the betrayals of history. . . . The important novelists are always precise and informed historians, their ears are as fine and sharp as their pens, and they possess their own knowledge and style—that divine blessing."
—Philippe Chauché, *La Cause littéraire*

OVER SEAS OF MEMORY

OVER SEAS

FRENCH
VOICES
FRENCH
VOICES

Winner of the French Voices Award
www.frenchbooknews.com

OF MEMORY

A Novel

Michaël Ferrier

Translated by Martin Munro
Foreword by Patrick Chamoiseau

UNIVERSITY OF NEBRASKA PRESS   LINCOLN

Originally published in French as *Mémoires
d'outre-mer* © Éditions Gallimard, Paris, 2015
Translation © 2019 by the Board of Regents
of the University of Nebraska

French Voices logo designed by Serge Bloch

This work received the French Voices Award for
excellence in publication and translation. French
Voices is a program created and funded by the French
Embassy in the United States and FACE Foundation
(French American Cultural Exchange).

Cet ouvrage a bénéficié du soutien des Programmes
d'aide à la publication de l'Institut français.

Library of Congress Cataloging-in-Publication Data
Names: Ferrier, Michaël, author. | Munro, Martin,
translator. | Chamoiseau, Patrick, writer of foreword.
Title: Over seas of memory: a novel /
Michael Ferrier; translated by Martin Munro;
foreword by Patrick Chamoiseau.
Other titles: Mémoires d'outre-mer. English
Description: Lincoln: University of Nebraska Press, [2019]
| "Over Seas of Memory was first published in French as
Memoires d'outre-mer. Editions Gallimard, Paris, 2015."
Identifiers: LCCN 2018046957
ISBN 9781496213204 (paperback: alk. paper)
ISBN 9781496216021 (epub)
ISBN 9781496216038 (mobi)
ISBN 9781496216045 (pdf)
Classification: LCC PQ2706.E775 M4513 2019
| DDC 843/.92—dc23 LC record available
at https://lccn.loc.gov/2018046957

Set in Fournier by E. Cuddy.
Designed by N. Putens.

For my father

Long after the days and the seasons, the living and the lands
—Arthur Rimbaud

I am of no nation recognized by the chancelleries
—Aimé Césaire

FOREWORD

Patrick Chamoiseau

Whoever knows Mr. Michaël Ferrier knows this: that he is woven of the same matter that he explores in his sumptuous writing. A man of faraway and nearby lands, of a thousand belongings and scrupulous fidelity, his life, his choices, and his movements reflect an experience in the world that cannot be summarized in a simple family tree. It is therefore not surprising that to lead us in the footsteps of his grandfather Maxime, he will take with him almost the complete totality of the world.

His quest will see him dive not into the branches of a somewhat everyday familial relation but into the dizzying mystery set up from the outset relating to three graves ("Three tombs; three persons; three islands") and the *mise en abyme* of one of them. An inaugural cemetery: as if he first had to make a blank slate of all that common sense can imagine for a life, a country, a nationality, and moreover and especially, of our understanding of the world in which we live.

If his grandfather is the central reason for this exploration, the theme is what Édouard Glissant calls "Relation." By means of the wretched workings of Western conquests and colonization, the world has become the *Tout-monde*, the world as one, everything. In our consciousnesses, our lives, our individual experiences freed from the old restrictions relating to identity and belonging, the world has been opened up to its own diversity. At the same time it has achieved a form of unity that is impossible to define. Our cultures, civilizations, and imaginaries flow in interactive, unstoppable, unpredictable ways. As a result, our individual destinies have been liberated, even propelled, into a chaotic and open planetary alchemy. Over and above communities and nation-states, individual formulations have become determinant. Everyone finds themselves having to organize their lives (their ethics, their values) on a basis that is no longer that of "my land," "my parish," "my language," "my ancestors," "my history." For each of us everything is connected to everything; everything is now shaped in unpredictable multiple ways in a coming into contact of cultures and visions of the world, national histories and old phenotypes. This unprecedented mixing, far more unpredictable than a simple form of miscegenation, produces a human reality that is at once apparent and opaque, that we live day by day, but that most often we do not see, that we struggle against sometimes in ourselves and all around us. "Delectably interwoven!" says Michaël Ferrier, who embraces the phenomenon.

He is right.

All it would take would be for everyone to sit down and consult their own archives, as the narrator does here with what he has left of his grandfather, to collate the wanderings, proliferations, and uncertainties of contemporary lives. In the wake of Maxime Ferrier, the world will reveal its colonial horrors ("But for now, what you have is the waltz of euphemisms: the conquest is 'pacification,' revolts are 'incidents' [or 'troubles' when there are too many casualties], and the great wars of independence are grudgingly afforded the status of 'events'") but also the new complexities that testify to what we are today. The protagonists know that "origins mean nothing": what really makes a person is how the world has formed and shaped them. They know that the major languages are constantly in contact with a thousand other languages, that they have all derived and evolved, and that they testify to a relational alchemy that cannot be denied.

Therefore, the point of departure is not especially a strain, nor simply a wound as it might have been, but it is a completion, like the flowering of a bud: "At the same time, they retained the memory of their origins—in the form of scars or else as sweet souvenirs—and carried it proudly on the open seas." The seed opens onto itself, and the fruit, the fruit opens onto the world.

In this novel "we climb back into time but also descend it; we cross it and take it up again," and not only time but almost all of the Indian Ocean, this intertwined space whose multi-millennial scale is that of an opera. Around Maxime Ferrier, the enigmatic grandfather, "there are knots, many levels of time set against or layered on top of each other, pieces of memory that demand to rise again, resurfacing in a great tempest from the bottom of the abyss. You need to know how to move around in there, in this enormous archive, to listen out, be on the lookout: certain memories are trapped, others blocked, others still recalcitrant or vindictive, and they try to place over the top of them all as a kind of cover a great unified memory, with a single resonance, monotonous, and supposedly national."

We are here in the chaotic matter of the *Tout-monde*.

This impulse toward an open, inexhaustible, even indefinable totality is inaugurated by a small act of alphabet terrorism committed by the grandfather. The original name, *Février*, is transformed into *Ferrier* with just a distortion of the single letter *v*, like a bolt on a door that you throw off in order to escape—not just from the indignity of bearing the name "of the shortest month of the year!" but from that of having to stay in one place with a solitary national history, from vertical, proud languages, from closed and fixed identities . . . The grandfather is curiously free. He walks in the mobility of his name that comes to structure his being. He chooses the land of his life: Madagascar. He resists oppression and is largely consumed in love. He remains all along a person able, at the most crucial moments, to "choose something else," as if the plasticity and fluidity of Relation were the page on which he wrote, sketched his body, the story to come, the grave that remains always in the making, to be completed.

It is not surprising that just like his name, his body itself, an acrobat's body, is inscribed in this plasticity as in the refusal of any rigid authority over the skeleton and the bones, of the gravity of the Earth itself, or of the poverty of the single relationship with the land: "Acrobatics, beneath its festive exterior, is not just entertainment: it is a very special way of being in the world, a form of aerial combat, as well as a hidden, secret battle." Thus, he enters into other coordinates of space and time, another state of the body itself. He has his own tempo, a sort of organic music that leads him to the other side of things, their invisible source. He will hold on to that time, which is his own, until his dying day.

Finally, the novel highlights an unexpected effect of colonization: "When it comes down to it, the native peoples are no longer Malagasy, French, or anything. They are left there, in sufferance, on the overseas shore. Because nationality is never a right; it is a favor that they are awarded. The native people slide from the rank of inhabitants to that of onlookers; they disappear bit by bit from their own country. Absent, phantoms, they are a décor, an ambiance, a picturesque but also exploited and taxpaying ornament in the grand spectacle of progress and colonization, a background canvas. They are there but not there: specters in their own country." Specters also in the matter of the world. The destiny of Maxime shows how these specters are richer than those who damned them, that they are enriched by many lands, names, stories, by a horizontal presence in the world, the only one that allows us to live in the full splendor of Relation.

But in what is almost an instruction manual for the world, the human quintessence remains. Maxime can be divined, without really being fully revealed to us, in his outbursts and wanderings but also through those who bear witness to the tracks of his journey: "When

I meet older people, I see clearly that they have come into possession of a secret, which transforms life definitively into destiny and which makes them shift into another dimension. Their very body is not the same; they float in the atmosphere as if they have been extracted from the rock of time and yet are completely caught in its flow: they are lookouts, at the edge of another world, which is not death but the renewed power of life, its permanent passage." It is from the edge of this other world, in an enthralling acrobatics of writing and vision, that this text stands, overlooking, radiating.

OVER SEAS OF MEMORY

In Mahajanga cemetery there are three tombs. They gleam, inconspicuously, in the midday sun. All three are almost identical: same height, same color, same dimensions. They are simple and sleek, like in an artist's sketch: with neither sculptures nor engravings, neither flowerpots nor ornaments, the three stone rectangles seem placed on the land like ships cutting across the water. Facing southwest, turned toward the sea, they are set at the same level, placed together in a geometric structure, and connected by paths overgrown with grass, over which lizards cross, their eyes keen, their tongues agile. On top of each stone there is a simple cross with no inscription, a cross like you would find on a road rather than in a cemetery.

In their sober and discreetly wrought elegance, the three graves provoke immediately the greatest confusion. There is nothing lugubrious about them, nothing that sends a shiver to the soul—nothing sinister or sepulchral. The stone is pale, carefully painted and polished, and absolutely denuded of details. It forms a flat, bare, unadorned surface and is made of a material that absorbs light. The whiteness of the three tombs catches your eye as soon as you enter the cemetery: the people who live nearby call them the "Trois Lumières," the Three Lights. Each gravestone rises up from a four-sided vault and is constituted of three tiers that build gradually to the sky in ledges placed one on top of the other—like so many additions to the initial square mastaba—that seem to intensify and propagate the luster of the mastaba and to give out a strange luminescent power.

Then the eye is drawn like in a painting to the strange network of contours that the tombs create: according to the time of day and the position of the sun, the shadows' shapes, and the passage of the wind, the movements of the branches sketch on the bright stones a series of multiple, ever-changing motifs—an anchor, a fishing boat, a fish . . . The whole thing gives out a feeling of grace in its lines and contours, a sense of lightness and space in the positioning of its various parts. The affinity between form and material, structure and proportions, and depth and perspective gives a unique impression, at once inexplicable and inexhaustible: the angles and edges of the steles appear to bring about a strange conjunction of movement and immobility. You approach, you go back, your gaze moves from one tomb to the other, the three crosses dance in the sweetness of the sea and the faint perfume of the mango trees.

They are never more beautiful than now, at midday, with the sun at its zenith—vertical illumination . . . We like to speak of cemeteries as being places of silence and melancholy, where all the terminal rot and decay of life comes to rest, as if our lives are destined to end in degeneration or, at best, in the mausoleum. But no, it is not like that here. There is a real racket going on in this place, sound and dust . . . To the right I hear the furtive hiss of a heron rising up from the coast. Farther away, over the ocean, there is the humming sound of an aircraft. And over there, way down low, there is a whole hidden orchestra of little movements in the grass—frogs sliding, crabs pattering, spiders crackling, curled up in their web making . . . They are the denizens of the in-between places, invisible and musical: you have to listen carefully to hear them, beneath the clicking of the ants loaded down with pieces of straw and other derisory treasures—the noisy junk of cemeteries.

The more you look at them, the more you hear circles of music that seem to rise up and spread around the three tombs. Shadows tremble. White-headed vanga birds twitch; corncrakes and lapwings take flight, whistling through the bamboo. Stonechat birds provide the rhythm, snakes dance, getting munched at sometimes by dogs rummaging around in the grass. From time to time there is a solo by a dragonfly or the improvisation of a white butterfly . . . Now the slightest movement sideways opens up another angle in your vision and brings to life a multiplicity of breathing sounds, bodies, accents, and characters that are so many open trails or tracks that never close over again. Maxime, Pauline, Willy, Francis . . . Nuñes, Beau Bassin, Maurice . . . All the names of long ago. Aunt Émilia, Marie Adélia d'Albrède . . . Éliane . . . Is there no one left to listen to their story and to gently gather again the leaping sounds of the conch shells and of humans in the nighttime?

These people were adventurers, *Outre-mer* in the French phrase, or people from the overseas regions. They came from faraway places, from India or Africa, Europe or even China. You could say they came from even farther away on the spur of their desires and dreams: they came from forever; they left for everywhere. They were explorers, romantics. They could read maps and hearts, wield their sex as well as their sextants. Inclined to free morals and free thinking, they switched in the space of a few years their country, their religion, their state and fortune. They remained, however, true to themselves through their trials and tribulations; they were masters of ducking and diving, experts in the art of navigation.

Descendants of slaves or free men, runaway Africans, indentured Indians, banished Chinese, exiled Arabs, excommunicated Jews, expatriated Europeans, displaced Greeks, dispersed islanders, they had long known that origins mean nothing and have no more worth or meaning than a chestnut stuck in its husk or a manuscript that stays rolled up in its case. At the same time, they retained the memory of their origins—in the form of scars or else as sweet souvenirs—and carried it proudly on the open seas.

Here are three of those people, now, before me. Three tombs, three persons, three islands. The grave on the left is the farthest from the path. It is the only one with a name, that of Maxime Ferrier, engraved on a copper leaf at the foot of the cross:

MAXIME FERRIER

(1905–1972)

The grave on the right is that of Arthur Dai Zong, whose name is not on the stele but is found written in the register at the entrance to the cemetery. The name is broken down thus, in Chinese characters: 阿手 (Ha Chou, or Arthur), 岱宗 (Dai Zong). It is a strange signature, and we have not yet understood all that it has to say.

As for the last tomb, in the center, it has no distinctive marks. No date, no name: and yet it is this one that has taken me here.

Farther ahead on the right lie soldiers from the colonial expedition led by France in 1895 and, a bit farther still, British soldiers from the capture of Mahajanga in 1942. The French dead are entitled to a monument, "to the memory of the soldiers and indigenous auxiliaries who died in the service of France." The British dead are entitled to nothing. It is, however, they, here as elsewhere, who were more or less alone in standing up to the French troops of the Vichy government, on this island where the stakes were as much strategic as symbolic as, from the nineteenth century on, fervent anti-Semites, dreaming of yellow stars on the Red Island, had thought of it as a place of deportation for the Jews of Europe.

Land of slavery and colony, land of exile and relegation: in the humble cemetery of the Corniche, memories do not so much tear each other apart; rather, they reinforce each other. They are not muted by pain, but neither do they talk much; they do not question each other, they don't chat away their misery. They know that each time a tomb disappears, it is the whole cemetery that is damaged.

*

The breeze picks up. The trade winds blow in from the open sea, and the three tombs seem now like three frigates in battle formation, accompanied by the cries of sea gulls and the murmuring of the rain. Time accelerates and returns to its source. On each of the tombs I can track time's displacement volume, as it were, passing from green to blue and from blue to gold. I see the hatchings and the contours, the slices and the grooves—the immense embroidery of time into which death sometimes weaves a little piece of black velvet.

I hear the sounds of crossings and great migrations, the enormous passing fancy of the current and the everyday, the journeys, the wanderings carried on the arms of the sea and the shoulders of the wind. I listen. What I hear is a musical score of rocks and foliage, of Indian cloth and British candies, a music so incredibly light— the acrobatics of butterflies, forests, and voices superimposed on each other.

All that remains for me now is to follow them. I make my way down the road that falls gently to the sea. I have scribbled in my spiral notebook the few words inscribed on Maxime's tomb. Under his name, in italics, an epitaph scrawled in the form of a Malagasy inscription in the stone:

Ho velona fa tsy ho levona

It is a strange phrase, which I will understand more fully only later on. It plays on two words that echo each other and that reverberate endlessly the similarity of their three syllables, *velona* (living) and *levona* (destroyed). All that the following story tells, all that it says of life, is there in those few syllables, in their delicate shifting, in the unfurling of this little phrase in a foreign language and what it signifies:

So that it be living and not destroyed

A MAN LEAVING

I have had some trouble finding the trail of Maxime Ferrier. That is no real surprise, as he did everything he could to cover his tracks. We are in November 1922; the International Court of Justice has just been set up in The Hague. In Genoa the basic principles of the Gold Exchange Standard have just been defined: the U.S. dollar is indexed against gold, while the rest of the indexed currencies are set against the dollar. In Russia, Stalin is elected general secretary of the Communist Party before signing, at the very end of the year, the treaty that founds the Union of Soviet Socialist Republics, the USSR. In Stockholm, Einstein receives his Nobel Prize for physics, which was awarded to him the previous year, "for his audacious hypothesis on the corpuscular nature of light." He will be succeeded by Niels Bohr, for his work on the structure of the atom. In one year, all the elements of the twentieth century are put in place, with their various tones and colors, their explosive force and their contradictions.

In France the first stone of the Paris Mosque is laid, while in Marseille a colonial exhibition begins. In the Netherlands the new Constitution suppresses the word *colonies* in favor of *overseas territories*, but the Indonesians remain Dutch "subjects" . . . There are some years like that, which seem like whole centuries, moments where everything speeds up and condenses, a kind of temporal crest where things take their thread, their shape, their speed, their clearest curvature. Suddenly, itineraries and routes are sketched out, affirmed, refined; everything rises up and becomes knotted together in the blink of an eye. The past, the present, and the future come together as one: it is like the grand finale of all the centuries revealed in a few days. Soon that whole sense of things coming together is going to be lost again, disappear, and fall apart . . . The end of clear sight. But for the moment, it is there, and I grasp the cogs, the gears, and see how it is all connected.

The same year, in Paris, ironically detached from the century's great clamor, Sylvia Beach publishes Joyce's *Ulysses*. An Irishman in his bewildering style suddenly revisits all the myths of Greece. In Egypt, at the end of a set of stairs dug out of the rock and down a little sloping corridor, Howard Carter and Lord Caernarvon discover the tomb of Tutankhamun, hidden behind a varnished door covered in the seals of the royal necropolis and defended by two statues of black sentinels that symbolize the hope for resurrection. In November this resurrection takes place, though no doubt not in the way the Egyptians had wished for: brought out again into the open air were toys and games, chairs, stools and beds, wine jars—a whole little mass of objects and practices—as well as aristocratic missiles, such as bows, arrows, and boomerangs.

In the funeral chamber they find thirty-five model boats and a statue of Anubis, a god with the head of a black dog and an enigmatic smile: he has a key in his hand, and around his neck hangs a cornflower necklace. The walls are painted with scenes representing the ritual of the "opening of the mouth" and the solar ship on which is taken the journey to the beyond. To windward there are the mummies: the reopened echo chamber vibrates once again. At the same time, as if he had heard of the discovery, Marcel Proust (who, in the first pages of *In Search of Lost Time* evokes in passing the spinning mystery of metempsychosis) dies in his cork-floored bedroom, after a long-running dispute with death. "Dead forever? Who can say?"

Maxime Ferrier knows nothing of all this. But certain people are like that; they can sense what is in the wind, smell the messages of the time, decode its signals. Something inside warned him that he would have to leave, depart the family circle and enter the crucible of exodus. He had to leave, run off, slip away, leave behind the notions of inside and outside, become as foreign as possible: nothing or no one could stop him.

He will show it many times from this point: Maxime has the nervous system of a cat, a particular interior disposition—a vegetal inflorescence, a cavernous body, a tactical sense—an ear particularly attuned to the vibrations around him, all that one describes normally in terms of intuition and that is in fact an extraordinary sensitivity to the waves of time. He is a fluid, a feline or a wolf, a body radar. From that basic state all the rest joins up as in a chain: journeys, encounters, projects, disasters, the fragile happiness of being alive, but everything will have been thought of from that original state or condition, from this sensitive body and its fine tunings, like a gigantic interior map indicating ways of thinking and, according to circumstances, the attitude to take.

Now the boat turns off toward the west coast of Madagascar. It is a little cargo boat loaded with rations, men, animals, and flowers: it is called *L'Étoile*, or *The Star*. The inventory that I have been able to find gives a fairly precise idea of its cargo: sugar, textiles, clothes, spices, perfumes, herbs, gold and rock crystal, Bombay flour . . . In another document are also listed dates, camel butter, furniture, and carved doors—the strange commotion of the world.

The crew is multilingual, men who can do a bit of everything in the powerful and deliberate disorder of the sea. On board you hear French, Malagasy, Mauritian Creole, Reunionese Creole, English, Hindi, Urdu, Telugu, Chinese, and Italian . . . In which language do they communicate? French, for the most part. A French flavored with several other languages, open, fluid, undulating, but formidably precise, not the flat and hardened language that they now want us to have as the only one possible. They say, for example, "Alors, vous aussi, vous avez sauté la mer?" Which means literally—today it has to be translated—that you have "jumped the sea," or in other words, that you have left your country. And one cannot forget the universal language of smiles, threats, chants, and gestures.

It is a timeless opera. Human exchanges have been taking place on the Indian Ocean longer than on any other maritime space—for more than five thousand years it has been so, while such exchanges have existed on the Atlantic Ocean for five hundred years and on the Pacific two thousand. The Comoros, the Seychelles, the Maldives, the Mascarenes: a whole network of islands of varying sizes and diverse populations. Since the dawn of time, people have been exchanging here looks, glances, and words; currencies circulate, ambitions come face-to-face, rules and rituals are imported and exported—contracts, returns, compensations. Traditions are swapped and beliefs passed on. Men with Spanish grammar, crazy travelers, Hottentots, Ngunis, Malagasy, Senegalese, a whole world of faces and voices, coming from India, Africa, Europe, Asia, the Middle Kingdom, and the Land of the Rising Sun, all of this shifts around on the rippling sea, in the rolling currents and the sliding wind.

This particular cargo boat is all the more singular: it is carrying two special loads that give it a slightly crazy yet poetic allure. First of all, there are whole armfuls of flowers, cut or in pots, mostly orchids, vanillas, vandas, cattleyas, carefully placed on the deck so that they encircle it with their perfumes. Waiting already at the quay is Hassan Ali, the region's big landowner. This man is mad about flowers. It is not by chance that he settled in this town: Mahajanga is one of the most important cities in the west of Madagascar. Situated on the Virgin Islands coast, people call it "the city of flowers," and you see bunches, bouquets, and sprays from Africa, Arabia, and Asia arranged on the Quai aux Boutres.

All seems calm on the boat as it sails toward the town. But in the ship's hold there is stowed away another, strange cargo. Under the waterline, in a dark stench of wild cats, pieces of folded blue cloth sit beside steel rods, ropes, and hoops. The smell catches your throat as you approach the cages, while your ears fill up with growling sounds, murmurs, and grunts. The piercing cries of monkeys; birdsong in the commotion of the seas . . . Your eyes get used to the darkness, and you discover a speckled and growling gathering, like the reverse of the fragrances on the deck: there are panthers from Asia, leopards from Africa, jaguars from the Americas, a whole population confused and churned up by the movements of the sea. Huge tiger heads roll across the wood.

In a corner there is a red-and-gold sign with the words, in glittering letters: *Cirque Bartolini*, the Bartolini Circus. Madame Bartolini is a strong woman who has made her fortune in the transportation of rare plants and stunning shows and spectacles: the Snake-Man, the Woman with Two Heads, the Rat-Child, and the Spider-Man. In this fairground troupe there is also, for contrast, a Hercules, a Cleopatra, and even—you can't have too much of a good thing—two Venuses: the "Venus of the Morning" and the "Venus of the Evening," two sisters with graceful features and impeccable bodies. The captain's journal tells us that during the crossing, a lioness gave birth to a cub: life is transmitted amid the absurdity and disorder of this journey.

Maxime travels without papers, with almost no money, and without the slightest worry. He is equally at ease with the flowers as with the monsters. At his age, and in his situation, he does not have the right to enter Madagascar, and he knows it. He grasped the opportunity offered by the circus to leave Mauritius in the most perfectly clandestine way: young, flexible, subtle, muscular, and slender, he didn't pass up on the chance to join the traveling circus. Madame Bartolini's eagle eye spotted immediately the potential of this young man and his "strange little body." Maxime has what they call in French "la caisse," that is, a highly powerful thorax supported by two long and slender legs, like a safe balancing on two matchsticks . . . "The ideal physique for an acrobat," notes Madame Bartolini in one of her journals at the end of his recruitment interview. "This funny body gives him at once power and fluidity," she adds in her fine, slanting handwriting, and ends by saying: "Enormous rib cage and suppleness of the limbs: he can do everything, tumble, turn, climb, perform sequences of movements, and manipulate at different speeds, moving forward with poise and balance. Excellent grip on the apparatus."

While waiting to dock, the acrobat looks at the approaching shore. I imagine him surrounded by his many companions, as they are described in the circus program:

The man who walks with his hands as he has no legs.
The woman who eats with her feet as she has no arms.
The skeleton-man who is the husband of the bearded woman.
The Aztecs with the pointed skulls.
The sword swallower and the knife thrower.

Each one of them has a particular body, a body that is unique in the world, a body that speaks and does tricks. Max's body is no less strange than the others, with his huge chest and his two slender legs, but in the only full-length photo we have of him at this time, he gives off a great sense of elegance in this very singular body: his white shirt, his flannel or white cotton pants, his little brown handmade hat. He is very well dressed but seems to be mocking his clothes in a way. His head is turned toward the sea, slightly in profile; you see a foot in a moccasin resting on the ship's rail. The open air blows all around this great body. If you did not know you were dealing with an acrobat, you would easily guess it: his balance is perfect; the point of his shoe is raised toward the sky. What is he thinking of at this moment? No one could say, but everything in his look and the way he holds himself suggests that he is happy.

All around him there are more flowers, a real delight of stems and stalks, branches and bulbs, leaves and fruits: behind the line of his shoulders, you can make out stumps and grafts, cuttings, roots and runners, small branches with buds on them. It is as if Maxime had become a flower himself, a strange and vegetal being, indifferent to the chaos of the world and growing as of that moment according to his own laws. Farther behind, in the dark part of the photo, there is a faint ribbon of sea-foam that rises right up to me and that I must follow now, a smell or a shadow, a vestige, a way, a path, barely a mist of footstep sounds.

*

Paris, on the rue du Fer-à-Moulin, I open a book . . .

It is authored by two delicious-sounding names: Kumari R. Issur and Vinesh Y. Hookoomsing. I like that solitary letter, planted right in the middle of the name, inserted between the first name and the family name. There is something that slides there, a pause, an accent . . . that rings differently . . . a possibility of syncopation.

I read aloud: "Since the sixteenth century authors have written in and about the Indian Ocean in French: travel writing, back-to-nature tales, utopias, fantastical works in every genre, and then you have exotic poetry, colonial novels, and finally indigenous literature and exiled writing. This rich and varied literary production remains largely unknown."

I could not have put it better. Poets and novelists from the Mascarenes? Forget it. Malcom de Chazal, the "extraordinary poetic meteor," adored by André Breton? Not so much . . . Rabearivelo and Rabemananjara? Come on, how do you even pronounce them?

Ah, France and its memory . . . Its memories, should I say: the complexity of memories, their torment, and their turbulence . . . It is very difficult to speak in France of anything other than France itself. And even then, it is a certain kind of France . . . It's not easy to get people to admit that France is more than metropolitan France—the Hexagon, as they call it.

This afternoon I saw Xavier to let him know I was leaving . . . Xavier is a friend, a writer, very well-known in Parisian circles. Blond and tanned, he has just come back from a literary festival in Corrèze, in southwestern France. It was the height of exoticism for him . . . A phrase comes to mind: "They think they are happy because they are immobile."

We were at the corner of the rue Bonaparte and the rue Jacob, the *Pré-aux-clercs* . . . Hemingway used to go there often, as did Breton, Bataille, and many others. A memory of place . . .

— But what are you going to do in Madagascar? A whole month at the end of the world!

— My grandfather's grave is there.

— Ah, I see, a family novel.

— No, it's not that . . . It's more like . . . how can I put it? An important anniversary, a happy one. We climb back into time but also descend it; we cross it and take it up again . . .

— Ah, okay? But, all the same, a return to your roots!

— Not at all.

— An exotic novel?

— No, in fact it's the very opposite. Madagascar, Mauritius, and the Indian Ocean are integral parts of the history of France: you cannot understand France if you don't include those places and a few others as well. You have there generations of men and women thrown upon the seas and who, some years later, would give birth to French people like me and you.

— How come, these three acrobats, what do they have to do with the history of France?

— Everything! It's all tied up together! I could show you. You will see . . . France, its history and origins, come from afar.

He raises his eyes to the sky. I see him balking at the idea, disagreeing . . . But here comes my friend Li-An, who arrives at just the right moment, with her mischievous, sweet face, tall and slender with black hair down to her hips, a living appeal for the crossing of cultures. Straightaway we speak a little in English, we *switch*, she agrees with me, we have him in a sandwich between two or three languages . . . Li-An is an épéeist, a member of the Chinese Olympic fencing team, and it's for that reason she is in Paris, for a tournament in Bercy. She starts up again, flirting and jousting with him!

— Yes, yes, she says in English, it is very difficult to speak in France about anything other than France.

— and yet, to understand France, it is necessary to include other countries. You have to look elsewhere to understand what France really is . . .

— Other countries, yes, yes, she says in English. There is a drastic memory loss regarding certain subjects: no more memory, no more memory . . . she says, again in English. Xavier is now in agreement with virtually everything. His eyes are on Li-An's legs . . .

We stood jousting there, reinventing the place, to the west of St. Germain Abbey and its old town . . . Li-Ann has to go to her training session; she leaves, leaving in her wake a final smile and a faint smell of flowers. Xavier looks a bit disappointed that she cannot stay any longer. I feel that he is ready to be even more profoundly convinced now! He flicks through a literary magazine absent-mindedly . . . I have a drink of my Perrier and turn my head gently toward the sun.

*

In Paris I live on the rue du Fer-à-Moulin.

Formerly, it was the rue des Morts, the Street of the Dead. It was known as such, for there, right below my window, stood for a long time the Clamart cemetery. Few people know about it: it was the biggest cemetery in Paris. It has nothing to do with the suburb that now has the same name: it is found at the site of the old gardens of the Hôtel de Clamart, the property of the lords of Clamart, near the former place Poliveau, just next to the Jardin des Plantes. The history of France interests me. Almost forgotten today, this cemetery was famous for having received the remains of those condemned to death and, in particular, those guillotined during the Revolution. Mirabeau himself, when his body was removed from the Pantheon, was thrown into the Clamart cemetery: his remains have never been found. On the rue de la Clef stood the Sainte-Pélagie prison, where many singers (Bruant, Béranger), rogues, and poets were locked up . . . Everyone who thought a bit freely ended up spending time in the prison: Daumier spent six months there, for his caricatures; Nerval spent a few days, for causing a row at night. The Marquis de Sade was also there, and this was for him his final stay in prison before going to the Charenton asylum. Madame Roland, a reader of Montesquieu and Voltaire and the muse of the Girondists, spent some time in the prison ("I, the only woman in this jail! How horrific and what an honor")—just before they cut her head off.

There is a whole nation of the dead under there. And it is from there that I am writing to you.

The Clamart cemetery was the graveyard for poor people, those who could not afford the Cemetery of the Innocents. There was no money to pay for the wood for the coffin, so they stitched the dead into an old piece of cloth and threw them into a cart, before taking them to the communal graves. Louis-Sébastien Mercier describes the scene in his *Tableau de Paris*: "The bodies that the Hôtel-Dieu vomits out on a daily basis are taken to Clamart. It is a vast cemetery, where the burial pit is always open . . . This lugubrious cart leaves every day from the Hôtel-Dieu at four o'clock in the morning: it trundles along in the silence of the night. The bell that precedes it wakes up all who are sleeping along its route; you have to be there on the route to really sense all that the noise of the carriage inspires and the full effect that it has on the soul. People have seen it, at certain times of high mortality, pass by up to four times in a day: it can hold up to fifty bodies. People put their children between the legs of adults. The bodies are thrown into a wide and deep pit; then they throw in some quicklime; and this crucible that never closes says to the horrified eye that it would devour without any difficulty all the inhabitants of the capital."

The memory is a muscle; if it is not used, it wastes away. That is why I am looking to retrace the path of Maxime Ferrier. Maxime, my grandfather, the acrobat . . . In my family everybody knows the crazy story of this man, who left his native island, Mauritius, at the age of seventeen, joined a circus as an acrobat, and made his fortune in Madagascar, before losing everything because of the war, under mysterious circumstances.

I met Maxime when I was a child. But the only memories of him that I retain are very confused. I remember a tired old man, just before his death, while in the photos I have found or the newspaper articles that tell of his spectacular rise and no-less-brutal fall, he is a young man that appears very dynamic, almost scarily so. It is to fill in the gap between these two images that I have set out on his trail.

There is something else: before dying, Maxime had three tombs made in the Mahajanga cemetery, a town in the northwest of Madagascar, where he rests now. Three white tombs that are almost perfectly identical. The first was made for his friend Arthur Dai Zong, a Chinese man who had for some time been his partner in the most breathtaking acrobatic duo in all the Indian Ocean. The second was for him, Maxime. But the third tomb, who is buried there? No one knows. And what is the meaning of the strange epitaph that is affixed to the tomb?

So that it may be living and not destroyed.

At this point I have no idea what it means.

However, this is not just a matter of a familial pilgrimage. This evening the television is showing over and again the results of the latest elections. The "political leaders" appear one after the other: there are too many taxes, there is too much unemployment, not enough competitiveness, growing insecurity, an irresponsible judiciary, rampant immigration, state handouts at the expense of the taxpayer, it's all going on . . . What follows is a game of one-upmanship over who is the most French, the best French . . . Exclusion, homogenization, reorganization . . . People need to be taught again to become French, to think French, to buy French. How many of us these last few months, with ancestors of foreign origin and confronted with the delirium of today's France, how many of us have not asked ourselves if our ancestors could become French today like they were able to before? Li-An is right: it is very difficult in France today to speak of anything other than France. I say it again: to understand France, you have to pass through other countries, journey through other histories.

In particular, you would have to know more about the generations of men and women thrown upon the seas and who, some years later, would give birth to French people like you and me. Can we reconnect the chain of time? Do we have to reunify French history in a sort of grand narrative, which would go well beyond a simple family saga? Or else is there another way of paying homage to this mobile multiplicity of people and letting it speak? And what would literature be if it did not give voice to the silences of history?

By a happy set of circumstances, it was my turn to have a sabbatical from the university: I jumped at the chance and decided to set out on the trail of Maxime. Now, on the terrace of 24 rue du Fer-à-Moulin, directly opposite the square Théodore-Monod, that magnificent wanderer . . . October blows in. I have written all night, it is four in the morning: on the right is the Hôtel Scipion, the only hotel in Paris that dates back to the Middle Ages. Underneath: the dead. "The dead, the poor dead, know great pain," wrote Baudelaire.

They call to me. I return, pick up my pen, and write—unseen, I board the nightly cart of the dead.

*

We have never known exactly why Maxime set out to sea and signed up for the Bartolini Circus to get to Madagascar. The craziest hypotheses circulate on this subject. A story of love gone wrong? Family problems? But no . . . Snippets from newspapers, fragments of letters, a few oral testimonies, tell us that he left behind him a loving mother, who looked always for ways to see him again, and a young fiancée with the wonderful name of Jeanne Wilhelmine Bhujoharry, who wrote to him deeply moving letters right to the end of her life. Nothing would make him come back.

There is no trace of his father; it is as if he had also fled. We know only that he was a sailor. He recognized his son (you can still see the birth certificate at the town hall in Souillac, Mauritius), and then he took again to the sea. From that point no one knows anything else about him. It is tempting to wonder whether Maxime's act was a repetition of the father's own traumatic and essential act of abandonment, but I don't believe that at all. The modern way of thinking is so standardized, so impoverished by the procession of banal nonsense on TV, that people turn instantly to this kind of mechanical causality, as if the little familial psychological issue or the immense sentimental blanket of love and relationships could explain everything.

So, was it a desire for adventure? To try his chance, seek his fortune? Yes, of course . . . At the start of the century important gold mines were discovered on the Big Island, and after that all the adventurers in the region made their way to Madagascar: penniless Creoles from Mauritius and Réunion, Indians, Europeans, Chinese, people from the Comoros . . . The South and its high plateaus are full of gold-bearing quartz, manganese, platinum, and iron. The first oil discoveries were in 1911; numerous drillings revealed the presence of hydrocarbons all along the west coast. In the north there were the precious woods of the Antalaha region: specialists knew already about Madagascan ebony, which was—many forget this— the variety most used in French furniture of the seventeenth century, but they discovered also the immense reserves of rosewood, with its characteristic red and deep-black grained look, that was to gradually become one of the best wood varieties in the world for tuning pegs for violins, violas, and cellos. Great musicians knew this, and today still you only have to spend a few days there to *hear* it, that is, to understand it through the ear and the vibrations of footsteps on the land: Madagascar is an immense continent of sounds and songs. A hidden poem of timbres and tones whispers in its savannas and forests; it is a great musical storehouse for the whole world.

On the high plateaus the farming of silkworms was developing, an industry in which many invested great hopes. "Silkworm farming has a big future in Emyrne. Mulberry trees grow well there, and the Madagascan people, none too keen on heavy work, will find there a job suited to their easygoing ways," wrote a contemporary administrator. It is written there, in the book *Colonies françaises*, published by a big French publishing house in 1906, penned by "a set of writers, explorers, and administrators," a work supported financially by the French Ministry for Education and Fine Arts, the City of Paris, etc., with that parting shot on the indolence of the Madagascan people, in the instantly recognizable style of the colonizer.

Finally, following the discovery of high-quality rubellite in the Sahatany Valley, the word spread that the whole island is covered in gemstones: amethyst, garnet, topaz, striped sapphires nestling in the peaty boglands, sparkling rubies in the turbulent riverbeds. The *Times* correspondent of that period, a certain Mr. Knight, spoke of a "Madagascar boom": hundreds of thousands of coconut trees were planted at Analava, facing the island of Nosy Be. To think of a hundred thousand coconut trees waiting for him, in their happy ecstasy, with their heads so green and full, must have thrown Maxime into a wonderful sense of excitement and anticipation.

But can we ever really know why people leave? It is a banal question, normally the first one you ask of exiles whom you meet. The replies can be varied, by turns precise, succinct, or evasive, but they never get to the bottom of the enigma of leaving. From there a whole societal interpretative industry is set in motion, like the cogs and wheels of a machine. People get suspicious, they smell a rat, they guess, not letting it go, and where necessary, they make things up . . . they try to read the situation and surmise. They try to reconnect the chain of places and the precise number of links, to feel like they understand; they seek to uncover ruses and discover reasons, to untangle any contradictions.

In her film *Mémoires d'immigrés* Yamina Benguigui—whose parents, Kabylian people of Algerian origin, emigrated to France in the 1950s—also poses this nagging question that haunts the memory of all the children of immigrants: "Why did they leave?" She provides a response that suggests the scope of the mystery: "We never knew. It was a taboo subject; they never spoke about it." The whole of the film then turns around that mystery.

In the immense literature of exile, certain authors do, however, touch on the answer. J. M. G. Le Clézio, for example, by means of a simple story, sheds light on the issue. In his book *L'Africain* he tells the story of his father, a doctor who leaves one morning for the ends of the world so that he would no longer have to put up with an overbearing hospital manager who ordered him, at their very first meeting, in a ritual close to an initiation ceremony, to send him his cartes de visite, his calling cards . . . wait, could he have gone so far away just because of some small photographs, a few pieces of paper? Yes, he could have, to refuse the type of relation with the world that this practice supposes. He would leave then for French Guiana, then

Africa, because a map of the world is always bigger than a carte de visite. You think you have read everything on exile until you read a simple story like that, which touches and surprises you: every story is unique, but a simple resemblance is like a shared treasure. The following phrase, for example, which is very fine and which says everything about leaving: "He had chosen something else."

A man who leaves incites always a sort of anxious quivering, between desire and fear, and generally provokes the most unanimous reprobation. As soon as he leaves, the round of gossip and recrimination begins. Bad-mouthing colleagues, well-wishing friends, everyone has their say. But what is he doing, leaving like that? *He can't stand still.* A man who leaves breaks, for himself, the thread of time, the order of years and worlds, he shows that fixed times and places can be mixed up and broken, that the music of time is multiple and that he is free to live as he wants.

All of a sudden he is alone: the only one who knows it, who feels that he has to leave, to escape, and find the vanishing point of humanity's adventure.

Maxime was a man who left, departed. By all accounts he was a skillful talker, ready to rid himself of his bonds and ties, like the illusionist Houdini, a great star of the time, famous for his own spectacular escapes and whose picture Maxime had pinned to the wall of his dressing room. You catch a glimpse of him, he arrives, says a few words. Then he slips away, a bit like a fencer, whose sharp determination and elegance of movements he shares. Sometimes he has a rant; other times he throws a punch. But he never gets into a sterile argument, an endless discussion or—especially not—a lovers' tiff. He never lets the insult outwit the sidestep, the recrimination get the better of the leap. Besides, he has an inimitable way of leaving high and dry those who bore him and whom he leaves hanging literally in midsentence: he gets up, a little handshake or a quick nod of the head—hail the artist.

*

The boat is now at the quayside. You have to imagine this man, in the middle of the flowers and wild animals, stepping onto shores that he knows virtually nothing about. He has no papers; he seems to need nothing or no one. Straightaway the police, inevitably, take an interest in him.

On that day, around noon, as attested in the customs and immigration registers, there was a "serious incident" between "Maxime Ferrier, a passenger with no papers," and the police force. It was an old, nearly retired police officer called Coquillard who was in charge. He was famous for his name, which in French means "bandit" or "marauder." He makes it difficult for the young man to enter the country. There is a shortage of labor for sure, but you can't let in just anyone. You have to "ensure an increase in movements in and out but also maintain control of the country," as it says in the training booklet for overseas customs and immigration officers.

This marks the beginning of an almost uninterrupted altercation between Maxime and the forces of law and order, which would endure over time and different regimes and leave him with the reputation of being an uncontrollable hothead. On this occasion it is "thanks to the intervention of Madame Bartolini" that the problem would be resolved, but the police report, drafted in the dull, nonspecific language typical of this kind of prose, gives no more details. You can, however, easily imagine the scene. Madame Bartolini steps forward. Elegant, refined, voluble like an Italian woman who has crossed all the oceans of the world, she freely mixes business and theater. This year she has chartered the whole ship for her flowers and beasts. She vouches for Maxime and convinces the immigration officer he is an exceptional acrobat; resistance is futile.

Cheerful, always laughing, with a sharp nose and thin fingers that spin gracefully, she wears light white dresses that make it look like she is floating. She is blonde, almost white-haired, which is surprising for an Italian, but with the Bartolini Circus there is no end of surprises. She speaks, speaks a lot, mixing Italian, French, and Creole in her ringing tirades, punctuating it all with great bursts of laughter . . . She likes contrasts, provocative ideas, and audacious comparisons. In a contemporary interview, she declares that the circus was born in the eighteenth century by the coming together of two groups that society had apparently cast aside since the Middle Ages: "the descendants of the knights on the one hand, aristocrats, horsemen; and on the other, street artists and fairground people, who were the successors to the acrobats and wandering entertainers." She calls herself at once a socialist and a Catholic, a patriot and an anarchist, freely rebellious and deliberately reactionary. Her favorite phrase, which she made the motto of the circus:

Meglio vivere un giorno de leone che mille da capra.

It is better to live one day like a lion than a thousand days as a goat . . . It was quite an agenda she set herself! In the space of a few minutes, on that day, the Bartolini lioness devoured the goat Coquillard.

Madame Bartolini's family is a great commedia dell'arte family. For centuries they have worked in the live entertainment business. She has retained from that tradition the art of the gesture and movement and a love of music. On the circus program an operatic air accompanies every act. It is Vivaldi for the artists' entrance, Monteverdi for the acrobatics, and Mozart for the horse riding—lots of Baroque music. But la Bartolini is equally at home in improvised dialogues and musical interludes. Buffoonery even has a place, and she has classic commedia dell'arte figures like the Pantalone, the Captain, and the Harlequin . . . She knows by heart all these easily recognizable characters, she knows each part of their act, and has an ability to see the meanings of masks and situations. Starting with only a few retorts, she can construct hundreds of different situations: it will take more than a fussy immigration officer to throw her off. She carries the blusterer away immediately in a ballet of gestures and words that almost make him lose his mind. She seduces and threatens, she uses compliments and innuendo, and maybe she even slips him discreetly a few banknotes. And then Hassan Ali himself is on the quayside, becoming impatient, waiting for his good friend and his cargo. You can't keep flowers waiting. The immigration officer suddenly relents on his high principles, and the following day Maxime is registered.

Soon, after providing the required four identity photos ("facing the camera and with no hat," as stated in the immigration regulations), he will be given a "definitive identity card" for a set fee of forty-five francs (which is required for all males over eighteen). He will pay it in two installments, with an impressive array of one- and two-franc stamps stuck on a card that has on the other side drawings of a dog and a bird. He gets his change in tokens from the French chamber of commerce, in aluminum bronze, and a few nickel coins for twenty-five, ten, and five centimes.

The first residence visa is valid for a year in Madagascar and its Dependencies. Maxime Ferrier was to stay there for the rest of his life.

*

Of those four photographs there remains only one, which is sitting here on the table, facing me. Maxime has very short hair, almost a shaved head, which gives him the air of a resistance fighter, a deportee, or a convict. The dark shirt sets in contrast the face, a pure luminous oval. The shirt has a Venetian collar, just as he would always wear them, with the tips broadly spread. "Chic and relaxed," according to the Italian tailor I questioned in Venice, who added: "You see them already in Tintoret's paintings. It is the most classical style; it crosses the centuries."

The folds that you see shaped around the shoulders suggest the power of his thorax. Maxime looks straight ahead, almost in a hard, tough-guy way. You feel that he forced himself to look straight at the camera, and in fact, his left shoulder still leans a little to the back, as if his body resisted the image that they were assigning to it: it is as if he had a little ironic sign hidden in the shoulder. It looks like he is saying, "What do you want of me?" He is not posing for posterity; he is there, in the moment, you would not want to be in the place of the one taking the portrait—as they say—of this young ephebe with the neck of a bull.

*

To try to retrace the life of Maxime Ferrier at that time, the sources are scarce. There are three types: the circus programs—various, colorful flyers, decorated with drawings or, more rarely, with photographs; certain newspaper reviews of the time that mention in particular the incidents that pepper the circus tours; and finally, police reports that begin at the precise moment that Maxime sets foot on the Big Island and that from then were to follow him around ceaselessly. Otherwise, there are a few eyewitness accounts, which are not always reliable. I have all this in front of me, press cuttings, bits of paper, stolen words, uttered by someone else and displaced, moved around: it is up to me to make sense of it all.

Circus programs, newspaper articles, police reports . . . Bringing these three types of documents together gives a strange impression. The circus programs are full of life and color, the newspaper articles are glittery and dazzling, while the prose of the immigration officials or that of the courts is flat and repetitive. Maxime's life slides between these three styles of writing, none of which seem able to pin him down.

And so I wander. I browse. I rummage. I spend whole weeks in a dark bedroom, or anteroom, I should say. It is like wanting to trap a ghost . . . I don't sleep much, I write continually, morning, noon, evening, and night. Li-An passes by from time to time with a coffee. She tells me I should think about getting some rest, that

I should not work so much. I think about Kafka's phrase: "I am a memory come to life, which explains my insomnia." All of this to trace the path of a man about whom we know little more than his name. And so, let's speak a bit about this name . . .

*

We should try to clear up at this point a mystery, that of my own name. In fact, when Maxime arrived in Madagascar, he wasn't called "Ferrier" but "Février." That is in any case how his name appears in the birth register in the town of Souillac, in the Savane district of Mauritius, where he was born.

We know of many cases where migrants' names are changed—voluntarily or otherwise—in the course of their wanderings. To emigrate is often first and foremost to change one's name. In their *Récits d'Ellis Island* Georges Perec and Robert Bober recall the countless changes of family names that took place a few hundred yards from the Statue of Liberty, on the narrow sandbank at the mouth of the Hudson where were set up the services of the American Federal Bureau for Immigration and through which transited over many decades the immigrants who were to construct the United States of America: someone called Vladimir became Walter, Skyzertski became Sanders, someone from Berlin became Berliner, while Israel Baline himself was transformed into Irving Berlin . . . This little Jewish immigrant would become, a few years later, one of the greatest American musicians of all time, the composer most notably of "God Bless America"! Thus, that landing stage—a site that is sometimes referred to as the "terminal"—becomes for certain people a point of departure, a new beginning.

The following anecdote is the best known. It is once again Perec, who is, alongside Proust, the greatest twentieth-century French writer on the theme of memory, who tells the story: "They were telling an old Russian Jewish man to choose a good American name that the registrar would have no trouble in transcribing. He asked an employee in the luggage hall for a suggestion—the name proposed was Rockefeller. The old Jewish man repeated several times Rockefeller, Rockefeller so that he would not forget it. But when, several hours later, the official asked his name, he had forgotten it, and replied, in Yiddish, 'Schon vergessen,' which means 'I have already forgotten,' and it was thus that he was recorded under the good American name of John Ferguson."

The transformation of *Février* into *Ferrier* is of a slightly different kind, but it is just as instructive. On this transformation there are several versions going around, as if the simple shift of a single letter had itself opened up an endless round of commentaries and different accounts.

Some people talk of a simple writing error, during the recording of the civil status, between the *v* of *Février* and the *r* of *Ferrier*. The movement is more or less the same, and the hand can easily stray. Others bring up his status as a runaway and explain the name change by his wish to cover his tracks. But could the simple change of one letter fool anyone? Curiously, they don't give much credence to the explanation of the man himself, Maxime . . . Asked a few years later on his name change, he replied calmly: "There is no way I could have gone by the name of the shortest month of the year!"

What a strange joke to crack, and people generally put it down to his sarcastic side. As for me, I see in it the most pertinent and profound reply, in its very impertinence. Apart from its symbolic weight—which is quite simply that of a baptism, Maxime like Moses changing his name as they came out of the waters—the change from *Février* to *Ferrier* is also a neat way to write oneself out of the human calendar and its fixed temporality. By thus *forging* his own name and giving it a certain density (*fer* in French means "iron"), Maxime changes age and epoch, he breaks the biological chain and finds himself anew, the only one to carry his name, joyful, alive, filled with new life and a new experience of time.

The stories related to migrants' names are by turn comical and ridiculous, anecdotal or pathetic, and quite often moving. They are never insignificant. At Ellis Island, as Perec again recalls, "destiny came in the shape of the alphabet." A whole series of letters written in chalk on the shoulders of the new arrivals decided their destiny, their supposed illnesses and infirmities: *C* for tuberculosis, *K* for a hernia, *L* for lameness, *TC* for trachoma, *X* for mental debility . . . At the same time, on the other side of the world, a man all on his own reversed this logic and, by means of a simple change of letter—a delicate, fragile, *spirited* gesture—chose to give himself, by way of the alphabet, his own true freedom.

*

A man leaving: the fissure in the wall, the rip in the cloth. What grace but also what violence in that life . . . To leave, to throw everything up in the air. Above all, to never come back, to depart without leaving anything behind. To break free from the hypnosis, the sleepwalk of mechanical routines, to take leave of the horology of death . . .

There is a degree of cruelty, of course, in this border crossing. For example, leaving his mother to die alone, over there, in a forgotten little place, in order to know everything about the crime of existence. Maxime, who was seventeen years old when he left, was never to see his mother again.

Also, to take on his name fully, to forge it—a single letter to free himself—to carry it, export it, import it, impose it . . . It's the grand gesture of all migrations, their secret motivation: to at once forget and affirm one's name.

Migrate and multiply . . . Migrations are a "displacement of parasitical individuals in the course of their metamorphosis," according to the lexicographer Bouillet in the *Dictionnaire universel d'histoire et de géographie*, in his very nineteenth-century style . . . Today there are reduced, miserabilist visions of migration: they emphasize political dangers, wars, economic constraints. The stories told about the immigrants themselves often insist on sadness and nostalgia. And yet there is also the joy of leaving, the great unfurling that the departure opens up to the imagination and memory . . . One cannot understand anything about migrations without a little musical sense, of canons, stretti, and response . . . The freedom of the fugue, the art of improvisation . . . All these passing people, these oblique people . . . They undo fusions and collections; they *play* dissensions against recensions and slip, musically, into the spaces in between.

It has always been the same, in fact, since the dawn of time. Since the Greeks, since Homer, the Africans, since the black man who stood up in the Great Rift Valley, the Jew who dragged himself out of his slave plot . . . Suddenly, there is nothing that hangs on to you or blocks the way, nothing to hold you there. Arthur, Maxime, Madame Bartolini . . . Each one of them with their own history, trajectory, their own style like a projectile.

Every departure is accompanied by a sense of clarity. To leave, leave far away, to lose oneself in order to find oneself, to pass by or through the other to free yourself, the great dive into the abyss and the release that you had dreamed of . . . The novel is finally nothing but a means of finding again this rhythm, breathing freely, rediscovering acrobatic memory and sharpened perception.

*

Who is Maxime Ferrier? Why did the Bartolini Circus, stopping over at Mahajanga, never leave the island again? What became of Madame Bartolini and Arthur Dai Zong? How was Maxime able to become so rich in so little time and then lose everything in the space of a few years? Why did he have three almost identical tombs made in that old cemetery on the Corniche? Who is in the third grave?

And what is the meaning of that enigmatic epitaph inscribed into the stone on Maxime's tomb?

So that it may be living and not destroyed . . .

Memory is like the sea, obscure and full of the bitterness of algae. Certain traces are lost, buried, or indeed vanished. Others remain, but they don't speak to us, or only vaguely, confusedly, like the murmur of the ocean that you don't quite know if it is coming toward you or slipping away into nothing.

There are many obscure, hidden parts to this story. You have to search, go back to the archives and eyewitness accounts, go down in the libraries and the cellars, check everything, even in the police stations. And then you have to sift through all these boxes of old newspapers, photographs, and leaflets. I need to understand who these people are; they are so close to and yet so far from me. I need to return to their lives, to how their days played out and the silence of their nights, so that I might find it all again, right down to the accent, the very tone of their voices.

For that I need to leave, leave again—and it is thus that I feel, already, the imprint that they have left in me, the movement that they impress upon my life from the depths of their tombs, like an immense ascent of time itself.

Next stop, then: Madagascar.

FRANCE AND ITS OFFSHOOTS

— Oh!

— What? What's up?

— Oh!

— What now?

— Listen!

— More of your newspapers? Oh no.

— But yes, listen.

— No.

— Twenty lines.

— No.

— Ten.

— Nothing. Why don't you just come to the beach with me?

— We'll go later. But you are wrong . . . It's worth hearing this.

— I feel sorry for you.

— Why?

— You're like a rag-and-bone man.

— How do you mean?

— You are shuffling around this mass of papers, newspapers, letters, and notebooks as if you were rummaging through a basket of peelings. It's all so random . . . Do you think that helps understand anything?

— Absolutely.

— And you are suffocated by the whole thing!

— With joy.

— Ok, if you insist. Go ahead, then . . .

— Listen: "Will the fear of politicians to undermine the bases of a weakened national identity, the taboos of the collective unconscious, the lack of motivation in the universities, the routine nature of scholarly programs, and the interests of textbook publishers conspire again to kill at birth the interrogation of the anachronistic configuration of national historiography? All of the histories fabricated in the nineteenth century to celebrate the emerging nation-states have more or less erased any stains on their reputations. But the intellectual context and the ideological project that have conditioned the construction of a History of France from its origins to the present day, made official and transmitted by the education system of the Third Republic, are key to understanding today's malaise concerning questions of identity. Republican historians, who saw France as the light of the world, as a messiah nation, drew up an outline of the past that was intended to nationalize the French people and forge their patriotism. The historical narrative instilled into the imaginary an idea of France as homogeneous, one, indivisible, a metahistorical essence mysteriously present in an originary mythical Gaul. This narrative ignored the mix of peoples and cultures that in fact was at the very heart of the geopolitical space forged in the aftermath of the Capetian conquests and annexations."

— A multicultural France? . . . Who would have thought? And why not multilingual too, while we are at it? You are joking?

— Not at all. Listen to the final part: "Invented for and transmitted by the education system of the Third Republic, our multicultural and multiethnic history must be rewritten in today's France, a post-Vichy, postcolonial France, tied to the heart of Europe, an integral part of the complexity of the world in the twenty-first century."

There it is, written by Suzanne Citron, a nice name that makes you think at once of crepes and fruit, of sweetness and elegance.

*

The French don't know where to put me. We don't have any idea of how to be French in that way, they say to me. It's too complicated, all your mixed parts! What a joke . . . The French are united only when under attack—and even then it doesn't last long, you only have to see how they are at each other's throats afterward. *Français de souche*, as they say, where *souche* means literally "stump," as if there were no other way to be "truly" French . . . Anyway, what is a stump but a piece of dead wood, a tree trunk with no depth, an amputated limb?

In Molière's play *L'École des femmes* Mr. Stump is Arnolphe, a bourgeois gentleman who took his aristocratic name from a rotten old tree trunk on his little farm: Monsieur de la Souche. It is written there in black and white, from the first scene. The only women he likes are ugly and stupid. And people want to make of this some kind of example for France?

What a waste, to forgo the real name of his forefathers,
To want to take another built on chimeras!

So, you can be French by trunk, by wood, by stump . . . by stub or by stem! So, why not by branch or offshoot? . . . by leaf? by paper! What a wooden, pompous language, it has to be said. None of that really exists anyway. I am French by ear and by conviction.

On board the flight to Madagascar, I flick through the newspapers and magazines and watch the television news . . . What confusion, what a jam, it's all messed up . . . So many mixed-up memories! As soon as you touch down in France, everything becomes confused, complicated, opaque . . . History, geography, and time itself are from that point uncertain. There are knots, many levels of time set against or layered on top of each other, pieces of memory that demand to rise again, resurfacing in a great tempest from the bottom of the abyss. You need to know how to move around in there, in this enormous archive, to listen, be on the lookout: certain memories are trapped, others blocked, others still recalcitrant or vindictive, and they try to place over the top of them all, as a kind of cover, a great unified memory, with a single resonance, monotonous and supposedly national.

Today one would say that the cartography of France stops at the borders of the Hexagon. I have taken with me *Le Tour de la France par deux enfants*, a kind of official guidebook of the Third Republic . . . Now, nearly 150 years later, we still have not left it behind.

You are French, you know the story: André and Julien are two little boys from Lorraine, what are called "Optants" in French, as they opted to leave the territories annexed by Germany in 1871 to keep their French nationality.

Here we are, then, in their company on the byways of France: on foot, on horseback, in a coach, in the depths of a forest or on a mountaintop, in a dairy or a paper mill, a factory or a cheese maker's . . . In the 1877 edition there are no fewer than 120 illustrations, 196 etchings, and 19 maps, all to describe France and its heroes.

The meandering of the two children is punctuated with poetic landscapes, geographical insights, historical reminders, and common sayings. From the fair at Épinal to the foundries of the Creusot, from the hills of Auvergne to the Rhône Valley, passing by the Artois, Orléans and the ports of Marseille, the journey is pleasant and varied and, above all, instructive. They explore Rouen and its cotton, Versailles and its columns, the circus of Gavarnie, and the mountain streams of Pau. We discover the glass, crystals, and mirrors of Lorraine, the great plain of the Limagne and its candied fruits.

One day we find ourselves in the Jura Mountains, in the company of "great flocks of villages, led by a single shepherd." Another day we discover the logging industry and the great steam power hammers. Here and there the journey is enlivened by lessons on various things, including moral issues: we learn about "honesty," "the economy," the "way to gain someone's trust," and the "way to look after horses."

But it is not only geographical landscapes that we find in this traveling epic. The book is also overflowing with historical tales: Joan of Arc; Vercingétorix and ancient Gaul; Desaix and the Battle of Marengo; Bayard, the brave and irreproachable knight; the expeditions of La Pérouse . . . We also meet mother Gertrude and mother Étienne, father Guillaume (makes you think of Balzac and *Le Cousin Pons* and *La Cousine Bette*). At the end everyone ends up at the idealized farm of the Grand'Lande, which reminds you of Rabelais and Thélème Abbey.

The France that people love is made up of hardworking farmers, industrious workers, meticulous clockmakers, courageous soldiers, prodigious artists, daring scientists, and fabulous writers!

Here's what they say about La Fontaine: "He is one of the writers who have immortalized our language: his fables have traveled the world over; they are read everywhere, translated everywhere, and taught everywhere. They are full of verve, grace, and natural things, and at the same time they show men the faults that they must correct." That is so true!

Certainly, the maxims cited in the epigraphs of each chapter can be in turn amusing, tiresome, or irritating: "Be clean and decent, the poorest people can be so" . . . "Those who work are always held in esteem." But certain pages are full of marvelous poetry, like the description of Provence, with its "woods forever verdant with their orange, lemon, and olive trees, which descend from the high mountains to the sea." And what could you add to this piece of disarming wisdom: "All you need is to know the twenty-four letters of the alphabet and to want; with that you can learn the rest"?

It is an admirable text, at once broad and precise, pedagogical and precious. It is a discovery of the country through the land, the air, and the light. It is a whole poem, a whole country in a single sweep.

Along the way the frieze unravels a childlike series of games and toys, touching scenes of vineyards and foundries, mulberry trees and silk farms, swing bridges, guns and ribbons, and not to forget the noble landscapes of orange trees in the environs of Nice or the silkworm lace on the reed trellises of the Dauphiné.

This history does, however, have its shadowy parts and even its blind spots. Julien is—rightly—"very proud of France" when he recalls that "it was France that was first to abolish slavery in its colonies" (chapter 87), which alludes to the decision of the Convention, on 4 February 1794, but he says nothing about its reintroduction by Napoleon in 1802. There is also this little phrase in chapter 76, on "the white race, the most perfect of the human races," which is terribly typical of the time. In short it is France, with its improbable nuances, its paradoxes, its contradictions.

It is, moreover, a strange book, written by a man, G. Bruno, who was in reality a woman (Augustine Fouillée, née Tuillerie), in a very refined language, even if it is addressed to children, and which tells of the search for an uncle Frantz, whom they think they will find in Marseille but who left for Bordeaux . . . Ah, Bordeaux! It is always there that France finds its refuge, between the blue of the ocean and the clarity of the wine, so close to the shores, the threshold to the overseas regions. And what is the family name of these two French children? André and Julien Volden . . . a Norwegian name! In short it is a strange muddle that underlies the clarity of the overall book.

But the great absence in the *Tour de la France par deux enfants* can be summed up in a single word, superb and luminous in its very opacity: the *outre-mer*, or the overseas regions. You do find in the later editions a few passages on what was still known as Annam (chapter 122), or the "agricultural tests in the colonies" (chapter 123), but those "four million square kilometers, populated by thirty-eight million people," that "France possesses or protects" (strange ambiguity in that phrase) are each time dismissed in a few lines . . .

This is because the book is underpinned by a single idea: "the resolution to remain French and to live in France." You can therefore be French only in France, and this is what is drummed into you in the eight million copies that were sold over a hundred years of this enduring best seller.

One could, based on this nineteenth-century model that is now completely outdated, imagine a permanent rewriting of the *Tour de la France* through the ages. André and Julien would stand aside successively for:

Michel and Martine in the 1950s,
Philippe and Catherine (or Anquetil and Poulidor) in the 1960s,
Christophe and Nathalie (or Stone and Charden) in the 1970s,
Nicolas and Céline—not Louis-Ferdinand to be clear—in the 1980s,
Kevin and Élodie in the 1990s,
Thomas and Léa in the 2000s,
Emma and Nathan in the 2010s, etc.

You would, of course, take into account urbanization, industrialization, and the most recent technological changes. In the twenty-first-century version of *Le Tour* the Engravings Gallery would be completely photoshopped. The Maps Index would be digitized and put on a DVD with interactive features. The Technical Index would be expanding rapidly, and the Famous Men one would have *people*. The Moral Index would have more or less disappeared.

Or then again, let's dream a little: you could also sketch a different history of France, made up of intervals and crossings, a whole series of cracks and crevices and sidesteps.

Instead of the panorama, you would have a view from above, with multiple and renewed vistas.

You would replace the circular logic of the *tour* of a single, unified France with that of the detour and the unpredictable.

In other words, you would take apart the norms, reintroduce a more playful approach, explore France's blind spots, that which it has always considered its outside or its extremities, its offshoots and *outgrowths*. You would go to the heart of things, bring out everything that has so often been put to the side and closed off—and presented in a very singular way.

This alternative itinerary would pass through, for example, all the French overseas departments and territories but also all the territories where the history of France was formed, deformed, transformed, and recomposed: colonies, trading posts, protectorates . . . To mention only the most obvious ones, you would have: Guadeloupe, Martinique, French Guiana, Réunion, Mayotte, Polynesia, Saint-Pierre and Miquelon, Wallis and Futura, Saint Martin, Saint Barthélemy, New Caledonia, the Southern and Antarctic Lands . . . And not to forget the well-named Scattered Islands: Bassas da India, Europa, the Glorioso Islands, Juan de Nova, Tromelin . . . (which are all currently subject to competing territorial claims).

And then there is Clipperton Island, which is twelve thousand kilometers from France but which is nevertheless part of France since 28 January 1931, by the arbitration of the International Court and King Victor Emmanuel III of Italy. Did you know that? We have compatriots in the heart of the Pacific Ocean, in what is, according to the expert calculations of the International Union for Conservation of Nature, the most isolated atoll in the world, in that little heap of gravel, coral sands, and guano, populated by reptiles, crustaceans, and fish, just as French as you and me.

How could this be? A multi-territorial France, existing in different times that are unaware of each other, that are related, intertwined, superimposed on each other? . . . It is a disconcerting topography, an improbable encyclopedia . . . Endless surprises. It would no longer involve "learning France through the sole of its shoes" but remembering that it was also forged by men and women with the wind at their backs, poets and politicians, migrants and travelers. That France has more than one side to it.

This shift in perspective—which is not possible even now as I speak to you; it's barely a hypothesis—would reveal many other sides to France: transient and resistant, fragile and indubitable, so alive and so French. It would also create a parallel geography, land based and maritime, sensual and intelligent, on the move and moving, in an emotional sense. You might then succeed in showing that variety has constantly accompanied the historical creation of France, inside and outside, in Europe as in the Antilles, in Africa as in the Indian Ocean.

Thus, the idea of plurality would return, in names, places, and memories. France would become again what it has never stopped being, a heterogeneous yet also coherent zone, at times antagonistic, of course—as in Haiti, when the colonized people appropriated the words and ideals of the French Revolution against France itself, to give full voice to the most stirring ideas that France had pronounced in that century. You would speak about Fanon and Vivant Denon, Molière and Césaire, or even the Chevalier de Saint-Georges, that incomparable fencer, not so much the "black Mozart" or the "Voltaire of music," as he was called in his time, as quite simply one of the great French figures of the eighteenth century. And then there would be all the others, the invisible ones, the anonymous, the dead with no gravestone, those without whom France would not be France.

Basseterre and Marigot . . . Cayenne and Saint-Denis . . . Mamoudzou and Gustavia . . . Mata-Utu and Nouméa! A kind of import-export process, another model, other nuanced perspectives . . . Thus the epigraph in chapter 53 that I am reading just as the plane begins its descent to the Antananarivo airport would take on its full meaning:

"There are few countries as varied as France: it has every facet, every climate, and produces almost every crop."

THE RED CIRCUS

Here it is. It begins here. It is steep, very steep. It rises up out of the earth: an infinity of rocks and summits. Antananarivo is born here in the fury of the mountains; it is an event in itself.

Antananarivo is a city that rises and descends. As far as the eye can see, it continually reinvents itself in a succession of lines and dashes: streets that rise and streets that turn, the roofs like pointed hats, the serious-looking palaces, the almost vertical footpaths, the breathtaking slopes that skirt disheveled neighborhoods. One can only say that the city unfurls along an extraordinary landscape of hills and rocks, "a rough sea whose immense waves seem as if they were suddenly fixed during a storm," as Paulhan said. To begin with, the city covered three mountains, then twelve, and today it is eighteen. It is as if the city were born from a decision taken at a meeting of the mountains in a faraway land.

What a surprise! What a joy! At first look a great wild laugh rises in you as you stand before this beautiful capital city. From the lower part of town (which begins at the Analakely market) to the higher part (from the Isoraka district to the ruins of the Queen's Palace, which overlooks the southeast of the city), all you see are little cobbled, sloping streets, gray basalt staircases on granite hills that are pink at dawn, orange at sundown, and crisscrossed with changing light, with roads and pathways cutting across them, riddled with little rammed-earth houses next to sumptuous dry masonry tombstones. Here and there you see fences made with wood shaped like circumflexes. Everywhere there are tiled roofs and wood balconies, little shutters opening onto immense ravines, verandas overlooking the wonder of the empty spaces below that are devoured by trees, people, and gardens. The staircase steps are full of vendors and beggars. Crippled men follow you for a coin or two, to sell you a hat, a bracelet, a car tire, or a glass of water, while little girls in white dresses sing hymns and shine in the distance like little gems. Young people themselves look like overhanging rocks, and the old are like trees at the edge of a precipice.

In flights of stairs and flights of sparrows, the little streets descend, hopping in small steps, from the full sun of Ataninandro to the red coral of Andravoahangy, then fork off and broaden toward Anka-ditapaka, where opens up the whole plain of Ikopa and the green squares of its rice fields. For a mountain girl, Tana, as the city is known, is the queen of the rice fields. According to the season, she sits above a vast landscape of hens and scarecrows, sheaves and bundles, sowing and hoeing, to the rhythm of the precise gestures and songs of the pickers.

At every step the pedestrian is taken aback by the high-wire act of the roads and alleyways. They scamper, gambol, slam, jump, climb back up to the sky, or throw themselves into a neighboring ravine. Here nothing waits or stops, nothing arrives late. Let's move on . . .

You pass by the little forest of Analakely, cross the village of the skylark, go across the ditches dug by the people (tiredness gives you wings), and find yourself in the place where all your questions are answered. All around you it's a whole circus, a spectacle, to say the least: summits, crags, thorns, tufts and crests, furrows and railings, braiding, headlands, overhangs, chasms, sewers, valleys, vales, cuts, and mountain needles . . . And then suddenly, out of the blue, you see a rock decorated in flowers like a fine bell tower.

It is a complete nightmare for cars, which create terrible pollution low down in the city, but it is a delight for walkers: a whole city to climb up or hurtle down. "If you go against the current, you are the prey of the caiman; if you go with it, you are the prey of the crocodile," says a Malagasy proverb. That says it all, there is no way to escape: Antananarivo has caught you in its delicious trap.

The whole city seems to be on constant alert, exposed as it is to the clouds and the winds in its rocky setting. So, one obviously wants to find things out, get to know the city; you move around from place to place. You climb and climb, walking close to the sky. Near the fourteen hundred–meter highest point of this superb site, behind the remnants of the Queen's Palace, is found a viewpoint indicator. It was here during the monarchy that those condemned to death were executed, decapitated by an ax or stabbed by an assegai. It is to the piling up of all those bones, swept away by the rains after being gnawed at by birds of prey that the place owes its terrifying name: Ambohipotsy, or "the white place." Today, taken over by ferns, trees, and dahlias, it has one of the most beautiful wind roses that you could find anywhere in the world. You stop for a moment, you sit in one spot and then another. From high up on the viewpoint, the view is uninterrupted. You say to yourself that you are going to finally grasp what it is, this city.

At first view it seems to be set out in the shape of a Y; oriented from the southeast to the southwest, the two upper branches of this Y turn toward the west so that they encircle the whole city, which was built on a vast hollow that was more or less leveled out. Historians and geographers will tell you that at the beginning of colonization, the new district, a grid of streets, avenues, and businesses, rose up in the lowest part of town, in the branches of the Y, which gave it a semblance of order and organization. However, you never really get over the initial amazement, its explosive impact: very quickly, as the other streets and districts take shape randomly, set against the natural escarpments, you see other letters pitching, forming, then separating: the *P* of the Mahamasina stadium and the road that leads there, the twin *E*s of Isotry and the neighboring plateau of Isoraka, the slightly proud *R* of the former Colbert square, the slender *C* of Ambadinia, and soon the shapes, for a long time foreseeable in their very irony, of a *M*, an *F*, or an *S*. The city unfurls its alphabet: it is a *claybook*, a book of land and signs.

It is an unpredictable, undulating journey, made up of twists of phrases and changes in tone, modulations that seem to adapt to every change in the surface and sensibility, music, a score of bricks and branches, churches perched like cliff sides, rugged, studded here and there with a tuft of laurel trees. Aerial and voluble, fragile and willowy, there is a permanent improvisation that underpins this inopportune topography. One has the strange sensation that the city disappears at the same time as it appears, that an immense harmony is hidden there and, despite everything, is present everywhere. As soon as you try to explain it, you lose its movement, as if the city wanted to leave everything to its proper rhythm and momentum.

That sense of joy is inevitably unsettling; there is so much insouciance in the midst of poverty, so many treasures in penury, so much efflorescence in the architecture that could not fail to excite the verve of moralists and censors. Such a beautiful array of Italian palaces and French chateaus, an explosion of styles—neoclassical, baroque, colonial, Anglican, Moorish, Sakalava, Mahafaly, modern, contemporary, neo-Roman—provokes almost inevitably a call for fastidious and fussy order by the official artists. Thus, you have the architect of the central government under Gallienei, Anthony Jully, completely overtaken by events, who writes in an article of the official bulletin of 1898 (the island has been a French colony for two years): "Out of diverse architectural styles, Gothic, hybrid, classical, Hindu, thrown to the mercy of the natives, arises a chaos without character. That was what struck us on our arrival in Tananarive in 1890, and that is why, in building the residences for our senior officials, we sought a single outcome: to make it in French architectural style, as much in the outward appearance as in the interior layout. The period that best characterizes our art being the Renaissance, it is in the works of that period that we have sought our inspiration, while trying to inspire in the natives, in form as in the details, the French ideal."

Mindful of installing order in this strange muddle and of foregrounding the "positive role" of French colonization, Jully is a stickler for the rules. Clearly, the residence in question only added all the more to the hybrid, polyvalent style that he excoriated with his starchy critique . . .

One day, maybe not so far away, people will see that in its very disorder this city is one of the most beautiful in the world, that it carries the world's memory in it, as a hub of the Chinese, Indians, and Westerners, and people will come from all over to enjoy this marvel. The city will enter into a new era. But for the moment, as no position of mastery is possible (and is certainly not required), it is already possible to follow it like a lover's gaze follows their sweetheart and to begin to know this new kind of city.

Thus, it is only the sunrays, the perfumes, and the colors that seem to have any value. Antananarivo is one of the only cities in the world that can rival for color Venice or the paintings of Titian. *Colorito alla Malagasy!* It is an open delight in an inexhaustible palette of blues, reds, and grays . . . At noon the city is completely ochre, as if burnt by the embers of the cliff sides and irradiated from the interior by the pulsar of the quartz and the faint hue of iron oxide. In the evening the rumble of the city eases up, and on a café terrace you take an aperitif with friends in the softness of the twilight, your head bathed in luminous burgundy, dappled in orange and cherry colors. Above you there is the lush green foliage of the mango trees. Near the table's leg there is a little strip of wonderful golden color, impalpable like a reflection and superimposed like a luminescent carpet.

Also, you become sensitive to the movements of the wind, the delineation of the details, the form, color, and perfumes of the flowers. You see zinnias with multicolored shades, red, pink, and white cosmos flowers, the wild and incalculable richness of the violets, geraniums, and palm trees. You admire the impressive bearing of the camphor trees, their shade, the quality of their perfumed wood, with its light-brown grain running through it.

You listen to the delicious names of the ferns with their spread-out curved fractals: *adiantes* (maidenhair fern); *polypodes* (polypodies); and *cornes de cerf* (staghorn fern).

You learn that the biggest orchid in Madagascar is called *la comète* (the comet): it is decorated by a bouquet of flat white stars and equipped with long green spurs. This is important; I will try not to forget it.

Proust writes in *Lost Time* that "flowers divulge in some way one of nature's secrets: they betray the fact that somewhere in this world must be found life, hope, light, and color." But who still knows how to see, describe, and name these flowers?

You learn the ways to write about lilacs, guava trees, the sweet and heavy smell of vanilla, and the slightly spicy smell of the mulberry trees.

So, time begins to vibrate differently. Sometimes the city is decked out in the most beautiful clouds—journeys of white cotton tripping across the blue sky. The fiery sun takes hold of the rooftops. The balconies, transported by the light, seem to float in front of their houses like clouds of gold. Everything is covered in all kinds of fruits, flowers, and birds.

At other times there are storms swollen with lightning, and the city is surrounded by the rumbling sounds of the rolling thunder, gaping chasms, and sinister portents. The cracking sounds of the wood have a searing depth and intensity, the lizards scamper at top speed, and the rain comes in battering downpours in a riotous, cavernous sound.

Through the pages of this landscape, of this almanac of rocks and foliage, the Malagasy people walk around, in suits, in rags, in hats. Their way of walking is famous the world over: people see it as nonchalant, slow, and sometimes even slouching. There is a word that goes around, that even the tourists know, which sums up this light, fluid, and harmonious bodily rhythm:

mora mora

It is sometimes translated as "slowly" or "gently." There are, however, sometimes sudden accelerations, gestures of incalculable precision—that of the children who, on the bumpiest terrain, roll along with a stick a metal hoop with the care of an acrobat, that of the domino players who hit their tables with their little wooden tiles. You have to allow yourself to fall into step with the country itself, to get with the rhythm of the city, its yellowy pulsation. You then understand that *mora mora* does not have much to do with speed or slowness (or that which we name as such) but that it reveals, instead, another way of moving in time, outside of one's frames and resistant to their contours and coordinates: you have to leave the human calendar and its stifling strictures to enter into the energy of the body, its secret histories, its vibrating freedom.

Something is in the air, quite simply, to which one would give the following name: Antananarivo, joy, grace, or elation—take your pick.

*

The Antananarivo-Ivato International Airport is quiet: there are only six international arrivals and six departures every day.

Flights arrive from Bangkok, Mauritius, Paris, Réunion, Johannesburg, and Dzaoudzi.

They leave for Paris, Réunion, Mauritius, Johannesburg, Réunion again, and Paris again.

Georges has come to the airport to pick me up. Georges, a friend of the family, is an old Indian Creole, with bronzed skin and catlike eyes. He is a car salesman. Most important, his father knew Maxime, was acquainted with Arthur Dai Zong, and even went to the Bartolini Circus when he was very small . . . He was mad about the circus and left on his death a collection of papers, newspaper cuttings, leaflets and posters, articles, and tickets. I have high hopes that this pile of papers, which Georges tells me he has put into two cases and a three-drawer chest, will teach me a lot about this period. Right there at the airport, however, he warns me:

— Your grandfather Maxime was a one-man secret society. My father's papers will be of use to you, but if you want to understand him, you have to go all the way to Mahajanga and speak to many different people. I will lend you a car.

— Thank you, but do you have any idea who is buried in the third grave?

— No. When you told me you were coming, I asked many people, but nobody seems to know. Some say it has something to do with World War II, but I don't know if that is right. On the other hand, in the pile of papers I spoke about, there are numerous newspaper articles and circus programs. There are also Madame Bartolini's notebooks. And a chest that belonged to your grandmother, Pauline. Perhaps you will find something in there . . .

*

The following day, after a good night's sleep. The day rises over Antananarivo. I hear first the wheezing of cars and bursts of voices. Then, in the corridor, I hear someone polishing the parquet floor, people debating, cars, and everywhere a slight air of sharp mockery. Mopeds pass by endlessly, their motorized humming interspersed by the songs of the birds.

I get up and open the shutters. Georges lives right in the center of town, in a charming and agreeable old wooden house that smells of beeswax and pine resin.

To the left I see the walls of an old brick house with all the shutters closed. However, the lower door is open, and I have seen someone move around in the shadow of the staircase, whose guardrail I can almost make out. This house is very nice, but it blocks my view of the Queen's Palace. Yesterday a teenager was playing there in the courtyard with a kitten.

Below people pass by; mothers take their children to school. A white-tailed tropic bird crosses the sky. Far away a tree welcomes a flock of birds.

At the corner of the street a woman selling telephone cards (two thousand Malagasy francs per card) has just set up her rickety stall, a little shaky table under a leaning parasol. She must be about twenty years old and holds in her arm a baby no bigger than a little sausage.

Farther away a cobbled, steep street like you only find in Tana directs my gaze to the orange-tiled rooftops and the sinuous outline of a mountain, over there, very clearly sketched out under the pale strip of a cloud.

*

Georges, who is exquisitely kind and thoughtful, has brought me the newspaper.

In Malagasy astrology I learn that my sign is *Alahasaty*. It is the fifth month of the year in the astrological calendar. On the seventh page I come across the most concise and relevant horoscope I have ever read:

> *Work*: Don't be intimidated by people who are weaker than you.
> *Love*: You will find it easily. Don't waste your time talking.
> *Health*: Drink lots of water.

And there you have it—it's all true and so well put!

Georges has also given me the documentation that his father gathered on the Bartolini Circus. Two cases and a little chest of drawers—not forgetting the chest from my grandmother Pauline. I cast an eye over the cases—pages and pages of old magazines, articles cut out and set in old yellow cardboard folders, held together by a metallic strap.

Now I can get to work.

*

As soon as he arrives in Mahajanga, the circus sets up. He moves in with the circus, which makes sense. Space is required for the cages, the trailers, and the blue canvas big-top tent. A little outside of town, there is actually an area of low hills encircling a round red arena, which is crisscrossed by many ravines cut out by erosion. Its successive layers of earth are distinguished by a fantastic palette of pastel, ochre, and blood-red hues, which make it today one of the must-see places in the region. In Maxime's time the place is empty, populated only by a few lizards and the eagles that fly overhead: they call it the "Red Circus."

It is a stunning site, a former delta sculpted by the centuries and the unending erosion of the hillsides. The wind swirls in gusts; it opens, catches, devours, rises up again in columns along the brush-covered slopes, and then crashes even more strongly into the highest peaks. Above there is the burning sun of the Boina, immobile, directly overhead . . . For the sun time is not time, it is nothing but an immense silvery constant. It scrapes the rocks, erodes them, detaches them, transforms them into copper, iron, and lead . . . On a yellow, pink, or even red backdrop, speckled formations stand out: you see in them clear sections devoured by quartz, silver areola, and ruby rectangles. The sea so close by splashes its spray into the mix. It moistens the plants and flowers with its salty sweetness.

The colors are varied and powerful. Here you have ferruginous concretions, limestone wells, and anthracite sumps. There a dazzling succession of layers of sandstone, each one with its color, its own vibration, each one with its own style. There are sections of black, red, and yellow that slot together and are layered on top of each other, shielded by the blue sky. In a series of brown rocks, there is sometimes a sliver of tinplate, a strip of glistening mica, like the remains of bits of armor or scraps of shields, vestiges of ancestral combats . . . A palette ground down by typhoons . . . It is to this landscape—which no one knows whether to call wet or dry, land or sea, lunar or equatorial—that the circus brings its wild animals, artists, and monsters.

Maxime feels fine straightaway in this place deserted by the babbling of men and with its inexhaustible colors. Finally, following the trepidations of his flight from home, the short breath of the pursuit, there is nothing before him but pure space and the season. And when the day ends, there is the silence of a night broken only by the cry of eagles, a unique night, always the same since the beginning of time, a night of great vintage.

*

The Red Circus has clearly not been chosen randomly. Not only is there space, but one can imagine that the city's population prefers to keep at a slight distance the strange Areopagus of the entertainers. What is more, the word is that the circus's Venus figures were not averse to exercising their talents outside showtimes, under the tolerant—not to say approving—eye of Madame Bartolini . . . The two sisters always work as a family: lesbianism, sadomasochism, and even zoophilia (the whips and the wild animals must also be of use *outside* the show) . . . in those cases the scenes are played out behind closed doors and information on them is scarce. It appears that a certain number of town councillors and colonial officials are implicated in this mini spectacle and its previously unseen acts. According to some, Madame Bartolini, a fervent Catholic, gives her blessing. According to others, she draws from it payments that amount to a tidy sum . . . Across the country these meetings are known under the delicate name of "soirées Bordelini," a play on *bordel*, the French word for "brothel." Everyone agrees that she sees nothing wrong in a little of what you fancy so long as it does not upset the smooth running of the circus and stays within reasonable limits. The eyes light up, the blood sings, and the bones grow larger: nothing wrong in that, is there?

Did Maxime lend a hand (and his athletic talents) to these unapproved pirouettes? It is hard to say for sure, but it is likely. He is young and free, has just left without ceremony his family, his country, his worries: for him it is now or never. It would be hard to dream of a situation better suited to finally let out that which families repress, the intense secrets of the body, its volatile energy. You have to imagine him also in the midst of this life of trapeze and ropes, of silver and bronze costumes, of gold and steel figureheads leading their lives to the great galloping of twenty circus horses . . . But who could describe today, in the era of the banality of screens and omnipresent entertainment, those free, carefree, monstrous, wonderfully insolent acrobats and entertainers? Our time sees itself as right thinking, egalitarian, and open, but you only have to look at the destiny it has mapped out for the festive revolts of the circus to measure just how sad it really is, how elitist it is without knowing it, hateful, afraid, and terrorizing. What has happened to dance, juggling, and performance? Mime and music? The bravura of men and the respect for the animals? They have disappeared from sight and from most of the circuses themselves. That death is also our own.

Even at the end of the nineteenth century, Rimbaud himself knew that: "In improvised costumes, with a taste for the nightmarish, they play on the laments and tragedies of outlaws and spiritual demigods in ways that history and religion have never done." Or again: "The master jugglers transform the place and the people there and take playacting to its extreme." Maxime and all his entertainers are therefore demigods as much as they are outlaws or bandits. The French word is *malandrin*, and it sits beautifully between *marin* (sailor) and *mandarin*. For three years they will regale the inhabitants of the region with their acrobatics and magnetic, alluring jokes and pranks.

*

The circus is a kind of canvas womb; you enter it only at night. You have to wait for the silence of the twilight all around, the slowed-down pulsation of the blood and the unfurling of the black ink over the world, to enter into the real lives of men and women, their desires, their secrets, and their real presence.

It is the night of the circus. There is a sense of joyous expectation; the great canvas theater is filled with a colorful crowd, Europeans with white hats and veils, Malagasy people wearing lambas (those fine cotton togas that make them look like ancient Greeks), and Indian women in red and blue saris . . . The men smoke, the women laugh, the children shout or chat excitedly.

In the Bartolini Circus there is a giant, a dwarf, and a ventriloquist. There is also a bearded woman, a woman with no arms, and a man with no limbs. Real circus freaks. They are the ones who open the show: with music, magic, and juggling, they warm up the crowd, carrying it into the mysteries of nature and the depths of laughter.

No, life is not that which you think, there is another side where you can live more fully and be more alive, full of song, more real: that is what all these monsters demonstrate—the admirable precision of the word's etymology. Balancing acts, contortionists, drag artists, high-wire acts, antipodists . . . you find a bit of everything, a veritable rabble of people, acts, and characteristics. They have an admirable sense of farce and an astonishing bodily ingeniousness.

Amanda, the woman with no arms, lights a cigarette with her feet . . . a jumping pit placed in the ground allows her to throw herself in the air thanks to the leap of a human torpedo at the other

52

end of the plank. The dwarf Groseille, perched on the shoulders of the strongman, catches her, and then he juggles in quick succession plates, glasses, knives, and forks . . . Dexterity, concentration: the items fly about in an unending, ever-changing loop.

From the shadows to the left, here comes a horsewoman in red livery, with her hair a wine color and her crimson smile. She mounts her trotting horse in a single leap, then jumps on to another's neck like a rubber ball. A second horsewoman joins her, wearing a large hat and swirling her lasso. These are the Bartoletty sisters (are these Madame Bartolini's daughters? It's a mystery . . .). Brunette and blonde, the two Venus sisters: with them everything is reversed. The one called "Brune" is blonde and is the Venus of the morning. The other is called "Blonde," and her hair is jet-black; she is the Venus of the night. The first mounts a snow-colored thoroughbred, while the other has a dark gray mare. They say that Brune is blonde up top but dark elsewhere and that Blonde . . . is the opposite. The two have veritable lionesses' manes, and you feel that they are none too familiar with the rigors of the hairbrush.

"They have nothing to envy of the perfect little daughters of the Countess of Ségur . . . ," notes a journalist mockingly. Indeed! A photo from the time shows them with their legs spread wide, a generous décolletage, their chests prominent, and their avid mouths . . . "A fresh, refreshing, sunny show," as the program notes say.

They were put in the saddle almost before they were able to walk, tiny little girls prancing on the backs of huge Percherons or standing upright on Anglo-Arab sorrels, the horses' heads and necks appearing flimsy as they thrust their long backs nervously. They are fully grown now . . . Blonde, with her legs crossed and very bare, in white muslin, smiling radiantly, gives a big wave to the circus, sitting on the edge of a staircase, surrounded by balls. Her smile leaps from her lips to those of the audience: she enflames the whole place. As for Brune, she is wearing satin short pants decorated with red feathers: distinct makeup, lips luscious, red and lustrous like a cherry. Her dark eyes are lined in blue, and she has on her biceps a tattoo of two bracelets—the blue of which recalls that of her eyes— entwined like two snakes. She smokes a cigarette, a scarf wrapped around her neck, and her gaze glows like her lips. Her white, firm, and taut stomach catches the eyes immediately, the little bulge in her tummy, silky and soft to the look as it must be to the touch, as if it and the delicious curve of her ankle contained all the softness of the world.

The "Queen of the Night" aria plays when the second Venus, the one of the night, makes her entrance on a black mare in the act called "Étoiles filantes," or Shooting Stars: her body is supple and taut, balanced on her mount, she sings while throwing small glass cups that appear like stars. Everything is done with extreme skill and precision at every stage . . . Dance, parade of the chariots, everyone rolling, climbing poles . . . The complex manipulations and the diversity of the acts offer to the eyes and ears an extraordinary conflagration.

*

Some very solid jesters . . . Eyes dazed so that they look like summer nights, red and black . . . The cruel allure of the eccentric characters . . . The posters and articles pass before my eyes, poems of ink and satin, inundated with light and with the smell of dung in the air. Nothing exposes like the circus does the sweet, happy and cruel truth of existence.

The most surprising thing in the newspaper reports on the Bartolini Circus is the general impression of grace given off by all those deformed bodies. In the trampoline act, for example: "As they bounce into the air, the monsters execute graceful figures that delight the spectators." Or when the human skeleton coils around a narrow bicycle wheel, to which he holds on with his feet and hands: the curious slender athlete with the cone-shaped head and rubbery limbs, of whom there unfortunately remains no photograph, as if he was too *fine* to be caught on camera, carries out a series of pivots and maneuvers while balanced on a suspended wooden board . . . "There follow some amazing aerial tricks, then some gracious landings on the stage," notes the journalist . . . There is grace in the art of leaping, grace in the landings, always grace, starting from any point in space, the whole thing a greater marvel than the skies above.

At the heart of the show are the clowns. No need for animals for them—they act like dogs, birds, and monkeys . . . Cowboy movies, the epic, exotic wonders . . . all the genres are mixed together, and the plot is but a pretext for their fantasy, without the slightest care for coherence. Sometimes they tumble onto the wooden floors . . . Then the very small kids hide themselves. The little boys roll their fearful eyes, while the little girls bite their lips . . . But the clowns always get up again, laughing. People scorn them, but they don't care: while the whole world succumbs to death and stagnation, they are the last bastions of laughter and poetry, a spectacular narrative with inexhaustible japes and exploits.

But the highlight of the show is the acrobats. They fly through veils, swirl through and devour the draping materials. They hoist themselves with the strength of their wrists up to almost inaccessible platforms; they leap over broad and deep chasms; arms added to arms replace the ropes, and the shoulders serve as rungs, while all the others remain down below on the sawdust. Miss Tamara and Miss Julia . . . Miss Julia is all about suppleness and skill on the vertical rope. "An act full of grace and daring . . ." Miss Tamara and her hanging fabrics, suspended more than ten meters from the floor by a silk banner . . . And then there is Axel the tightrope walker . . . His act is "the most stupefying high-wire act in the whole circus world."

These are aerial artists, they are known as the "icariens." Like Icarus, they climb as high as they can, to the stars, to infinity. Even if they do not remember it, they know—with a form of knowing almost as ancient as the body and more ancient than knowledge itself—that the word *circus* comes from *circulus*, a term from antiquity that goes back to the orbit of the planets. Up there, then, in orbit, they turn in the spotlights, a vast spinning revelation. They curl up and stretch out; they constantly reinvent themselves. They puncture space, step across time . . . It is a rite of agility, an aerial poem, a great open wheel in the sky that you can name in your own way: a living, ephemeral, irregular spectacle; but also intelligent.

*

Here, for example, is a circus program, which dates from 1925 and covers four pages of beige paper: the back is faded, there is tape on the inside folds, it has a few traces of rust on the central fold and some little tears on the edges, but it is perfectly legible, all these years later.

In the center, at the top of the page, there is a medallion photograph of Madame Bartolini: she has her arms crossed, her eyebrows raised, and a long scarf around her neck. Her blonde hair swishes around her oval face. Her nose is pointed, her bust leans slightly to the right, her chin is raised a little in the same direction as if her whole face were drawn forward. Madame Bartolini is smiling. She must be around fifty years old; her skin is marked around her eyes—laugh lines—but her eyes have retained an astonishing sense of freshness. They seem to come looking for you after all these years, to enter into the room, jump up the walls, rebound in a funny way to the edge of the photo, and the message is clear: time is in the midst of tearing up her face, bit by bit, but she is not going to give up.

The central medallion photo is overlaid with a banner that says, in large black letters, BARTOLINI CIRCUS and is surrounded by two pieces of information in smaller letters, also in black ink: "30 tigers, 120 acrobats." In the upper left-hand corner, some more information, framed this time: "Founded in 1856." Underneath the

56

medallion there is a phrase in capital letters that announces proudly, in French and English:

LE PLUS GRAND CIRQUE DE L'OCÉAN INDIEN

THE LARGEST CIRCUS IN THE INDIAN OCEAN

Farther down there is a large rectangular photo of the circus floor, a slightly blurred panorama in which you can make out a big audience, a tangible sense of noise and action, kids perched on the shoulders of adults. The floor is round and measures a bit more than thirteen meters. The circus has around a thousand seats: it takes three whole days to set it up and take it down. The tent is filled to the rafters; the laughter of the children rises up and gives life to the tight space that is filled with ropes, poles, and apparatus. Dancers dressed in split skirts reveal their rounded hips, their delicate ankles, and pass by like shadows between the poles.

Inside, in a riot of music and laughter, the artists unfurl the unending ballet of their exploits, their dialogues, and their personalities: Coralis is on the ropes, and Vitalis is on the beam, Igor trains the monkeys, while Hercules tames the tigers . . . You get to meet Anna the balancing act and Olga the drag artist, Régis the tightrope walker and Éliane the woman with the sword . . . You come across Kate Storm's chimpanzees, Saint Cyr's trained mules, Amédéo's elephants, and the Java tigers led by Maia Landwoska. And not to forget the troupe of horsemen and women with such delightful names: Honorine, Apolline, and Rosine . . . A list of wildly eighteenth-century names. When Madame Bartolini needs a name, she searches for it in Choderlos de Laclos or Restif de la Bretonne. Sometimes she opts for a little Molière: Célimène, for example. She opens a book and transposes it immediately onto real life, a constant circulation between the stage and the show, business, exchange, movement, the endless rolling of the novel of life.

As Georges tells me, it is quite likely that these programs were to a large extent fictional. In fact, the circus seems to have had no more than a dozen or so animals and around twenty employees, but Madame Bartolini knows how to expand time and multiply people. In a white, always elegant, outfit, bare arms gloved to the elbow, the body that appears so exuberant highlighted by a long white fur, she smokes cigarettes constantly. She smokes and smokes and smokes; she responds offhandedly to every request, and she smokes, she clouds all of her replies with puffs of white smoke emanating with infinite grace from her long delicate fingers.

— Madame Bartolini, where should we put the apparatus?

— Well, right here, no let's see, over there, wherever you want . . . [*sweeps her hand to the left—a plume of smoke rises from her gloved hands*].

— Madame Bartolini, the manager is complaining he has not been paid.

— Next week I said I will pay everyone. Right, be off with you! [*a little gesture of her wrist, the cigarette throws a few sparks to the right*].

She drinks, she drinks a lot, punch and Campari "con limone e ghiaccio": she "can really hold her drink," says the strongman, who fears her like the plague, but no one has ever seen her drunk. All she has to do is walk into a dressing room and the artists make themselves busy, hurry around, bump into each other, the horsewomen suddenly do their makeup more carefully, the gymnasts do their stretches more methodically, and the jugglers do their exercises as meticulously as possible.

She always has new ideas. It is she who, one morning, takes back from the market a funny-looking teenager of indeterminate origin, his body all long and relaxed, his eyes haggard, his nose sharp, and his skin pale. This kind of walking skeleton will become the "rubber man": his terrible thinness, his gaunt face, and his protruding cheekbones, all of which, accentuated by sumptuous makeup, will make him one of the stars of the circus. Another time it will be an eccentric sailor, hired on the quayside at Les Boutres, that she will transform in a few days into a crazy, chained, and padlocked diver in a box covered with dark velvet at the bottom of an aquarium encircled by three alligators.

She thus manages the daily life of the troupe, advises the costume designer, spurs on the trapeze artists, reprimands the show director, and gives a tongue-lashing to the decorator . . . With her everything is carefully planned, and yet the unexpected is everywhere. She is always prodigiously busy but never does anything. She walks her eccentric and sporting silhouette in the middle of these bronzed people, with their bizarre clothes and curious eyes.

Her passion for classical music is insatiable, unshakable. She wants Mozart for the horses and Monteverdi for the acrobatics. The diver, bound hand and foot and handcuffed, descends into the middle of the crocodiles to the sound of a Haydn quartet. In the confused and disordered agitation of the circus, she infuses everything with a unique rhythm mixed with a strange elegance and an aristocratic benevolence.

In her grand white dresses she improvises the impossible. She transforms a consumptive old monkey into a triumphant gorilla; she turns four smiling children perched on a horse into a spinning carousel. A gray elephant that looks dried-out and thin, with red eyes, its hair worn by rubbing up against its cage, is metamorphosed in a few instants into a great white elephant, a sacred pachyderm come straight from the kingdom of Siam, its robe the color of snow and its eyes the color of honey, its triangular ears deployed like wings! She adapts, she moves things around . . . she modernizes, she modifies . . .

What about the artists' clothes? The leftovers of old clothes that she transforms into saris seeded with flowers, crab-green or shrimp-red kimonos, one-of-a-kind tunics, sumptuous purple dresses where birds run across the branches of the sleeves . . .

The musical instruments? In the midst of the violins and strings, you can pick out some panhandles, the spouts of coffeemakers, pipes . . . a whole ironworks of cymbals and domestic items escaped from the kitchens. They say that one night, on her command, the orchestra musicians took down the gates of the public gardens and transformed them into sistrums and triangles. In the Bartolini Circus nothing goes to waste; everything is created and re-created. She reworks things, renews them, renovates, and switches them around, she transforms—she transposes. She knows all the secrets and the metamorphoses.

All of that incites at once disquiet and wonder: it is after all this mix that characterizes the circus, and it is why it stands alone among the arts.

The audience sometimes scolds the artists, realizing that it's a con trick . . . One evening a magic nautical operetta cobbled together with three extras recruited at the last minute draws a hail of cursing, a storm of protests. Called in as a backup, "Rex the king of the clowns"—an elderly worn-out maniac in a white undershirt and suspenders who looks like a poor devil with silvery features—goes out to a chorus of boos and a hail of rotten mangoes. The audience is terrible! . . . When their discontentment explodes, the most diverse set of objects is thrown from the stands, pebbles from the beach, stones from the mountains, banana-missiles, pineapple-bombs, spiky-feathered live chickens . . . They boo them, they shout them down, accuse them of thievery, rape, of buying drink and not paying for it, of kidnappings!

But the people come back, ten times, twenty times, in a row. When the white elephant act comes out, they have to lift the barricades to keep the crowd penned in.

"As white as snow—only his penis is pink!" the program points out blithely. The line stretches back a hundred meters; an endless murmur rises up on the night of the circus, a burlesque din that has a dizzying effect and is punctuated by men spitting, the piercing cries of women and children's laughter, a procession of feet that trudge through the muddy puddles and the dust of time.

The artists, the dancers, the animals . . . the acrobats . . . the musicians, above all . . . the people hate them, but they cannot do without them. It is their little reserve of life in their rotten existences . . . For deep down inside, the people know that they have only that to live by, that after these wonders, they will assume again in the darkness of the night all the worries of their lives, the weight of their torments, and the despair of their children.

And that is how, every evening, the little Bartolini Circus is transformed into the "Largest Circus in the Indian Ocean."

IN PRAISE OF THE ACROBAT

It is Sunday. A volley of church bells rings out as I wake. The white curtains, the little bedroom eaten up with all my papers, the smell of wax, which the sun that comes in through the window breaks down into specks of dust that smell faintly of resin, gypsum, and pitch.

Like every morning, Georges brings me the newspaper. I tell him how much the Malagasy horoscope delights me. Three calendars rule the lives of the Malagasy people, he explains to me: the official (Gregorian) calendar; the agricultural calendar, linked to the solar cycle that measures out the field work; and the calendar of destiny, which has 355 days. It is the latter, the lunar-solar calendar of Arab origin, that is used by the soothsayers to decide the best time for each activity and to draw up the horoscopes. These people straddle time and stride across the planets.

This morning's horoscope gives me particular delight, so full of advice, as simple as it is wise:

> *Love*: You have to know how to get on with
> things and forget the bad moments.
> *Health*: Tidy your garden well and empty your
> bin. Repair the roof of your house.

But above all, this one, which gets right to the heart of my preoccupations:

Work: Do not neglect the details even if
you don't like the little things.

The Malagasy astrologers, the famous *mpanandro*, are right. Do
not neglect the details. Georges's chest of drawers is in the corner,
waiting for me. I open a drawer . . . I open a second drawer . . .

*

Among the artists of the Bartolini Circus, three stand apart, and they
are always placed at the climax, at the end of the program. These are
the most striking figures, those upon whom the newspapers write the
most detailed articles. Honor where honor is due: Arthur Dai Zong.

Arthur: it is he who is in the first tomb, the one farthest to the right,
against the wall, as if it were seeking to escape from the cemetery.
A little leaping Chinese gymnast, with slender hands and muscular
calves, whose name rings like a gong: Arthur Dai Zong.

Arthur: slanted eyes, pointed nose, his mouth crossed by an indefinable smile ("a kind of Chinese Mona Lisa," Madame Bartolini
says of him). His very long chin has a little beard that he caresses
constantly. But the most striking thing, which is noticed by all those
who know him and comes back like a refrain in the eyewitness
accounts in Madagascar, as in China, are his hands. Arthur's hands
don't stay in one place; they flit around constantly from his chin
to his eyebrow, from a cigarette to the ashtray, they trace in space
innumerable curls that seem to have no end. A knife, a stone, a
pen . . . Arthur's hands are never empty, they can leave nothing in
place, they are always working to move things about, to make them
fly around, to balance them, place them on the edges, in suspense . . .
People say of him that he has wings in place of hands.

Arthur was born south of Peking, in the region of Wuqiao, on
the border between the provinces of Hebei and Shandong. His real
name is Ha Chou, but everyone calls him Arthur: like Maxime, in

changing his country, he changed his name. For over twenty years the Dai Zong family had multiplied its journeys to Madagascar: it was originally his uncle who settled there at the end of the nineteenth century to flee the first Sino-Japanese War. Then it was his father, who arrived in 1905 to, like thousands of other Chinese, build the railroads. Left alone with his mother, the young man grew up with the legend of this traveler father. When he was barely twenty years old, he also left for the Indian Ocean. It was on Mauritius that he was recruited by Madame Bartolini as "cook and acrobat."

You have to know a bit about China to understand. I went there two years ago. I have a wonderful memory of the visit because it is a very beautiful country and also because it was there I met Li-An. Two years ago, then, I made my way there in stages—I left from Tokyo, stopped over in Paris, then went to New York for a conference, and then I transferred to China . . . Wuqiao County . . . the port of Changhzhou . . . the plane, then the train, then increasingly narrow roads, Xiaomachang . . . I carried on, passed through some kind of hole in time coming from New York to a hundred years earlier, in the immense countryside, where the sky seemed to rest on top of the trees. It is there, in the perfume of the rice fields and among the people who speak of the coming harvest, after an hour of walking in darkness on a path of yellow sand, that I found Arthur's track, his imprint, in the middle of the vast plain of northern China.

Bathed in the east by the Bohai Sea and backing onto the Taihang Mountains, Wuqiao is a land of beaches and plateaus, of mountains and vales. The region has been known for millennia for its acrobats: they say that in its villages every family is a troupe in the making. I saw, in a hamlet in Xiaomachang, some graves covered in frescoes dating from the Eastern Wei dynasty. That takes us back to the sixth century before Christ, where you already find girls juggling with plates and boys walking on their hands. Costumed musicians accompany them, with zithers, bells, drums, and wind instruments.

In the center a man dances, a cross balancing on his forehead, while two young people around him imitate the flight of the swallow so that they might squeeze into very narrow rings: the joyous and attentive body transforms itself; it passes, it seems, through the hoops of the species, tumbling and rolling, and becomes wind, dragon, and bird.

All of this to say that it is not to a Chinese person, and especially a native of Wuqiao, that you will be giving lessons in acrobatics. The district registers make reference to a piece of writing by Fan Jingwen, an advisor to the Ming cabinet and himself a native of Wuqiao. Entitled *A Visit to the Garden of the South*, this text describes an equestrian show at the Terrace of the Wind (the southern gate of the city): "Some horses gallop across the floor as fast as lightning. The horsemen adopt all kinds of postures: lying on their backs or on their stomachs, curled up on themselves or simply crouching, on sidesaddle or straddling, their hands holding the horse or in the air, leaping or standing still, their feet touching the ground or at the side of the horse; sometimes they let the reins drop and come out of their stirrups. Just when you think they are going to fall to the ground, they climb back on to the horse with incredible skill."

It is no surprise to find so many horses in these exercises of skill. For the province of Shandong is also the land of Sun Tzu, the author of *The Art of War*. Acrobatics, beneath its festive exterior, is not just entertainment: it is a very special way of being in the world, a form of aerial combat as well as a hidden, secret battle. We should perhaps read in that regard the final pages of Sun Tzu's book, the famous chapter 13, in which he insists on the importance of secret agents and draws up a typology of them . . . In the magical network that he puts in place—the "divine labyrinth"—a special place is reserved for certain spies, who are called "living agents" or "flying agents": underneath a common or even disgraceful outward appearance, these are "nimble, vigorous, tough, and brave men." They may well have a slightly gauche or inoffensive air, but it is they who are sent to collect information at the right time. They have the acrobat's furtive ways and rapidity of execution, the glance and the intrepid nature. In contrast to suicide agents, they return to make their reports following their mission. The paradox is that these sons of peasants, for all their lives attached to the land, have given to the world—in addition to juicy pears and little jujubes with red skin and yellow flesh—the quickest acrobats and the most subtle strategists.

This secret agent side will serve him well later, as we will see. But for the moment Arthur is ahead of the game so far as horse riding goes; he is a flying horseman. In his acts, in a nod to his peasant origins perhaps, he uses a set of agricultural objects—vases, containers, pitchers, cooking pots . . . But he uses them only to make them dance through the air. In the *Jar Act*, for example: "earthenware jars destined to be used to store harvested grain are no longer heavy vases—they fly off his feet and land balanced on the back of his neck." Porcelain, pottery, earthenware, fortified enamel, everything works for him: with every material, he draws on an infinite reservoir of movements that seem to come out of the utensils themselves, suddenly liberated from the tyranny of work and returned to their quivering, leaping, spinning lives . . . On his touch, the tools pick themselves up; the ornaments take on a magical quality.

I carry on flicking through the programs . . . There is not a description for all of Arthur's acts, but their very titles are enough for me to imagine the contours of a swirling landscape that is at once poetic and athletic. As if to signal that he is going to get your own head spinning, Arthur begins often with a *Pagoda*. What is a *Pagoda*? Bowls are seized in his toes and placed on the soles of his feet, he passes them from one leg to the other, hops, the bowls run along the ankles, then go back up to the toe, balancing there, following the sharp notes of an accompanying bamboo flute. The acrobat goes around the circus on his hands. You need to know how to live like that, with your head perched, an oblique look, and an offbeat perspective.

A Pagoda hand balancing act, using bowls and the support of the hand, a Pagoda using bowls with the two swallows in full flight . . . Suddenly, a *Pagodan using a flower basket!* Why is that called a "Pagoda"? Because, like in a pagoda, the rhythm rises regularly, the acts form a chain or build on one another, you move from apparatus to the rings to the ropes to the ladders—and you find yourself, without realizing it, up high, way up high, in the blue of the sky.

Some nights, however, Arthur gets bored of tumbling and pagodas and takes out his bicycle. It is his specialty, his secret weapon: the acrobatic bicycle. Everything that works in cycles and circles propels him along on his joyful journey. Perched in turns on a unicycle, a bicycle, a tricycle, and even a push-bike—there is a whole set of bikes in the Bartolini Circus—he spins like a top and does endless pivots and maneuvers, pirouettes and turns . . .

In the *Act with Bowls on a Unicycle* there he is undulating on a round table: his left foot pedals while his right foot throws bowls, forks, and spoons that fall with uncanny precision in the basket placed on top of his head. Arthur can do anything on the bike: stand still, reverse, pedal backward, drop suddenly under the bike frame, move onto the bracket, and rise up vertically . . . The crowd's eyes never leave him all through his convolutions. Standing on the handlebars, crouching on the wheel guards or pedaling backward, he is at once strength and suppleness, height and inversion. On the ground, on a plank, on a wire, nothing stops this encyclopedist of the velocipede, who unfurls in the round of the circus his living catalog of virtuoso exploits.

The circus round is free; it has no beginning or end. At the end of his act, almost at a halt—arms spread for balance, victory, and saluting—he spins to the right and left in a thousand turns, never tiring, never stopping.

*

The second main attraction of the Circus Bartolini is Axel the tight-rope walker. He is a quite pale and fragile-looking boy. The oldest of the three acrobats is also the most easily influenced: you could bet money that it was Maxime who set him on this journey. Axel, who is the oldest child of a notable family in Mauritius, does not get on well with his father, who is too bourgeois and too serious in his eyes. He likes the circus and poetry, he dreams of becoming an artist or performer. When he meets Maxime, he is immediately fascinated by this ball of energy from a family well below his on the social scale but who derives from that poverty a great surfeit of freedom.

Languid, lanky, a bit effeminate, Axel has a touching sense of grace. But behind his slender appearance, he is a formidable athlete: they say that of the three acrobats, he is the most assiduous trainer and that he can spend a whole evening suspended on his wire prac-ticing an exercise until he is satisfied with it. "Who, if he is normal and of sound mind, walks on a wire or expresses himself in verse?" asks Jean Genet in his marvelous work "Le Funambule," or "The Tightrope Walker." "It is too crazy. Man or woman? A monster, for sure." Indeed.

In the Red Circus his act plunges the audience into a subtle mix of suspense, anguish, and happiness. Axel performs on a thin, taut brass wire, suspended high in the air and held up by two metallic crosses set into the ground. Down below is the arena, the vast stretch of sand. Up above, among the fire and air, Axel must pass through a series of circles, large ropes of braided raffia that are soaked in suet and ignite as he goes through them. He uses a pole to keep his balance; the pole is weighted down at either end with little bags of sand, which adds to and distributes his mass and gives him time to correct his position. He is there, between death and a miracle. Life hangs by a wire, and for once the expression means something. He has *aplomb*, that is for sure. He is a solitary dancer, a flaming wonder.

Toward the middle of his crossing, as several newspapers point out, Axel often has a difficult period: "You will know a bitter time—a kind of hell—" says Genet again (who truly recognized himself in the figure of the tightrope walker), "and it is following this passage through the dark forest that you will rise once more, the master of your art." It's a Dantean spectacle, then. At the middle of his pilgrimage, alone on his wire, Axel looks ahead, then he looks behind: there is no question of making an about-face, as the way back is as far as the one ahead, so you see it is the same, you only have to be hanging there to feel it, to know it, and underneath lies the chasm, the most simple thing in the end would be to let yourself slide into it . . .

The tightrope walker in the middle of his wire is like the swimmer between two shores—a citizen between two countries—at equal distance from both. Lost overseas. Don't think it is so easy to be a child of *l'outre-mer*, the overseas. The continents are no longer in sight, and your reference points and landmarks slip away . . . So, you are left with nothing but a fragile piece of greenery, cut across by the winds. The slightest breeze is to him a storm, the smallest puff of air a frightening whirlwind. Desolation lies in wait for him, the doldrums, fear. The muscles stiffen up; he is a little tired already. He feels the swelling overtake his fingers; stiffness climbs up the length of his calves . . . It would be so easy just to stop there, to crouch down on the wire, go to one side or the other—it doesn't matter which one—crawling . . .

But it is nothing; the best have felt the same. Axel's inspiration is Blondin . . . Jean-François Gravelet, the Great Blondin, the first to cross the Niagara Falls on a cable and who would repeat the exploit several times during the nineteenth century. When Blondin reached the middle of his 335 meters of rope, above the gaping precipice, in a halo of mist rising from the chasm below, he took out a bottle of wine and served himself a pitcher right there, above the abyss! Another time he took out a stove and cooked himself an omelet on the wire. Always at that point in the crossing, there is that moment of horror, to which he chose to respond with humor.

The Great Blondin was to cross waterfalls many times, each time increasing the difficulty of the exploit: once he was blindfolded, another time he had his feet in a bag or his hands in handcuffs . . . It was, of course, all about inventing exploits that were more and more audacious but also about increasingly setting himself apart, confirming with every step the infinite precision of his own person in the surrounding racket.

In doing that, he took along the whole world with him, his friends, his family, his agent . . . In London's Crystal Palace, in 1862, he pushed along at fifty-five meters above the ground a wheelbarrow in which he had put his five-year-old daughter, who, full of smiles, threw great handfuls of rose petals over the crowd below! It was an unreal spectacle, poetic and flowery, a wonderful affirmation of filial love: of course, it was banned right away by the Home Office, which was alerted by the press, which gave forth on the fate of the child. But what can you say to this gentleman who is up there on high as if he were at home?

Blondin's stage was the whole world. We have forgotten it, but the Niagara Falls were for a long time nicknamed the "Blondin Falls": he made the place his own, leaving it free and open for all but the inhabitant of his singular presence. A wire held between air and water, a great rush.

So, Axel sets off again, gently. His hips are back in place, his foot grips more solidly right along the taut wire. His breathing is once again fluid and silent. All of his joints are working, his spine, kneecaps, all the cogs turn, and his thoughts feed through his body, right to his bones. He crosses the chasm, the circles, the fire, and he reemerges on the other side, in the clouds of smoke and a deafening explosion. He smiles. The tightrope walker is an island who remembers the continents and salutes them from afar.

*

I stop for a minute and open the dictionary. The word *acrobat* is from the same family as *microbes*: it comes from the Greek, from *acro* (extremities) and from *bios* (life). The Greek acrobat was the one with the ability to move on tiptoes or on a wire, a pole, or an apparatus: at the extreme. In a word it is the ability to live on points, on edges. Maxime is the perfect example of this: he is stubborn and pointed in the sense of being sharp and refined.

The life of the extremities, the life of the fingers, the lips, the soles of the feet . . . The pride of the toes, the nails, the grace of the eyelashes. It is touch in waves, the word at the tip of the tongue. The hands speak, and the feet trace on the ground a strange calligraphy, as if one were physically posing the question of language.

They often say that the art of the circus is that which consists in arranging all the other arts together. They are constantly straddling, *composing*. They belong to multiple places and disciplines. They have no interest in setting up precise borders to their sovereignty. In every one of these acts there is a certain relationship with knowledge ("one would say that knowledge has found its act," said Valéry about female dancers) and a great science of the multiple. Each one of their steps, every one of their gestures, opens up an in-between space, an alternative idiom, a science of the gaps that can be applied to numerous fields: language, cooking, music, medicine . . .

In the Bartolini Circus the horsewomen, who are the first to make your heart leap, *know* how to jump in many different ways on a walking or stationary horse. They can also kneel down on the saddle, sitting on the soles of their back-to-front feet. Arthur Dai Zong *knew* how to sing with his head held low, with a top spinning on the sole of his left foot and a saber balanced on the sole of his right foot. Axel the tightrope walker *knew* how to ride a bike on a wire and wave a silk scarf. They seem at each turn to pose a question to us: what about you, what kinds of crossings are you capable of?

*

But the most astonishing of this trio is Maxime.

There are those who know how to carry and those who know how to throw. Those who do the bridge and those who do cartwheels. Those who lift up, those who hold, those who launch . . . Specialists in balancing and those skilled in rotation . . . Maxime knows how to do everything; he was hired for precisely that reason. "The possibility of switching roles, carrier, acrobat, joker . . ." I found this phrase in Madame Bartolini's notebooks. She wrote it in haste just after Maxime's audition. It is the first written description that I have found of my grandfather, and I find it suits him well.

On the ground a carrier, observer, or acrobat . . . In the sky he is a high-wire walker, a ropedancer, a trapeze artist. He can replace most of the other artists at short notice. He is what they call, in circus vocabulary, a "joker." A young man, with a pyramid-like frame, a scintillating gymnast.

A sketchbook—perhaps also drawn by the hand of Madame Bartolini—shows him to us in all his talents. Maxime wears a superb ruby-colored costume with black flashes: he is a cherry elf, a Carmelite imp. When the *gardine* opens, the great red velvet curtain that separates the backstage from the arena, a whole range of intense situations and different sensations run through him. He enters into the private space of his attentive flesh, into the country that breathes and pounds beneath his skin . . . fingers-fingers, feet-fists, hands-wrists, hands-elbows, he is already thinking where, when, and how to place each of his supports.

He hits one hand with the other. Magnesia reduces perspiration and improves the grip, but it is also a kind of starting point, with its oxide smell, of a spectacle of white powder where all forms are dissolved. The blood flows, the door opens, and the body speaks. Then it is the joy of being onstage that kicks in.

On this point Madame Bartolini's notebooks are precious and

precise: Maxime is "alive, attentive," he "opens himself up like a corolla to take on the jumps," he also knows how to "close himself up again for protection."

The technical indications state: "alternation between fast and slow tempo."

Body line: "slender, elegant."

Posture: "vigorous."

She notes also the extreme variation of the speeds and the almost musical punctuation of his floor exercises, as shown in this astonishing notation, which is like the directions in a musical score: "Moderate, fast, strong, soft, merry."

There is a fault, however, that is spotted during his practice: "he doesn't like falling into line." On the other hand, he can take part in any combination, sitting, standing, lying down, static or dynamic, in a pyramid, in a group or a column, solo or in a trio . . . The joker's role: I help you to climb up and stay balanced atop the person who carries you. The aim is for you to stand alone, alone against the whole world if you have to. Then I help you to come straight down. I can also help you to come down acrobatically: I carry you, lift you up, throw you and hold you. I throw you into the open space, into the magic of the blue and white canvas sky. I exult you; I catapult you.

When it comes to Maxime's turn, he examines first the protruding bones, the muscular masses, their elasticity, their robustness . . . It is a strange rapport that this body has with itself and all the others. He feels the other bodies, wraps them up, flies above them, with the palm of his hand or the leap of his eye; he recognizes in passing the most solid surfaces for support, the places for strategic positioning, the best bits for taking flight . . . It is for him the great geography of the body.

Hands on the pelvis, hands on the shoulder and the pelvis, hands on the shoulder: the first thing to do is to foresee the various ways of making contact with the other. Then, very quickly, he passes beneath the skin, as it were, detects the veins and the joints. He taps, he climbs up, he gathers himself and takes flight: the most important things take place there, in the gaps.

Can I put my foot here, my hand in that place? Where and when precisely and for how long? In what form is my partner this evening? Will I throw him for a jump, a double jump, or a twist? A good acrobat is first of all a great physiologist: he x-rays his partners' bodies, he crosses them bit by bit, and all of that must be done very quickly, *in an instant*. The eyes, the forehead, the lips, the tongue, the voice, the arms, the legs, the bearing, the color of the face, the salivary glands, the heart, the lungs, the stomach, the arteries and the veins, and the whole nervous system, shivers, heat . . . Everything is important. An internal and external sweep, a complete scanning: he knows the world through his five senses and through one further sense that he possesses. He knows what is going on in the body at all times.

And now you hear the endless drumroll . . . It is the last act, the climax of the show before the final parade: the trapeze. At the end, with all the others worn-out, he is the only one still standing; no one can follow him now. First he crosses his legs, then pulls himself up with his arms: there he is climbing; he is going to seek out the light, the projectors superimposed onto his body. He does the *corde lisse*, the cloud swing; he climbs; he is going back up to the trapeze . . .

The trapeze is a ship: you hear the sound of wood cracking, the ropes sway; you sense a breath of wind. The crossing is about to begin . . . A few moments of silence, two or three swaying movements, he begins with a few passes to test his balance. He does a succession of figures: the *Low Frog, the High Frog* . . . the *Front Stork*, the *Back Stork* . . . All of these animal spirits warm up, get into position, change position . . . he comes out of confusion, he puts things in order. He is synchronous. A tour of the ropes, and then, very smoothly, he continues with some geometrical figures: first the

Right Angle, then the *Square*. The muscles in his arms tighten, but his face belies no trace of exertion. A vertical climb . . . Waiting, stationary. A swing to the front, and there you have it, *The Siren and the Seagull*.

There is in the act the physical engagement with the apparatus, the muscular strength, but there is also something else: rhythm and breathing, a certain way of not being overtaken by the speed and energy he builds up, to be always present at the right pulsation. Balance is a constant disequilibrium, a play of forces and movements. Above all, do not force things. On the contrary, back off . . . . Know-how here lies in letting go: compression of the muscle and detachment of the mind; breathing is everything. It is all in what the French call "détente," which signifies at once impetus and rest. Thus, the body adjusts itself, the leg around the rope, the hand on the bar . . . Suddenly, all the supports fall in just the right places, and in this exactitude lies beauty itself.

Maxime smiles, climbs back up his rope ladder, grips another rope . . . A short rest, and here is the *Hammock* figure. Suspended five meters up, he stretches out between the two ropes nonchalantly. Madame Bartolini plays a little tune on the harpsichord . . . It is by Couperin, a banal sarabande. The audience laughs; they also catch their breath. Quietly, as this goes on, the tent has been transformed into a great cathedral of silence. High above, the flying archangel starts up again: the *Ship*, the *Escape*, the *Flag*, and—a complete reversal—the strange figure of the *Arc of Time*. Finally, the *Airplane* and then, very simply, the *Cross*. He hangs there for several seconds, his arms like two great white wings.

Then, suddenly, he flies into the air.

The dangerous triple turn with twist is Maxime's specialty: in a single movement he passes from one trapeze to another situated a few meters below in the religious silence of a crowd that seems to hang onto his shoulders, arms, and the hollow of his knees. He does three turns in the air in his red costume, looking like a burning wheel. It is a strange moment, where time does not stop—as the common cliché goes—but is instead unfurled in all its wild diversity.

There is a single photograph of Maxime carrying out his famous twist; I found it in Georges's papers. It is a poor-quality photo, with a blurred background and fuzzy composition, his face in motion. But there is something moving in seeing this man alone, thrown into the immensity of a sky of blue canvas, suddenly rendered in the slightly faded darkness of the paper that has been devoured by the years. The photographer must have clicked the shutter shortly after he jumped and, given the speed of reaction of the subject, Maxime was caught—or more precisely, intercepted—at the highest point of his loop, his arms stretched out into the darkness, a bit like the Olympic divers just before they dive. In spite of the poor quality of the photo—or, in fact, because of it—you understand right away the extraordinary graceful strength of this flying madman. He is standing in the darkness, his arms open, his hands reaching for the sky. There it is as if he breaks the circle of his kind, his species, he extracts himself from the cycle, he eclipses himself—and it is like each turn allowed him to cross an infinite number of degrees of freedom. It is a new space-time, threaded by light, carved by matter, an elastic time untrammeled by rules and laws.

*

Maxime the acrobat: a peaceful bird that flies in reverse. When he is not flying, there is no salvation. He has to make himself fly, by means of a long, immense, and reasoned deployment of all the senses. There is nothing predictable in his movements and, at the same time, nothing that has no use. Bird, monkey, fish, plant—he has become unclassifiable. He is the world, a world suddenly knowable through the body, decomposing and recomposing. It is the acrobat's victory.

Thus, he enters into other coordinates of space and time, another state of the body itself. He has his own tempo, a sort of organic music that leads him to the other side of things, their invisible source. He will hold onto that time, which is his own, until his dying day.

On that last point I have a very precise memory. It is toward the end of his life, Maxime is almost seventy years old, but every morning he still does a series of stretching exercises on the floor and a few turns on the wooden bar that is curiously suspended above his front door . . . (So that no one may enter here if they are not in some way acrobatic, that is no doubt what he meant by putting it there.) The memory that I am speaking about—I am five years old—concerns one of the rare conversations I had with him, our knees touching each other gently, on the little bench at the house at Mahajanga, on the other side of the boulevard, facing the sea. I still hear his very distinctive voice, a serious voice, a bit sarcastic. I can smell his cologne and its subtle lemon scent. As I bombard him with questions about the circus, Maxime tells me that at the moment of the dangerous leap, he always closed his eyes.

— All you need is to close your eyes.

— Close your eyes? Up there?

— Absolutely. At the right moment. That allows you to find the trapeze, with the eyes closed, from the inside.

He is not trying to pass on to me a piece of knowledge—he is not interested in that—but at that moment he is extraordinarily jolly and serious. Without stopping on the trapeze, he doubles himself up and mutates, transforms himself, changes weight and speed. He escapes ceaselessly, endlessly coming back to the same point of his own space, with the rope loose, in a sequence that repeats itself many times. And the secret—so he tells me—is so simple that even a child of five years can understand it, before the whole of his adult life tries to make him forget it. The secret is to close the eyes, that is, to substitute all the usual visual markers with a sort of internal vision that is sharp and ruthless. He is a resistance fighter to the core, an indefinable worker who reinvents himself by the day. In him everything is breath, sound, muscle, music, and voice.

Even today in my dreams, I can see him, sitting on his trapeze in the darkness of the hoists and ropes, red among the shadows. He is far away. People say to me that we are separated by dense layers of time, and it would be vain to try to connect with him again. However, he looks at me: then the whole enormous reservoir of things is open again, in every direction.

BOXING BY THE WATERSIDE

That little scent of a flower: that is what she is.

Li-An arrived today on the morning plane. The Olympic Games are over. She has come back with a splendid slice of lemon, from which she takes a big bite: it is only the gold medal for team trials! She is beaming.

The previous week her compatriot Lei Sheng also became an Olympic champion, the third in the history of Chinese fencing. To do so, he faced in the final the Egyptian Alaaeldin Abouelkassem, who is nevertheless the first African to win an Olympic medal for fencing and the man who beat the four-time world champion, the German Peter Joppich, and the reigning world champion, the Italian Andrea Cassara. That can't be bad! There were no Europeans on the podium, the bronze being won by the South Korean Choi Byung-chul . . . "Fencing continues to open up to the world," the morning paper rather soberly concludes.

How's your book coming on, then? Madagascar, that will never work out. Madagascar for people today is a cartoon . . . with palm trees, coconut trees, and loads of animals. Or else it is a brand of dark chocolate! Why are you going to even bother telling them that a brand of dark chocolate is part of the history of France?

Li-An always has little remarks like that, to lift my morale. It is the fencer in her, she crosses swords, spurs me on . . . It is her way of helping me, of telling me that I have to continue searching, looking in front and behind at the same time. Like they do in fencing: you set your markers while advancing and retreating. A game of parry-riposte—she knows what she is talking about . . .

*

I have, however, found something, a major scoop! Right at the back of Georges's chest of drawers . . . Nothing less than a copy of the *New York Times* of 9 December 1924 that dedicates a whole page to . . . Madame Bartolini. We learn there that her real name is Sibylle Aimée de Scarlatti, that she gives herself the title of Countess of Pichon-Janville, and that she is in the United States to negotiate the contract for a tour, which would be the first for the circus in this part of the world. The article's author, a certain Edmund Court, has clearly fallen under her spell:

> She has a large nose, and her blonde hair is slightly faded, but her body gives a sense of breezy elegance in her white, classy outfit—voluptuous and attractive. She speaks lovingly about the animals, about her horse, which crushes her feet but to whom she cannot resist feeding sugar cubes every day, about the cats that she adores, about the stray dogs of New York for whom her hotel bedroom has become a refuge. She states that everyone can be noble, all it takes is to want to be so, and as we were talking about food, she says that she likes only chops and soft-boiled eggs and that sometimes that is all she will have for lunch and dinner. She has left her famous circus on an island in the Indian Ocean, with her acrobats and dancers who await her return impatiently.

The strong man is the first to depart; he leaves to take up a cook's position on a liner heading for Europe. Axel the tightrope walker follows him shortly thereafter and decides to return to Mauritius, his native island. I have to say something here about the extraordinary destiny that awaits him there and which I could write a whole novel on. I believed for a while that Axel was the one at rest in the third tomb: I thought it made sense, the three tombs of the Corniche bringing back to life, as it were, the famous trio of acrobats of the Red Circus. It was a seductive hypothesis.

But there was no truth in that, as I learned through numerous press cuttings that I found in the files of Georges's father. Axel did not die in Madagascar, as he had returned to Mauritius. In a few years he was to go back to his studies (English, Greek, and Latin) and, following many ups and downs, take over again the school founded by his father, the Bhujoharry College, which was to become under his leadership one of the best boys' schools on the island, rivaling even the Royal College of Curepipe. He was also to have a brief but remarkable political career, as he became the mayor of the capital city, Port-Louis, at the beginning of the 1950s. He remains today the one who allowed thousands of young Mauritians to discover the metaphysical poetry of John Donne, Milton's *Paradise Lost*, and Chaucer's *Canterbury Tales*. The young tightrope walker from the Bartolini Circus was therefore to become one of the great figureheads of intellectual and political life in Mauritius . . . There are some remarkable, stormy, tempestuous lives, some that burn with the beauty of fire and which create in turn a desire to live through reading about them.

But for the moment it is the Venus sisters' turn to vanish into thin air: they take with them all the circus whips and, no one knows for what perverse intentions, the dwarf Groseille! This marks the end of the Bordelini soirées. Is it a coincidence that at exactly the same moment administrative headaches begin to rain down on the circus, which has lost the support of Hassan Ali, who is furious for having been left high and dry by the one whom he will refer to from now on only as "the American," refusing until his dying day to pronounce her name. There follows the nonrenewal of the parking permit at the Red Circus, the refusal of entry and access to certain parts of the country for the traveling show, which will continue nevertheless in a much simpler form, before fading away completely near the end of 1925 . . .

As for Madame Bartolini, from that moment on, there is no trace of her. Is it her, under the pseudonym of Sybille-Aimée Bartleby, that one finds at the head of the Bartleby Circus in the 1930s, then working for the prestigious Barnum and Bailey? It is possible, but I can't be sure.

As for Maxime, he does not appear to have been surprised by the turn of events. As a good acrobat, he has the sense of anticipation. As soon as the circus begins its decline, he has already bought a little store on the coast where he sells soap, rice, fabrics, and especially alcohol, which he distills himself in a copper still. "When a starfish loses an arm, it grows back," he likes to say to his clients.

In a few months, profiting from the fame he acquired in the circus, he transforms himself into a skillful merchant. He sells a bit of everything—all his life he will rebel against "specialization," that way of doing only one thing at a time, as if a man had only one hand, one eye, one hemisphere . . . In his store are found bottled sands, basketwork in raffia and *satrana*, or dwarf fan palm leaves, bouquets of dried flowers on palm leaves, rosewood model ships, fossils, and celestite, which he cuts himself to make ornamental stones. He also sells bucrania, those carved ox heads used for tomb decoration. In all it is a whole artisan industry of wood and horns, leather and coral.

Maxime's store is located not far from the Red Circus, in Mahajanga, on the beach at Amborovy. An immense stretch of fine sand, between yellow and light gray: a place of sewers, bushes, trails, mixed with various colors of gravel and land . . . It is not, however, the landscape that interests Maxime so much as its location: Mahajanga was then Madagascar's second busiest port. At the mouth of the Betsiboka, the most important waterway in the country—a river with tumultuous waterfalls, tainted with red due to the considerable quantities of water it churns up—the town is the hub for coastal navigation and is accessible to ships in every season. It is situated at the crossroads of all the maritime routes: Arabia; the east coast of Africa; the Comoros. The Chinese have for centuries sent their ships there: as early as the tenth century, thirteen ships, each one loaded with a thousand men, had sailed across the region and had drafted maps that were far more precise than those of the Europeans and which Marco Polo would still marvel at three centuries later.

At the time Maxime establishes his business, there are four big companies competing with each other for the market: the Messageries Maritimes; the Havraise Péninsulaire; the Chargeurs Réunis, and the Deutsche Ostarikanische Gesellschaft of Hamburg (DOAG). There are also other, smaller operations, such as the steamboats run by French companies like Mantes and Borelli, Americans like Ropes, German like O'Swald or Soost and Brandon, and especially, British companies like Procter Brothers, Porter Aitken, Troucht, Laroque, and Dupuy . . . And not forgetting the Indian dhows. Maxime buys and sells to all these operators. His accounts book, maintained with a certain indifference, is a cave of ink where are aligned multilingual company names and various products in the middle of elliptical scribbling: sardines, polish, perfumes, cotton and linen fabrics, metals and ironwork, flour, sugar, mineral oils, glasswork and crockery, lima beans . . . You would search there in vain for any coherence or a carefully planned business strategy: it is the joyful disorder of the world. The heavy and the light, the dense and the diffuse, rice powder, coffee beans, and tobacco leaves dance across the pages.

What is striking in reading Maxime's accounts book is that he can buy and sell anything and everything: precious stones, fabrics from all over, molasses, cut flowers, food, chemical and petroleum products . . . In the registers of the time, his is described pithily as an "informal business." I can imagine him today—he would be selling electronic goods, with a cell phone attached to his ear working on a deal in Europe and another in Asia, resourceful and determined, exchanging products with the whole world.

Alcohol has an important place in these registers, just as it did in Maxime's life: spirits, rums, tafia, fine wines from Bordeaux . . . He has already a hell of a liking for the bottle, which will only increase with time and not be good for his reputation. Above all, he has a precious possession—how he got his hands on it is a mystery—a large copper still in which he distills the alcohol from fermented fruits and even, when demand is strong, from eau de Cologne. The customs office obviously does not like this: on many occasions he will be chased by its motorboats—the policeman Coquillard was replaced by the customs officer Deschamps, then by a certain Ortolan—who will never succeed in pinning him down. We should say that Maxime knows the region like the back of his hand, the direction of the currents and the winds, and that he has two perfectly streamlined dhows at his disposal.

On 12 July 1928 he very nearly gets himself collared, but he gets away with a charge of escaping the police. The police report, with a touch of unusual lyricism, which says much about the customs officers' admiration for this new Mandrin, brigand of the seas, notes that their boats managed to get within a hundred meters of him but then suddenly: "The wind picked up, almost miraculously, and the suspect, hoisting the sail with exceptional speed, made it to the open sea supported by the arms of Neptune and carried by the wings of Aeolus." They'll never catch him!

The same report is accompanied by two photographs of Maxime's dhows: "two dhows with Greek sails, a square one to the stern, and a pointed one to the aft." What chance do the clapped-out police boats (the Malagasy people call them "chouk chouk boats") have against these wonders come from the depths of time and which seem to obey only the wind and the sun? They are quite simply unbeatable when the dhow sails close to the wind: with the sails in line with the boat and optimizing velocity made good, he flies across the sea . . .

*

During this time what is Arthur doing? He thinks first of trying his chances in a big European circus: China is in fashion in circus arts, it is the era when Chester Kiesling—aka the Great Kingston—also adopts a Chinese costume and, under the name of the "Chinese Puzzle" or the "Human Puzzle," performs a series of contortions and dislocations as well as a stunning variety of balancing acts on his hands. His wife, Marthe Liesling-Debussy, draws on paper the various figures in his act: she is the niece of Claude Debussy, a very beautiful woman (she will be the first Miss Paris). You can still see her drawings of the Chinese Puzzle today, at the Museum of Popular Arts and Traditions, in Paris.

But Europe is very far away, and the journey is expensive . . . Arthur decides, then, to go up to the capital, Antananarivo, to open a boxing school there! He tries briefly to get Maxime to go with him, given he is such a great athlete, but he is tied up already in his business, his dhows and pirogues. Arthur leaves alone for the high plateaus.

On arriving in Antananarivo, the acrobat gets by for a while: he survives first through little jobs—street crier, peanut seller, rickshaw puller . . . In fact, Arthur is looking for a big building, a hangar or depot, to transform it into a gymnasium, which must be big enough to hold fights there and have large windows so that the place can be ventilated. He makes a list of several places that more or less fit the description, but they are expensive. One evening as he returns from a soccer match—he tells the story in a letter to Maxime—his attention is suddenly drawn to a sign in the district of Isoraka: "House for rent" . . . It is a solid, two-story building with a large backyard, big windows, and good parquet flooring. The rent is ridiculously low. A godsend!

Mahaiza manararaotra izao fahamaikana izao mba hananao tany

as it said on the notice, of which Arthur sends a photograph to his friend: "Don't wait around for this chance to own a piece of property!" The deal is concluded the following day. The boxing hall will be set up on the first floor, and Arthur will occupy the second.

Madagascar has many forms of traditional wrestling: the *ringa*, the *moraingy*, or the *savika*, a sort of rite of passage rodeo that pits young Betsileo fighters against zebu cattle, in a sort of barehanded athletic ballet that resembles dance as much as boxing. But the techniques taught by Arthur, while borrowing at times from these indigenous forms, are completely original, as they include Chinese martial arts. In fact, Arthur's techniques are to quickly become quite successful and popular.

The school is called the "School of the Five Styles": the presentation brochure that remains explains that it placed itself under the patronage of a legendary doctor of the time of the Three Kingdoms, the creator of a method of physical education inspired by the movements of five animals—the deer, the monkey, the crane, the bear, and the tiger—and a monk from the temples of Shaolin. The latter, after having witnessed a fight between a bird and a snake on Mount Song, one of the five sacred mountains of China, had developed in the third century a method based on the movements of animals. After the fall of the Han dynasty, China was in an extraordinary state of uproar and confusion in which everyone was trying to take power: in that time of uncertainty it was essential to know how to fight.

Arthur placed himself in this long lineage of masters of warfare. He describes superbly in his book the various types of kicks and punches and the art of the grip, the placement of the hand—long hand, sun, slicing—the techniques of the palm and the fist, detailing successively the combat of eagles with their talons, the praying mantis, monkeys, snakes, tigers, cockerels, dogs . . . Halfway between martial technique and therapeutic gymnastics, Arthur insists a lot on the imitation of physical stances but also on the "state of mind" of the animals . . . For him health comes from combat, style is a question of movement, and animals have minds: it is as simple as that.

Arthur's specialty is "Boxing by the Waterside," which uses blows from the fingers, which are specially hardened by appropriate exercises, and favors the circulation of the blood by "slow and quick, supple and energetic, full and harmonious movements." Arthur recommends it particularly for civil servants and teachers, "the members of the intellectual professions, journalists, teachers, writers, those tied to their seats behind an office desk." Spread the word!

"Boxing by the Waterside" is explained over several pages in the brochure that I now have in front of me: I learn there that it was born in the province of Hubei at the time of the fall of the Ming, when six brothers in arms found refuge in a river gorge . . . From there they observed for a long time the maneuvers of fishermen setting their nets and the extraordinary feats of the fish trying to escape them, which inspired them to create this new discipline. "Just as a fish in water moves easily in all directions, so the expert in 'Boxing by the Waterside' knows no limitations or constraints," states the final page.

The conclusion is sublime: "It is an art of evading and hitting wholly designed as a defense of freedom."

At the School of the Five Styles they practice, above all, "short boxing," which is founded on a great economy of means: three to five displacements and a dozen movements. The postures are low and fluid, the techniques simple and lively. There is very little of the fancy and unrealizable aerial techniques that you see popularized in today's martial arts films. On the other hand, there are many brief sequences and twirling combinations, in which you see the imprint of the former Bartolini acrobat.

Added to that is a whole mysterious and fascinating numerology system. "Boxing of the eighteen curves" lists, for example, eighteen separate sequences, then eighteen combinations of 387 shapes, before closing with a two-man combination. The teaching insists also on the techniques for kicking and falls. Balance is the supreme attribute, the element to be conquered and then overturned to master it better: "You must know how to maintain balance during complex movements but also to break your balance and fall while remaining calm," writes Arthur. For that there is a cardinal method: improve breathing. Respiration is at the center of this strange practice that mixes movements and judgment, the athletic and the zoological, physical culture and poetic observation.

The program of daily exercises is impressive: it is made up of "six forms of training, five uses of the hands, five uses of the elbows, five uses of the arms, six forms of movement and eight uses of the feet." You could say of Arthur that he has three hands and eight fists. He practices a sort of meteor boxing, in which the body is no longer anthropological, clinical, or mechanical but a series of multiplying movements, a set of doors that are in turn open and closed beneath the skin.

The body's well-being, control and discipline, mastery and propulsion of the blows . . . Arthur's style is axed on rolling, or coiling (it is what he calls the "spinning silk system"), and the techniques are executed continuously. The style has more than seventy forms for the bare hands, thirteen with weapons, and a half-dozen training methods.

His strategy: incessant changes in movement of the legs and a variety of jumps, the dominant use of the left hand to surprise the adversary.

His preferred combination: the cannon blow in three directions, followed by a rotation and punctuated by a last swipe of the hand . . .

His secret weapon: in the low horse stance, apply the powerful hand technique.

He takes all of his examples from the slightest acts and movements of daily life: thus are born—or are remade—"Boat Boxing," which came out of the tradition in the province of Zhejiang, of attaching two boats in order to install a platform for fighting; "Lame Boxing," or "Infirm Boxing," inspired by the movements of a handicapped person; "Drunk Man Boxing"; "Way of the Fish Boxing"; and that of the wild goose . . .

These are beautiful systems of combat: you could sit dreaming for hours looking through this brochure, which is at once sensitive and reasoned in its understanding of movements and postures, this repertoire of techniques of admirable grace and precision. Several pages are missing: I would have liked to have known more about the technique of the powerful hand, the eight variants of the "Lost Trail Boxing" (which come, he tells us, from a twelfth-century Chinese novel), or the "Way of the Words Boxing," a style from south China that dates from the end of the Qing dynasty and which emerged from the teachings of a monk and his daughter: a "series of techniques linked to the characters of the Chinese alphabet and combined by the combatant as he would write a sentence."

QUEER-LOOKING SPECIMEN

My horoscope for the day:

> *Work*: Keep your distance from troublemakers and
> put the finishing touches to your projects.

That's what I'm doing, that's what I'm doing . . .

> *Love*: Your amorous relationships are fluid, and
> tender friendships are coming to the fore.

That is so true. Since Li-An's arrival, things are looking up.

> *Health*: Hard to be in good shape when you have slept so little.

That is also so true! The papers from the case and the chest of
drawers have now invaded the whole space, like wild grasses surging
up from the past. Spreading out like ivy on the bed, they literally
prevent me from getting to my mattress. But in spite of the fatigue,
time is pressing: I have to move ahead, I have to continue.

It is today that I begin to dig into the chest that belonged to
Pauline, my grandmother.

When she died, Pauline left a little chest of leather and rope,
with black metal hinges. Inside, I find on large sheets of paper her
course syllabi. For her French class: Montaigne, of course but also
La Fontaine (the greatest, according to her), Rabelais, Ronsard,

La Bruyère, La Rochefoucauld . . . All the big names. I also find a large, well-presented book, bound in brown sheepskin, its title embossed, with flowers in between the letters: *Historiens et chroniquers du Moyen Âge*, Historians and Chroniclers of the Middle Ages, subtitled "Studies, Analyses, and Extracts," which contains the chronicles of Villehardouin, Joinville, Froissart, and Commynes. It is illustrated with numerous etchings, to which time has added a few red marks on the cover.

On another sheet she has copied by hand a Shakespeare sonnet:

> You still shall live—such virtue hath my pen—
> Where breath most breathes, even in the mouths of men.

I myself also take a breath. I look at the mass of documents that awaits me at the bottom of the chest . . . They deal with the whole period after the circus, when his unstoppable social ascent began. I brace myself and dive in . . .

*

While his friend boxes, Maxime takes flight. His business goes from strength to strength. Time passes, the money comes in, and the customs officers tail off. In the eyes of polite society the tightrope walker from the Bartolini Circus is gradually transforming himself into a respectable man: it wouldn't take much for him to become socially acceptable. This progressive change in reputation comes in part from his fortune, which grows steadily—and then allows him to grease the administrators' palms—but also from his participation in several scientific expeditions.

Since the end of the nineteenth century, in fact, with the development of evolutionary theories, the number of maritime expeditions has been increasing rapidly. Certain scientists are convinced that they can find in the oceans the origins of life or at least its most primitive forms. In the depths of the ocean would be found protoplasmic masses in great numbers, forms of early life from which are per-haps descended all living organisms. Perhaps life did not so much descend as rise or escape in great numbers from the seas to populate the land and the skies. The secret of life, they say, was to be found in the overseas regions, deep in the oceans.

In the great scientific competition to discover the primitive forms of life, the Indian Ocean is particularly coveted. Extending from the south of Asia to Antarctica and from East Africa to Australia, it accounts in fact for no less than one-fifth of the world's seas. More-over, it is connected on one side to the Pacific Ocean, through the passages around the Malaysian archipelago, and on the other to the Atlantic Ocean, by Africa and the Suez Canal. Finally, it extends to the Arabian Sea (the Red Sea, the Gulf of Aden, the Persian Gulf) as well as the Bay of Bengal and the Andaman Sea. Thus flow into it waters from the Zambeze, the Tigris and the Euphrates, the Indus and the Ganges, and through the River Irrawady climbs the waters that stretch back over the vast central plain of Burma, right up to the Chinese border. For the scientists, then, it is a veritable mine, of water and salt, fish and rocks, seaweed, coral—a submarine repos-itory. It is a vast stretch of water that at its surface penetrates land and, in its depths, pierces time.

Maxime is very much in demand by these explorers of the hidden depths, at first for his skills as a diver—his monstrous rib cage is a wonder in itself—but also for his knowledge of the winds and currents. Maxime knows the language of the ocean and the sky, the thousand tricks of the air, the ruses of the local climate. He reads and interprets objects, the color of the ocean, and trees. He knows, for example—it was he who taught me—that when the sand in an hourglass does not flow well, that means it will rain. He sees in the shapes of clouds the routes of hurricanes and the approaching winds. Many years later, just before his death, it was again he who explained it to me—with a perfect memory and an uncanny precision in the details—the great systems of currents that cross the Indian Ocean: the one that goes in a clockwise direction and drains the currents from south of the equator and Western Australia; and the other, the Monsoon Drift, that varies with the seasons. Twists and turns, whirlwinds hold no secrets for him. He narrows his eyes for a moment and remembers . . . At almost seventy years of age he forgot nothing of the current of Somalia or that of Mozambique. His eyes light up still when he talks of the warm waters of the famous Agulhas Current that, when it meets the cold currents from the west, gives rise to the highest waves in the world.

But Maxime does not content himself with diving and seeing. He also *transcribes*. No one knows the origins of this passion of his for drawing, which seems to have emerged at the beginning of the 1930s: he had very little schooling and certainly none in the fine arts. Perhaps it is the influence of that young musician, Pauline Nuñes, who is an increasingly regular visitor to his store and who loves the piano, books, and painting? Maybe it is quite simply that he sensed a business opportunity, conscious of the needs of the scientists crossing the region. Color photographs were still rare at the time, and there was a need for watercolor artists on deck to catch the colors and hues of the fish.

Without a picture of the animal drawn on the spot, it is impossible to describe and therefore classify it. So, with paintbrush, sponges, cotton, and a rag, there he is trying his hand at sketching and then at wash drawing. I have before me the unlikely equipment that he uses for the sketches: the paintbrushes are made of chicken feathers or goat hair; the pigments are all natural, made from plants or shells. Here and there, there are dashes of ink or watercolor. He uses his own saliva as a binder. He spends long hours on the deck of the boat, offers at first his services for free, then makes them pay, at increasingly high rates as his technique improves and his talent is recognized.

Sometimes he restarts two or three times on the same fish, until he is happy with the outlines and the color is just right. When evening comes, he arranges the drawings in pairs and places those that the scientists did not want in a large cardboard folder wrapped in pieces of string. It is this large folder that I now have before me, saved from all the successive house removals of Georges's father. On each drawing is carefully detailed the place it was taken (often the Ramada Islands or the Mitsio Islands) as well as the name of the fish in question and its measurements, at the bottom right-hand corner, in pencil.

There remain, therefore, a few pages of this marine encyclopedia, and I have them here, in front of my eyes. What I see is a whole bestiary, a whole *pesciary*, as it were: red carp, tropical sea bream, flying swordfish, turtles, yellow tuna, dogtooth tuna, black marlin, and striped marlin. All shapes and sizes are there: from the tiny goby fish to giant, arborescent sea fans, moray eels as long as ribbons, and huge blue rays. The fish are most often caught alone, immobilized in the whiteness of the paper, but there are also several sketches in which Maxime draws them in groups, schools of narwhals and triggerfish, groups of fusilier fish along with little barracudas. On one of them there is a splendid ballet of silver anchovies.

The annotation on each picture is precise, careful, and concise: you can clearly distinguish each species. A simple glance in passing is like leafing through the underwater world and initiates you into its plural, infinitely colored panache. It is a pleasure to read it, when the colors rush into each other and the words correspond precisely to the broad palette of the eye. Yes, the shark can be silvertip or blacktip, hammerhead or guitar. Yes, the rays cross the whole area of the earth and the sky, eagle rays and leopard rays, great manta rays and mobula rays . . . One learns also that there are all sorts of groupings and professions in this enormous industry of the deep: parrotfish and scorpion fish, angelfish and butterflies, lionfish and surgeonfish, fusilier fish and demoiselles, clownfish, dancers, and captains! . . . From time to time, annotated by hand, a few mysterious inhabitants pass like branches, like those juvenile fish or these nudibranch fish.

Maxime's style is perhaps not that of a great artist, but it is assured, dynamic, detailed, and astonishingly varied in its use of colors. It is no surprise that the scientists fight over his drawings: these are not runny or decorative watercolors, and Maxime does not paint to make something pretty, but there is a prodigious precision in the execution of his brushstrokes. He concentrates for a long time, then he draws very quickly: he has a predilection for fish with bright silver bodies—flat, lively, slender, their very bodies say it, they are traveler fish. Evidently, he particularly likes the moray eel, no doubt because it moves in waves and sends out from time to time an electric discharge. He delights also in the dance of the sea anemones, those underwater vahines carried by the fluxes and refluxes of the tides, and sketches many times the dragonfish, a sort of fish seaweed that no one really knows if it is mineral, vegetable, or aqueous. Maxime says that it is the sea personified, floating, rippling, undulating . . . Finally, he excels in painting the skipjacks, with their elongated heads and split mouths, blue jackfish that come from the deep and bring to the surface the violet jewels of the overseas regions, the red-and-pink snappers, whose facial features make you think of the makeup of the Japanese Noh theater.

Fish are like a series of darting enigmas, carrying all the colors caressed by light and, at the same time, are lively arrows from the dark. It is life thrown into the deep and the silence of dark meditation. Is that, therefore, what life is? This silence, this obscurity of marine life, this kind of ferocity at the end of pincers and claws? Maxime dives whenever he can and goes to rejoin the ultramarine world, its depth, weightiness, and paradoxical delicacy. He gets to know the lobsters, the sardines; like them, his eyes are also alive, his gills light.

*

In these fish-filled waters, for millennia studded with the passage of these unknown species, a modern-day Saint Peter can still bring in a miraculous catch. In December 1938 it is in these waters that a South African fisherman, Hendrik Goosen, caught in his boat's nets a fish that was impossible to identify. He thought initially it might be a grouper, but a grouper has small eyes and scales. The fish in question weighed nearly sixty kilos and was one and a half meters long, covered with three sets of scales, and had a powerful jaw equipped with terrifying teeth. Born out of the rock, it seemed made for combat. Its scales were a mix of brown and blue, and when it was turned over on the boat's deck, the scales were a light mauve color and sparkled with iridescent flashes.

It is that bluish glow that attracted the eye of Marjorie Courtenay-Latimer, a curator at the Museum of East London, in South Africa, in the middle of a pile of rays and sharks. This unknown fish, whose fins resemble the beginnings of limbs, intrigues her enormously. It is neither beautiful nor ugly; its scales are of the same deep and changing blue that you see in the ocean. It looks like it is millions of years old. It is.

The research reveals, in fact, that it is an extremely rare species that existed before the dinosaurs and was believed to be extinct for sixty million years. Not only is its skeleton partially made of bone, but through the triple density of the scales (which the first witnesses describe as being like a suit of armor made of steel plates), under the spiny fins that are spiky like arrows, there is a pocket of air that is like a lung, which gives it a completely unique place on the tree of life. What this Nereid brought back from the bottom of the oceans, in the retinue of sharks and Poseidon, is that which the whole world will know soon by the name of the coelacanth. In other words, it is the "living fossil," the ancestor of land vertebrates, the famous missing link.

On its skin there are spots, curves, hoops, notches of white marble. Its tail is strange, unique in the world; it has three lobes, like the bay windows of Gothic churches, the arches of medieval abbeys or the windows of Venetian windows, as if everything that spans the abyss of time had to be a multiple of three and spread out like a rose.

There is a letter from Marjorie Courtenay-Latimer to Maxime Ferrier, which tells us of his excellent reputation as a sketch artist before the Second World War. In this letter the curator of the Museum of East London informs the illustrator of the Malagasy seas of the discovery of a strange fish, "the most queer-looking specimen," as she puts it. "I have drawn a very rough sketch but am in hopes you will be able to draw a better one." There follows an invitation to meet her at the mouth of the River Chalumna, where the fish was caught, so that she can take it to the taxidermist in order to have a portrait drawn of the mysterious specimen. The letter, written on the museum letterhead, is dated 24 December 1938, Christmas Eve, two days after the capture of the "queer-looking specimen," when Marjorie Courtenay-Latimer did not yet know that she had just made a discovery that would revolutionize the history of paleontology.

Maxime will therefore take himself to South Africa and sketch the first drawing in color of the famous prehistoric fish. As for Marjorie Courtenay-Latimer, she will pass the rest of her life in her little South African museum, collecting fish, stones, feathers, and shells. Toward the end of her life, she will write a book on flowers. She will not ever marry and will die at the age of ninety-seven years old, on 17 May 2004.

*

Since then, new species of coelacanth have been discovered, off the coast of Madagascar, in the Comoros archipelago, and around the coasts of Indonesia. No serious ichthyologist thinks today that the *Latimeria chalumnae*—that is its scientific name—is the ancestor of the amphibians or the missing intermediary between fish and humans. It remains, however, the most important zoological discovery of the twentieth century. In all likelihood Maxime would never have known that he had had the honor of sketching on paper the features of a fish that had survived in the depths of time for millions of years. For him the coelacanth was probably a fish like any other: fishermen catch them every year in their nets. In the corner of the sheet, bottom right, Maxime wrote the name of the fish, but in Comorian: *Kombessa*.

*

Maxime and Arthur lived all their lives *outre-mer*, overseas. A whole life under and beyond the sea. They are there, perched, at the edges. They are aquatic beings, their lives unfold in tributaries, currents of corals and reeds. They are almost always at the same place, and at the same time they travel abundantly. As soon as they can, they grab a boat and take to the seas. Boxers, divers, it is not the destination that is important to them but the crossing itself, in its fury, in its sweetness. It is the casting off, the movement that pushes them, the mad trajectory of the hand.

They retain at all times an astonishing capacity for opening up and bifurcating into new things, new ways. They are like the sea that endlessly tracks back on itself and, in the same infinite movement, carries you far away. In order to follow them, you have to proceed by resumptions, stoppages, gaps . . . In accompanying them in this manner all the way along their meanderings, I discover one thing: the frontier condition of every human being. Even when they stay their whole lives in a single, same country, humans are always about frontiers and passages, molded by limits.

Like the coral, the lives of men bristle with crests and bumps, are cut by mysterious hollows, and crossed by silky bodies, living forms, backward returns and delicate translations. And like the coral, currents cut across our words, our speech, our utterances.

MIXED-RACE MONTAIGNE

— I found this in Pauline's old chest.

— Let me see! What is it? *La Relation de l'île imaginaire*, The Story of the Imaginary Island . . .

— Yes. Yes, the island was already firing the dreams of Mademoiselle de Monpensier. She writes about it in this book.

— Mademoiselle de Monpensier? Who is she?

— The cousin of Louis XIV. The richest and most titled European princess of her time, the wealthiest heiress in the kingdom of France. The first princess by blood, the first peeress, and the first mademoiselle of France . . . Or if you prefer, the granddaughter of Henri, duke of Montpensier, and of Henriette Catherine, duchess of Joyeuse.

— Duchess of Joyeuse, of Joyous?

— Yes, you couldn't make it up! And do you know the name they gave to Madagascar in the travel writings of the Enlightenment?

— No, what was it?

— L'Île Heureuse, the Happy Island.

*

All of these years overflow with an intense happiness. Maxime loves every minute of it. Just like a fish, he constantly has the sea around him. Business is good, he buys some new boats, and for fishing with a net, he buys an outrigger canoe. His destiny is carried away by the feluccas and the dhows, his life is an open sail, a navigation. *Aria aperta.*

Just as much as the fish, the birds bring great joy to him. He can spend whole days looking at sparrows skipping along the path: they have light, delicate lives, lives as ignored as his own. From one stone to another they leap: suddenly, one of them launches itself into the foliage for a love parade, an amorous acrobat. At other times, on the row of stones that lines the boulevard, you can see him, motionless, watching the eagles from the neighboring forest that soar in circles overhead.

Every evening he comes to sit at the foot of the famous baobab tree on the Poincaré Square. The tree is more than seven hundred years old and protects the seafront with its twenty-one-meter circumference. It is the great baobab that stands at the beginning of the boulevard, massive, elegant, imposing, facing the sea directly: according to the legend, all the birds of Madagascar meet up there regularly. The people of Mahajanga head there too, near the end of the day, in the middle of the flower and peanut sellers. The old Malagasy people teach the young to distinguish between the song of the blue coua bird and the singing of the roller bird: these are great erudite and musical discussions! From time to time the sickle-shaped beak of a vanga bird snatches up a frog or a lizard.

In a corner of the foliage Maxime has spotted a little fody, those migratory birds whose plumage goes bright red in mating season. It so happens that destiny has brought him his own bird, with a marvelous song and soft and graceful plumage: she goes by the name of Pauline.

*

No one on earth remembers where or when Maxime Ferrier and Pauline Nuñes met for the first time. It was a meeting that might well not have taken place—he is a womanizing adventurer with loose morals, and she a discreet, educated, reserved young woman. Like all of the really important events, the meeting was unlikely and yet inevitable, an incalculable landmark, a star on the map of time. *Reserved*: the slightly somber, iridescent patina of this adjective suits her well. Pauline has the depth and tenderness of a wine cellar. You could say that she has for years been kept in reserve, kept away from the great rumblings of the world, preserved. It is like she has been sieved or filtered through time itself in the singular perspective of this meeting . . . Maxime, a fine connoisseur of wines and spirits and a great distiller before the Eternal, has no doubts.

One day or another, perhaps in a shop in town, Maxime noticed Pauline. Or maybe it was Pauline who saw him. But no, Pauline notices no one; she is far too serious for that. "Serious like the pope" is the expression that people always use when talking about her, for she is serious and Catholic. All of her family comes from Goa, a Portuguese colony in India, the town of Saint Francis Xavier. Pauline was born in Madagascar, but she has the look of Goa: she is Indian in her skin and profile, a beautiful dark-copper color with golden flashes. Her nose is long and fine, as if traced in charcoal; her features and eyebrows are slender, sketched in pencil. She has beautiful, shining lips with a light color. Her hands are long and well-groomed, her fingers slim: at first glance, if you can think of anything other than her big, wonderfully dark eyes, you know that you are face to face with a pianist.

Like Goa, Pauline is Catholic, obstinately so. Someone should one day write the history of this branch of Christianity, bronzed, adventurous, and metaphysical, its sublime architectural flair (Goa, that festival of churches), its hero Xavier, that visionary born in Europe, who wandered as far as Japan and came to die off the coast of China, and all those travelers dispersed between the East and the West, caught in the great scattering of the world. Even in death, they are between those worlds: the body of Francis Xavier rests today in the Jesuit Church of Goa—a silver coffin placed on a marble stand—while, since 1614, his right arm is in a reliquary in the Church of the Gesù, in Rome. Thus, he rests, between the Rome of the West and its counterpart in the East. A book written by a contemporary novelist retraces his travels right to the threshold of the Rising Sun: it is entitled, *L'Extrêmité du monde*, The World's End. It is a good title that speaks of the limits to which certain people fearlessly proceed.

Before Goa, Pauline's family came perhaps from Bombay. Others say it was Lisbon, where a street still has the name of a hypothetical and indisputable ancestor, who went by the common name of Nuñes. In fact, like Goa, Pauline is of mixed origins: a bit of Portuguese, a bit of Indian, a bit of Spanish perhaps . . . in Mahajanga they say that she is "a mixed guinea pig," like all the people whose mixed heritage is so ancient and so fully blended that you no longer really know where they come from; they oscillate there between the multiple song of their veins and the resources of their two or three cultures, they place themselves at the threshold of each tradition like so many mocking sentinels—what happens to their people is happening now to all of the people of the world.

Hers was a large family of tailors and musicians who, in Goa, prospered in the silk trade and then, at the start of the century, left for Madagascar in the hope of making their fortune there. In the east of the country they found a Malagasy *Bombyx* of a particular species, a wild silkworm living in the small branches of the tapia tree. They fed these caterpillars with large quantities of mulberry leaves, and they produced a brown silk that was very solid and had a unique look and which was particularly in demand for funerals. Then comes the weaving, spinning, and dyeing—all is done by hand and with great skill. The Nuñeses also make lace and raffia and very elegant straw hats to rival the Panama hats of Central America. They work the whole day, with all their energy and every fiber—raffia fibers, palm bark, and fan palm spindles.

Pauline is one of those women who attract everyone's attention right away: slender, holding her head in a majestic way, she has what they call "maintien," or bearing (Maxime used the same word to describe his position on the trapeze: "you need style, you know, *bearing*"). Every day, at the break of morning and the end of the afternoon, she passes by the boulevard. The young guys look out for her toward the Pointe du Sable . . .

There she is, she always arrives slowly; it is like seeing the top of a mast behind a rock—soon the sail will appear. In the twilight on the boulevard she shimmers like an apparition. She passes, regally, surrounded by her female cousins, sisters, and aunts . . . A pulsating gynoecium crosses the boulevard and walks back up it slowly, along the seafront, chatting joyfully up to the Quai aux Boutres. They are beautiful, they are young, and together they are like laughing flowers with their pistils swaying in the evening air. Pauline is radiant—the beauty of the white cloth on her Indian hemp skin. Her body tilts and stretches like one of the pirogues that sail along the coast. You hear her coming from afar: everyone knows it; it is Pauline who is coming when you hear a humming sound, she hums the whole time, poems, operas, Malagasy songs mixed with old French love songs . . .

Merle, merle, joyeux merle,
Ton bec jaune est une fleur,
Ton oeil noir est une perle,
Merle, merle, oiseau siffleur.

Blackbird, blackbird, joyful blackbird,
Your yellow beak is a flower,
Your black eye is a pearl,
Blackbird, blackbird, whistling bird.

She is not very tall, but the low-cut neck of her blouse shows a slender neck, and her slow, elegant walk does the rest. The people of Mahajanga say of her that she has the walk of a zebu with perfect hooves: the tracks left by the front hooves are followed naturally by those behind. As she passes in the morning, everything changes, everything grows more beautiful. The flowers rise up, the sun grows stronger. At the end of the day, on the other hand, after her the temperature freshens, the air is sharper. It is as if her walks are cuts on the fabric of the days: Pauline frames the days, brings them into sharp relief, exfoliates them. She is a landmark on the contour of the evening.

*

Then, from the first breath of nighttime, there is music. There is the father, Francis, the leader of the orchestra; the mother, Ascension, who has a superb voice; Aunt Émilia on the violin; and Uncle Pierre on the trumpet. The sisters make up the choirs; the girl cousins sing the hymns. Pauline is the youngest: she is on the piano. All of this merry crowd comes together in a Mahajanga hotel-restaurant run by the aunt, Chez Nuñes, which was to become over the years Chez Nénesse, then the Nouvel Hôtel, 13 rue Henri-Palu, not far from the town's Grand Market. Late into the night the musical notes fly around, and the young people from the town come to dance. You hear whispers and promises uttered in the shadows of the terrace, under the bougainvillea trees. Maybe it was there that they met, Maxime and Pauline, in the midst of the sharp notes, the quavers, the double-quavers, and the sighs and silences of the nights with their dotted rhythms . . .

According to the seasons, the group grows from three to five, six, seven, and sometimes even twelve people: a veritable musical flotilla. A group comes together, randomly, sometimes a trio, sometimes a quintet, between a dance and a concerto. On the program you have jazz, beguine, tango, rumba . . . The rhythms from Europe or elsewhere, which travel by boat or by radio, are quickly taken up and transformed, played on local guitars, drums, and the *valiha* . . . They replay the hits of Louis Armstrong, who has just hit the big-time in Chicago with the famous Hot Five, and the names of Johnny Dodds, Kid Ory, and Johnny St. Cyr swing through the brass and over the piano keys. There are also the standards of Fletcher Henderson and his Orchestra, such as "Carolina Stomp," from time to time a little detour through "Lucy Long" or Blanche Calloway, but it is Armstrong who has the lion's share, with "West End Blues" and "Tight like This," or hits with their vowels flying and their dentals dancing: "Georgia Grind," "Heebie Jeebies," and "Cornet Chop Suey."

Aunt Émilia plays along grudgingly. She plays the violin like no other but prefers waltzes to jazz. If pushed, she will play the tango and the paso doble. However, there is already a name going around of a Malagasy born in the United States who is writing some of the all-time classics of jazz: "In the Mood," "Ain't Misbehavin'" . . . He is called Andriamanantena Razafinkarefo, one of those clear and vocalic names that sing the generosity of the Big Island, with its delicate pronunciation. The American jazzmen, with their genius for abbreviation and syncopation, will call him Andy Razaf. When you hear the first notes of "Honeysuckle Rose" or "Black and Blue" and begin to hum their words, think about Andy Razaf—it was he who wrote them.

Soon it will be the music of Xavier Cugat that will be played, that native of Barcelona who emigrated to Cuba, then to New York, before returning to die in his native Catalonia. The musicians of the Nouvel Hôtel like these migrant, hybrid musical styles, these melodies born of the sound of the world itself. They are but a few émigrés lost in a corner of Mozambique, but they have already understood everything.

Maxime does not play any instrument, but he likes to whistle. He whistles to imitate the birds but also to attract the attention of the girls, which Pauline does not like, and she tells him so . . . He sometimes accompanies a few tunes with a whistling solo, but the two names from the orchestra that have remained in the local memory are those of Uncle Pierre, who plays the cornet and the trumpet (so passionately that his trumpet, a few people recall, left a mark on his upper lip, like a brass seal on the red flesh), and of Pauline, sitting upright and arched, on the piano. There, like on the boulevard, she is in permanent movement. Her bust does not move, but her hands are alive and slender: they say that when they see her play, she makes the spiders dance to her arpeggios. Her forearm and wrist are relaxed. The arch of her hand extends into her arched fingers and brings to life her playing, which is distinct, clear, and balanced. She improvises often, passes from the popular to the classical, pays little heed to categories: in the moment all of that turns around in the ear, music, dance, vibration . . . Every passerby with even the slightest musical inclination feels immediately their body reacting to the music, and every Saturday night the Nouvel Hôtel is full to the rafters.

To all of that is added the radiant physical presence of Pauline Nuñes. The daughter and granddaughter of tailors, she wears the finest fabrics: crepes, cocoons, and pongees wrap discreetly around her slender body and accentuate her fluid walk, her mischievous look. Under the fabric, however, things are happening . . . Her hips are two bombs, her breasts are two shells, her sex is a pink secret, explosive, one imagines, a mine of pleasures. Above all, she has a beautiful smell, a family secret that she will pass on to her children, a well-guarded combination of ointments and balms, an intoxicating legacy. Like her music, her perfume has high and low notes, sharp and swirling around the shoulders, more serious and arousing as you approach the throat and the opening of her cleavage.

On Saturday nights the party rocks until dawn . . . And on Sunday mornings all the family are at Mass, with Pauline at the front. During the week, all day long, she keeps under her velvet fist an armada of Malagasy, Portuguese, and Indian tailors. The fabrics that come out of the Nuñeses' workshops are known for their suppleness and solidity. She also gives classes in English and French, every evening from seven until nine o'clock. The rest of the time she dances her elliptical shapes all along the boulevard.

*

It is at the Nouvel Hôtel that Maxime and Pauline will see each other at the beginning, at first sporadically, then with increasing regularity. It is their musical den; they know they can find each other there every night. However, the first encounters are difficult, tense, mocking, and not without prejudices. One cannot imagine two more opposite temperaments: Maxime is a ladies' man, forever flirting with the girls. Who is this pianist, and who does she think she is with her airs and graces? Pauline is the soul of modesty and discretion. She hates raucous laughter, the guttural outbursts that signal the outpouring of general, cocksure stupidity. She knows that this is not the case with Maxime, but all the same, he hangs out with some characters, this zebra just escaped from the circus . . . She is a sensitive plant, a liana; he freely treats people like they are nothing. He is a storm, a typhoon. She is a flower; flower and patience.

So, they regularly cross swords. For the first time in his life Maxime is awkward, unsure. Ladies' man that he is, this time it is he who lets himself be caught in this trap of taut silk and swinging music.

He wants everything, right away. She concedes nothing.

If she is cautious? He gets mad . . .

He shakes, he gets wild . . . She grouches and gets haughty.

He speaks to her impolitely, hurtful and insolent. She gives him a look that cuts through him and refuses to be impolite back to him, speaking even more formally, to make him feel shame . . .

Their dialogue crackles, vibrates like a farmyard fence, like a fishing net stretched across the seas. He calls her a piano tinkler, and she calls him an old sea dog. He nicknames her the "old boor," and she names him the "bandit": they add on adjectives, looking for the rare and the precise, regaling each other in the dictionaries. It is a variation of the *hainteny*, those Malagasy verbal jousts that, at the time, interest no one, apart from that elegant young man Jean Paulhan, who published a collection of them in 1913, at the age of twenty-seven, for the great pleasure of another young man, Guillaume Apollinaire, who said he read them "slowly and fruitfully."

The tone rises, each one in its turn climbs up the verbal coconut tree by holding on to the notches already carved by the other:

— let the caiman snatch you up! she says to him.

— let your femur be broken by a falling tree! he strikes back.

She says to him that he is beautiful like Andriamihaja, the lover of Queen Ranavalona, and that like him, he will end up murdered and his body eaten by dogs. The words thus pass from one mouth to the other, like throwing a rope, like the canoe that goes from one shore to the other, like the monkey that perches on the highest branches. Soon there remain only themselves and the lemur who can follow them, branch by branch, on the journey of their shared invective—but these terrible verbal jousts, which liven up the end of the night at the Nouvel Hôtel, are the first forms of love, and they know it well.

Like all shy people, Pauline has moments of unexpected audacity. One day, when Maxime went to the Nuñeses' stores to have made a bespoke suit, she has his measurements taken by an assistant and then asks him a question out of the blue:

— Where do you wear them?

He is taken aback, thinks he does not understand but knows he does and yet doesn't. He stutters and stammers . . .

— What . . . what . . . What do you mean?

— *The jewels*, sir. To the left or right? It is for the crotch for the pants. I didn't know it was so easy to throw off an acrobat . . .

She smiles, a bit embarrassed by her own audacity. It is true that love beautifies. Everyone has heard talk of this quarrelsome and charming acrobat, and Pauline herself—who never, it seems, attended the circus—has seen photos of him in the newspapers. There is also sexual attraction itself, that is for sure. How could you resist this artist of levitation? He has a way of turning up there in space, a sense of rhythm, of vibration that suggests other rhythms . . . That's him, the strong guy on the ropes, the big man on the trapeze!

L'Intripido senza rivale nel trapezo

as Madame Bartolini would say . . . The unrivaled daredevil of the trapeze . . . He is—how to put it? . . . *Ascensationnel*, or "Ascentsational." It is Pauline herself who invents the word, in one of her early letters. She has imagination and dreams of another kind of acrobatics . . . She has seen, on her Sunday rickshaw trips, just after Mass, the statues that decorate the tombs of certain Sakalava hereditary chiefs along the western coast: with swollen sexes and prominent breasts, they are coupled in the most unexpectedly acrobatic poses. She sees herself as a beautiful young girl straddling the dolphins, seahorses, and other marine animals. Even at Mass, when the Host arrives, she waits for God with a sensual kind of pleasure.

Like all musicians, Pauline is acutely aware of situations. She knows well that this man, still young, who orders from her only the best suits, alpaca for the lighter tones and merino for the colors, has already had a turbulent life. She guesses that he is acquiring himself a reputation—if not a way of behaving and conducting himself—by clothing himself in the finest fabrics of the town. She knows that he is building, a little away from the coast, on an island at the bend of the river, an estate called "Anfelana" and that the town's notables, for a long time wary of this acrobat of uncertain race, are now welcoming him to their tables and asking him to take them hunting for caiman.

However, Maxime's adversaries always describe him as nasty and unstable. What a bad character! He is a *Beloha*, as they say here, strong headed. In the first letter that she writes to Maxime (at least the first that I have been able to find), Pauline says to him that he is like Montaigne: "shameful, insolent, chaste, lustful, talkative, taciturn, hardworking, delicate, ingenious, stupid, desolate, easygoing, mendacious, honest, knowing, ignorant and liberal, and greedy and generous." Maxime left school to join a circus, which is to say he is not what they call a cultured man. As regards literature, he knows only the Bible, which he reads and rereads endlessly all through his life. He knows nothing of this "nasty man."

However, he delights in that cascade of epithets. He will learn it by heart and, to thank Pauline for this discovery, sings to her from the following day an old Creole song:

Mon papa moutardié, mon monmon bingali
amoin minm batar moutardié, mi boir dolo ann kèr fatak

It is in Reunionese Creole, not that from Mauritius or Madagascar. Maxime is a skillful negotiator; he speaks all of the languages of the region. He translates the couplet for her:

My father is a weaverbird, my mother is a zebra finch,
I am a crossbred weaverbird, I drink water
from the hollow of Guinea Grass

It is a *maloya*, an ancient slave song, he tells her. Pauline tells him that Montaigne was one of the first Frenchmen to criticize slavery:

she is struck by that coincidence. She is also moved by the simple and profound poetry of this couplet.

The weaverbird has a bright-yellow plumage (thus its Creole name of *moutardier*, or mustard bird). The zebra finch is brown in color, the back an orangey red close to a wine color, a white mark underlines its eye. The two would go superbly together, Pauline had never thought about it. And she suddenly understands that this man has just entered her life.

*

Now it is the wild joy of their encounter. Every evening they bicker gently on the terrace of the Nouvel Hôtel. She plays him some piano or recites poems for him; he sings some old Creole love songs from Mauritius or some Malagasy songs. She speaks to him about Cézanne and Picasso, whom a Reunionese art dealer, Ambroise Vollard, had just introduced to Europe. He describes to her the wonderful fish and the dangerous caiman: every evening it is the coming together of Montaigne and the Creoles that starts up again. They alternate between *ban ʒolies ʒistoires*, tales and legends, *sirandane* riddles, short discussions of philosophy, and etymologies. Memory is thus shared, from the Gironde estuary to the mouth of the Betsiboka, passing by Goa. When one Sunday, shy, alarmed by the hand that he places gently on the frill of her white dress, she says she must leave for Mass, he smiles at her and replies with the Song of Songs, the song par excellence: he knows passages from it by heart and will recite them to her right to the end of her life.

From time to time you see them passing by together along the boulevard: Pauline leaves the babbling choir of her cousins and neighbors to walk with Maxime. At this point only they know it, but he already writes her some wonderful letters, with no punctuation, launched like an expression of love, carried away on the stream . . . All these letters lie sleeping today in the old hinged chest, on yellow paper, torn for having been read and reread, passed through the sand of their hands and the filter of their eyes. These are corniche-letters, cliff-letters, shredded like the coasts of an island and torn by time but written in beautiful blue, airy, expansive handwriting:

Pauline her name is like an oil that has been spread over her cheeks have the beauty of the weaverbird her eyes are like the eyes of the zebra finch she withdraws into the hollow of the stone in the nooks of the round stone she is a closed garden and a sealed fountain this bouquet of sea-foam the color of milk my girl my great love listen to what the water says to the pebbles

These letters move Pauline in the deepest part of her soul, without her being able to know who in her is the most moved, the fervent Catholic or the young woman in love. The two parts of her melt into each other like a mystical and voluptuous rose that burns with all its ardor for this sensual acrobat. It is a heavenly gift, an invisible music. It is love, that terrible thing, a love that has no need for explanations or justifications.

Then, one morning, for the first time in Mahajanga's memory, Pauline changes the itinerary of her walk. She is alone on that morning and has given the day off to her retinue of cousins and neighbors, her personal bodyguard of frills, petticoats, and laughter. Instead of going down to the Pointe de Sable in the direction of the port, she climbs back up toward the Pointe du Caïman, which is high up over the town and leads to the hospital and the cemetery on the Corniche. It is early, the wind blows in from the sea, and one can see the twinkling of the lighthouse at Katsepe at the edge of the facing coast . . . She looks like a Madagascan warbler bird in her brown dress with a white blouse underneath and a pale line above her eyes.

She has a rendezvous with Maxime at the Jardin d'Amour, the well-named Garden of Love, the square planted with shrubs and bushes to the west of the town, not far from the cemetery that overlooks the sea. In fact, the place owes its name to its architect, a certain Damour, but the site on which it stands, looking over the Mozambique Canal as well as the delicacy of its layout—its terraces and shaded steps—have long made it the meeting place for lovers. That is why people often add the apostrophe, upon which the desires of the young people rest: the Jardin d'Amour.

Maxime is late that day. She is waiting for him; the first walkers of the day recognize her and say good day: they note a particular vigor in her face. People are used to seeing Pauline in movement; this morning she has stopped by the little bench, more beautiful and intense than ever standing there in the full light of dawn, beautiful like the attack of a flower on the shoreline.

Finally, he arrives. They sit down one against the other. They sit à la Malagasy, that is, they sit back to back to speak to each other about love. Leaning back into each other, on the low wall of the Jardin d'Amour, they resemble a couple of Geminis sitting on the white stone: their silhouette takes shape in profile, parallel to the crest of the waves and the line of the horizon. The conversation goes on like this for a few minutes, during which they do not look at each other. Suddenly, she turns around . . . She is beautiful, more than beautiful, she is startling. The first time it is she who kisses him. Pauline, young, shy, serious like the pope, all of that is confirmed and carried away in a shiver, the enormous risk of a kiss.

Then she stands up, and you think you see the air take her shape, her breath, her step.

THE COLONIAL SPECTER

I could spend hours like this, reading articles and looking through programs, all that powerful life of the circus, with its artists like birds dyed in red and forever being reborn.

But I have to move on.

Li-An is right to tease me by comparing me to a great invalid surrounded by scraps of paper in a bedroom with a cork floor: if I want to understand something about the life of these people, I have to also follow their route, find again their trails and eat up some miles. The various places where Maxime worked, for example, or the last house that he lived in. I have to face up to places physically, their materiality, including the state of the walls, the faint smell of saltpeter and its little white crystals, the steepness of the staircase . . . I have to go to Mahajanga.

Georges does not appear to be in any rush to see me leave his house. But he says the same thing to me as Li-An.

—The documents, the papers, it's all very good. But you absolutely must meet Jean Pivoine, the old jeweler. No one knows anymore exactly how old he is, but he's probably close to one hundred. He knew all about that period, he is one of the few able to speak of it. If anyone can tell you who is in the third tomb, it is him.

Need to hit the road, then. Tomorrow morning we leave for Mahajanga.

*

In Madagascar every journey is like a battle. The roads are full of holes, smashed up, powdery, and often impassable. You come out of each journey exhausted and strangely reinvigorated, the body full of bumps and holes, as if the road itself gets under your skin. However, it is the best way to discover the country.

Georges has let me use his car. Well, if you can still call it a car, that is: it is an old white Peugeot with the floor full of holes and the rearview mirrors attached by string. The engine is almost new, he tells me; that is, it is not older than fifteen years or so. The gas tank light is constantly lit up, which does not exactly help in knowing when to fill up, but who could be put off by these details? From time to time the accelerator gets stuck, and that is very dangerous: I have to dive beneath the steering wheel myself to lift the pedal up by hand. As I do that, the car speeds away like mad, and as might be expected, with my head under the steering wheel looking for the accelerator pedal, my vision of what is happening on the road is rather reduced. The rest of the time, as Georges says, the car runs very well.

Li-An is sitting on my right, on the passenger seat, or as they say in French "à la place du mort," in the dead man's place, and when I say it to Li-An, she laughs, finding it quite appropriate, given the state of the car! We drive for a long time through a lively and colorful crowd, between the beat-up vans, cattle carts, kids running around, and women carrying heavy loads on their backs. Poverty catches your eye everywhere you look, as does life: a laugh, a friendly altercation, young people holding hands. I make mental notes of several signs that sketch out along the journey little portraits, colorful glimpses, of the country:

Dark and Lovely (hairdressing salon)

or this school with its tender and sweet name:

The Little Cherubs

but with a warlike slogan:

"Courage, ardor, perseverance."

We'll need some of that! Indeed, we have two days ahead in the car, first in the coolness of the high plateaus, then in the heat of the plains and the dusty tracks. Making the journey from the high plateaus to the coast feels like going from a refrigerator to a bread oven. Leaving the territory of the Merinas, the body trembles, the fingers are numb with cold. Arriving in the land of the Boina, the sun's rays transform the car's shaky interior into a sauna: the body gets cooked, you are like a roasted chicken turning on its spit. From time to time, we have to climb some steep hills and throw out a few cans of water to lighten the load.

On the approach to Mahajanga, there is a rumble of thunder: a storm crashes down upon us and leaves again as quickly as it arrived. Villagers run out: everyone lends a hand to push the car through the floods of mud studded with stone blocks loosened by the storm and the ravines denuded by the torrents of water. Li-An has been counting: we have passed fifty-two rivers in all, as many as there are weeks in a year.

Finally, stores start to appear by the side of the road; we are approaching the town. Everything is for sale here, nothing is wasted, everything is transformed into a joyous tumult: live chickens; cuts of meat; mismatched shoes; yellow bananas, looking soft and smooth; green pineapples with their tops fanned out . . . On the right a notice asks: "Are you selling a 403 half-engine?" Where did the other half go, then?

It is the joy of the marketplace and the great buzz of the world.

*

On arriving in Mahajanga, we have a mind-blowing tête-à-tête with the clouds. In its scale, its sweeping breadth, the palette of its colors, the variety of its clouds, the multiplicity of its light, the Madagascar sky is an astonishing spectacle. At the end of the afternoon, soaring over the Mozambique Canal, its tenderness knocks you over.

In the car, with its beat-up seats, we go to circle the baobab. It is the ritual, Georges tells us: going round the baobab that stands right at the end of the boulevard brings well-being to new arrivals.

Then we climb to the right, toward the Corniche. We go past the hotels and restaurants that overlook the sea, the provincial governor's house with its lanterns, the Jardin d'Amour, where Maxime and Pauline shared their first kiss, and we arrive at the cemetery gates. But night has already fallen, and the cemetery is closed. The three tombs are there, close by, hidden in the shadows.

We check in to the hotel. We are exhausted by the journey. Li-An falls asleep very quickly, her belt barely unbuckled, her long legs like two beautiful foils with flexible blades unfolded across the bed.

I listen: I can hear the rain arriving, passing, and leaving again . . . The rain always comes at night, with its overcoat of clouds, its blue storm. The feet of thousands of migratory birds land on the town's rooftops, scratching the zinc and the corrugated iron—all of a sudden, all the town's odors escape and wind their way through the alleys, between the tree trunks and the house foundations. It is the midnight meeting, the coven, between the wet leaves and the roofing, rust extending its power over the world. Clouds, alluvium, electrons, and iron particles, suddenly as free as the air: a magnetic force breaks free from each branch and spreads over the walls, women's dresses, and the hoods of cars.

The sky is unleashed: wind, gusts, and whirling rain. I take a look out the window. Outside, the backs of people's necks bend down, their heads disappear into their shoulders, they want to retreat into themselves to escape the rain and its thousand flashing blades.

And above it all, there is the wonderful smell of cherry and lemon from those little flowers that, a minute ago, seemed nondescript by the side of the road.

I will go tomorrow to see the Indian jeweler.

*

The jewelry store is clean and orderly. The main space is divided into four parts by two wooden display cabinets on which sit the precious stones and the silver bracelets and around which plays out the ballet of visitors, the commotion of the suppliers, and the comings and goings of the buyers. A bracelet costs between 260,000 and 300,000 Malagasy francs—that is a bit more than 10 euros. The gold is in another window and is dearer: around 4 million Malagasy francs, "but that is only 20 euros," as Jean Pivoine points out. No one knows exactly what age he is, but at around a hundred years old, he still juggles exchange rates, prices, and currencies. With a youthful spirit, he makes light work of continents, time zones, and currencies, he follows from day to day the price of primary materials, evaluates the geostrategic data, weighs up the political context, juggles from one currency to another, and converts everything into something else or its opposite. He is a kind of Ariel circulating and calculating— between the ages too: he speaks to you about the rates in the 1960s and the state of the market following independence, then returns in an instant to the current situation, working conditions, the difficulty of finding qualified workers . . . He is an elf, the personification of an age-old spirit, a commercial genie. Seeing him, you realize how several dozen Indians have been able in the space of a few years to build financial empires built on gold and silver, selected precious stones, and metalwork.

Jean Pivoine, the old Indian jeweler, at least ninety-nine years old if he is a day and with a face like a Noh mask, marked by the sands of time. His skin descends in waves to his chin, then spreads out in successive lateral slides toward his cheeks, his neck, and shoulders; it is just like standing before a melting caramel sponge cake. For some old people time stretches their features in a crumbling succession. His liquid skin is held together at the neck by a snug tie, which makes him look like a jabot: above the folds of the collar there are pockets, blisters that bubble to the surface in lumps. His face is like milk, butter, and flour—a doughy mass that slides downward. But in this face, right in the heart of it, there are two little lively, shining yellow eyes. They shine all the more as soon as we speak about Maxime Ferrier.

"Maxime Ferrier, Maxime Ferrier . . ." Right away, as soon as he knows I am Maxime's grandson, he moves around on his chair and stands up. His voice quavers, hesitates a bit in the lower tones, he gives a little cough, and begins again on a sharper note: "Come over here, we will have some peace and quiet. At this time there is not much business. It is the time for filling in tax returns, administrative forms: I have sent my workers home; they are on vacation for a month. All that paperwork has nothing to do with them."

We leave the main room, and he leads me to the back of the store, a dark windowless room that contains a set of scales and some precision instruments: glasses, iron fixtures, weights and measures. It is here that he weighs the metals, makes the alloys, checks the combinations . . . On the wall are two calendars, one with Indian scenes and the other with Catholic illustrations.

A lovely sweet smell floats through the air, of sandalwood mixed with musk and rose. Some incense emits a few rings of blue smoke. The light only barely penetrates this den, where sounds are made in the form of low hisses. As soon as I pronounced Maxime's name, he took on a mysterious air and led me to this back room. It is the farthest back room, the one that no one ever enters.

"The walls have not only ears, they also have eyes and a tongue. For those who know they are listening, in any case . . . Here we will be better." He pushes forward a chair. "Do not think that these inanimate objects"—he brushes an old bronze set of scales with his hand garnished with yellow rings—"are always mute. These chairs, these walls, these drawers, speak to me as clearly as if they were sending a message."

He begins to tell his story. His gestures are at once precise and ample, the ringed hands rise and fall softly on his chest—like a prayer—while he speaks about his youth, the card games at the Grand Hôtel with Nénesse, the Perrier-Martel, his favorite cocktail, brandy and soda water, which leaves in the mouth a lightly effervescent taste of peach. Later, in the 1960s, he will switch to whisky. Today it is rum . . . He pours one for himself and serves me a glass.

His eyes seem always to be fixed on some scene taking place a few kilometers away. He speaks softly and in slow syllables, as if the words were coming out of a pit, as if the phrases were climbing back up along a funnel. "These days I drink only on weekends. When you get old, you have to slow everything down to be able to go on," he says, moving his left hand, which is suddenly weighed down, solemn: you would think that it was crossing the ages to come and sit on his chest.

His gaze slides over my head, as if he was contemplating an exciting spectacle taking place on the other side of the planisphere. He searches a bit for his words and his voice, but his diction and ideas are perfectly clear. Now the little evening rum is lighting up his memory. I take out my notebook and pen and take notes . . .

*

It is precisely from the time he met Pauline that Maxime's fortune starts to grow exponentially. In a few years he establishes himself as one of the best businessmen of the west coast: by working in turns for the local colonists and for himself, he makes his way up the ladder of polite society in Mahajanga, "in less time than it takes to grill a grasshopper," as the Malagasy proverb says.

Maxime sets up first a plantation in Karankely, in the bush, for fourteen months, on behalf of the colonist Cavadini, the husband of a Delastelle girl, a well-known Franco-Malagasy family from the Big Island. In the previous century one of her ancestors, going by the resonant name of Napoléon Delastelle, had managed various establishments on the coast, working even with Queen Ranavalona. Maxime is at that point in charge of around thirty workers, who produce mainly coffee, vanilla, and pepper. In a year the coffee production has increased sixfold: the colonists begin to take an interest in this man, who is respected by his workers, who does not think twice about spending entire weeks in the bush sleeping with the Malagasy workers, and who, on weekends, accompanies the Nuñes girl on her promenades.

Then he works for someone called Berger, an Alsatian, proprietor of the "Transvaal Farm," who hires him from the Cavadinis by offering to double his salary. He goes from three thousand francs per month (and a fifty-kilo sack of rice) to six thousand francs per month (and a bicycle). He is now in charge not of thirty people but around fifty. Maxime stays there for a year or so, then he is once again poached, this time by Hassan Ali himself. The former friend of Madame Bartolini owns a dozen or so plantations on the northwest coast: he has never forgotten the young acrobat who arrived ten years earlier among the flowers and beasts. He puts Maxime in charge of the *métayage*, a form of sharecropping, on one of his estates and, in particular, his zebu farming. Maxime moves from six thousand to eleven thousand francs and then, after producing good results, from eleven to fourteen thousand francs. He also has at his disposal, by contract, several stacks of wood and an electric generator. He now has between a hundred and a hundred and fifty Malagasy peasants under his authority: he gives them plots of land that they cultivate for their own benefit, but at the harvest season they must give a *daba* of rice or corn (the *daba* is a tall and square gas can made from tinplate, the equivalent of around twenty liters). When they kill a cow, they keep the ribs but give the filet, the heart, and the brain to Hassan Ali. The mangoes, corn, cassava, and vegetables are for the proprietor, while the rice, *brèdes*, potatoes, and grains (broad beans, lentils, green beans) are for the Malagasy.

The estate's accounts are impeccably kept. He has come a long way from the time of the little store on the beach at Amborovy and its chaotic accounts ledger! From now on the legal and administrative papers are organized in bundles of thirty and categorized according to the nature of the certificates (leases, contracts, transactions, indictments, reports), by Pauline's expert hand. By bringing together the words of the old jeweler with the pile of documents I found in Pauline's chest, and which remain today like the dead skin of these successive moltings, one can get a quite clear idea of the colonial world in which Maxime lived, the difficulties he confronted, and the ways in which he tried to get around them. One discovers in particular an incredibly hierarchical republic, where it is very difficult for those who are neither French nor white to find a place.

*

On high, at the very top, sits the governor-general, invisible like God and, like God, omnipotent. In Mahajanga he is represented by the provincial governor, whose residence is found, symbolically, a few steps away from the great baobab. Then there is his court with, in order of importance: the senior officials, the officials, the military, and the colonists . . . The Malagasy, the most numerous, are found right at the bottom. Everyone is subject to a strict hierarchical order and a stringent official etiquette worthy of the Duke Saint-Simon. Covering almost twenty years, dealing with the most diverse range of subjects (legal forms, administrative missives, private letters), the documents reveal something of the life of the colony in its most ordinary spheres (requests for authorization, demands, tax inquiries) as well as in its most distinguished: jealousies, hatreds, unending rivalries in the shadows, viciousness behind the drawn curtains, looks thrown between the shutters, handpicked favors. Indiscretions? Theft? Espionage? You have to wonder how Pauline managed to get her hands on some of these letters, which sometimes have only a passing relevance to Maxime's affairs but which must have been of use to him as a means of applying pressure during difficult negotiations or delicate talks. A certain district official asks for a bigger house, one more suited to his position. A fawning magistrate asks the provincial governor for a secretary's job for his wife, as if it were a post as well connected as that of a royal master of the hounds working for a king with a passion for hunting. A Malagasy councillor, "at the height of his favor and personal consideration, with a reputation second to none," complains about being refused for a promotion: the reply says that he is guilty of not greeting the administrator during his last visit . . . A magistrate argues with an agency head over his wife's right to sit in the front row during a projection of the film *La Bigorne, caporal de France* on the school terrace . . . (Ah, wives: a constant source of discord!) In the mundane legal imbroglio that ensues, the seats on the terrace become the stakes of a bitter symbolic struggle, which would make the ladies of Soubise, the princess of Guémené, and the demoiselles of Montbazon turn pale with jealousy: they were to be all removed, successively, then put back, and finally painted in different colors according to the age and standing of the spectators . . .

It is the great colonial theater: sometimes comedy, sometimes tragedy, and most often a seaside boulevard. Desires and prerogatives, intrigues, resentments, calumnies, ill-timed malice: all of those high-flying officials and commissioners, assistant directors, and specially appointed private secretaries twist themselves like toque-wearing duchesses around an armchair or a chaise longue, adding to the brilliant education they have received an indisputable cunning and know-how in the art and degrees of procuring themselves little seats on the school terrace.

This vertical structure, governed by the culture of emblems and insignias and hierarchical protocol, doubles up as a horizontal structure, a sort of spiral thinking that functions according to the principle of concentric circles. Even among the French one distinguishes slyly—but carefully—between the French-born and those born in the colonies. Those who live in France are worth more and are better than the guy from Réunion, the type from Mauritius, and the old hand from Madagascar. It is from the metropole that come the best products, the most fashionable clothes, and the best French language. It is a Pharaonic society—and nothing indicates it has completely disappeared today—that only measures itself to the center and could be described as the unrolling of several cloudy lines around a fixed point of reference and rotation: the metropole. The society believes in the boundaries between social classes; the rounded, disconnected nature of the races; the incommunicability between different social spheres; and the truth of the pigmentocracy.

While preaching the virtues of "Eternal France" and hammering home the republican values, they create—in people's heads and on paper—all sorts of different and contradictory statuses, a gradated palette of differing degrees of citizenship. The colonial official himself, who lives in town, refers to the planter as "marécageux," or "swampy," and all the more so as he is not a French national, a status they are careful not to afford him. There are two schools: the "European school," for the Europeans and the assimilated (children of colonists and French officials, the odd offspring of rich Malagasy families); and the "official school," for the Malagasy. For the first school the principal comes from France, and the teachers are recruited locally. In the second the principal and the teachers are Malagasy, and the children go there barefoot and come out destined for modest careers and lowly jobs. In their speeches they talk of eliminating racial and social differences; in fact, they promote them. Finally, right at the bottom of the ladder is found the "most primitive stage of civilization," "the wretched life of the unclothed races," the "civilized primitives," as they say in the newspapers (or in their speeches at the chamber).

A certain idea of colonization thus comes to light across the pages, mixed with solicitude and profitability, alternating between the public powers and the private interests, including all political tendencies, from the Cartel of the Left and its epigones to the National Bloc and it successors: a permanent toing and froing between civilizing values and commercial strategies. It is impossible for the colonial not to be ambiguous: the great fiction of humanism and progress accompanies this enterprise of guardianship, which presents itself as a benevolent, civilizing force. It is the coming together of the rights of man and the law of the jungle.

*

Above all, language is the object of a maniacal attention, a deranged surveillance, as if they suspect everything comes from it, that everything passes through it and that one day it could call everything into question: so, it is examined closely and taken apart, selected and separated, delimited and distributed—like it is the most precious commodity.

There is on the one hand the florid French of France, festooned and of higher social value, and on the other the always-suspect locutions of the bad speakers of the *outre-mer*. People praise the flowery French of the metropole, delicate, ornamented, with its interlaced intricacies: its skies are of vair, and its land is covered in embroidery. Boxwood trimmings line the contours of its flower beds. Every path of grass trod upon by the white frost of its language is like a gold lamé train, every bush a radiant piece of silverware . . . Behind, rumble words emerging from the desolate swamps, from shunned lexicons, unworkable grammars, and from the dark, poison-filled pages of the Tropics. There are the cathedrals of high French, its lintels and tympanums, its arches, its columns (sublime, necessarily sublime), and the language of down below, a masonry of terrible words, crowned with a black halo, that smells of farts, red beans, and piss. The time is certainly not far away when the Patricks and the Raphaëls, kids with names of angels or saints, or the Simones and the Maryses, children with the names of nuns and aviators, will make the old edifice shake and topple over. Already there are rising up all over the place words from French Guiana, words from Guadeloupe, Africa, and Martinique, preceded by some splendid words from Uruguay, beautiful like the talons of birds of prey. Mulatto words, chabin words, mixed-race words, a whole set of phrases that for the moment are seen only as mortal emanations from the mangrove of languages.

But for now what you have is the waltz of euphemisms: the conquest is "pacification," revolts are "incidents" (or "troubles" when there are too many casualties), and the great wars of independence are grudgingly afforded the status of "events." The development of the conquered land becomes the "economic utilization" of the colonies. Naming is the most effective means of control: they remove vowels (the fabulous rainbow of vowels in the Malagasy language), they truncate, they amputate, they mutilate. Antananarivo is converted into Tananarive, they cut Toamasina to Tamatave, they reproduce Mahajanga as Majunga . . .

And they could have gone further! . . . In a 1902 issue of the *Quinzaine coloniale*, a reader wonders gravely: "Is it acceptable to let survive indefinitely these names that rebel against French minds: Manjakandriana, Ambohidrahino, Maevatanana, Andranogokoaka, etc., etc.? . . . Why not replace them with French names that mean something, such as Belle-Fontaine, Haut-Mont . . ."

If the relationship with the foreign language itself indicates the degree of welcome and resistance to the speech of the other, one can say that colonization was in most cases exceptionally deaf, unwilling to listen.

We should not, of course, make things seem worse than they are. We could also mention the enrichment of a certain local middle class, backed up by the medicalization, real, and the education, proven (although very insufficient), of the society. Yes, certain people are irreproachable: midwives, leprosy doctors, nurses mourning the deaths of children in shacks, administrators who learn the language and conserve the cultural treasures, teachers dedicated to their mission and trying to educate, train, and transmit knowledge. Certain ones perhaps succeed miraculously in combining the just with the imperial . . .

But as for the rest? Yes, there were sanitary improvements and mass vaccinations, but what about the spread of new illnesses and sometimes of full-scale endemics by the colonial conquest? People forget. Yes, there are many more roads and infrastructural developments, but what about the hellish exploitation of the workforce by the imposition of forced labor? People forget. The multiplication of rules and constraints, arbitrary sanctions, convocations, bullying, discrimination? The bans on free movement, collecting wood, requisitions, imprisonments? People forget. The censuses, the shattering effects of war, "the unlimited right to conscript black troops," permanent surveillance and generalized control? People forget.

Of course, we could always put all of that on one side of a set of scales and, according to one's history, sensibility, and ideals—or most often, the ideological interests of the present time—decide whether the scales lean to one side or the other . . . But the so-called *moustiquaire*, the "mosquito net," that young girl offered to the representative of the state, the administrator visiting the country? Quick, let's just forget about that.

People forget, too, about the native people and their culture, the multiplicity of regimes and specific codes, the incessant revisions and adaptations, the endlessly disappointed, improbable hope for citizenship, the legal dispensations written into the law itself. It is true that one gets a little lost in all the decrees, orders, mandates and conventions, observances and ordinances, rules and prescriptions, supposed to bring to the colonized their future status as enlightened citizens: assimilation, integration, association, accommodation . . . All of which passes into the tortuous dictionary of colonial language.

When it comes down to it, the native peoples are no longer Malagasy, French, or anything. They are left there, in sufferance, on the overseas shore. Because nationality is never a right; it is a favor that they are awarded. The native people slide from the rank of inhabitants to that of onlookers; they disappear bit by bit from their own country. Absent, phantoms, they are a décor, an ambiance, a picturesque but also exploited and taxpaying ornament in the grand spectacle of progress and colonization, a background canvas. They are there but not there: specters in their own country.

*

Ah, colonization . . . That's where we are. It is on this theme that readers scratch away at each other, prod each other, tear each other apart, and end up at each other's throats . . . The tone rises, the definitive truths fall; it all kicks off in the salons. Was colonization an opportunity or an error? Were its advantages real or supposed? Were its ideals false, or were they just led astray, betrayed? From these questions are born conferences, roundtables, sermons, lingering racism, and navel-gazing macerations . . . Chattering and drivel: on all the aspects of the phenomenon—positive, negative, laxative, dubious—minds go into overdrive.

Maxime's case could well add even more confusion to this complicated picture. Maxime is not an anticolonial, far from it. To a certain degree he participates in the system, he has some Malagasy people under his command, and he will do all that he can so that his children can go to the French school, in which he succeeds. However, he is also an escapee, an émigré, and as such, he will be subjected many times to the policies of the colonial power with regard to foreigners, the administration fluctuating permanently between the search for workers and immigration control, between the concern with favoring French activities and the necessity of finding a place for certain foreign activities that are indispensable to the economy of the Big Island. His acquaintances with the Malagasy are common knowledge: on that score there are many testimonies, and this solidarity will bring to him, as we will see, a good number of setbacks . . . Not only does he pass the greater part of his life in the bush—he sleeps, eats, and drinks with the people there—but even though he has the right to go into the *baȝary be*, the covered market reserved for "Europeans and those of similar stature," he is most often seen at the *baȝary kely*, the market for the indigenous people. He is, as is said of other colonists at the same time, *bougnolisé*, a vulgar term for "gone native." He has a real skill for entering into others' ways of thinking and taking on their mores. I think this is the only thing that really interests him at heart.

The color of his skin, above all, remains a subject of much conjecture—in those times, no more so than today, it is a not insignificant detail. Is Maxime "white," "tanned," or "light brown"? As soon as you go into the issue of his pigmentation, the question of nuances becomes infinite: his skin color seems to vary in time as well as according to his place in the social hierarchy. The descriptions of his skin color differ in effect according to the stage in his life and the state of his fortune. According to various testimonies (newspaper articles, police reports, oral accounts), his skin is variously mahogany and like molasses, plum or peach, cinnamon or caramel, sapodilla, pistachio . . . pinky yellow, ripe banana . . .

One detail recurs often: he has a white torso and tanned legs.

They also say that his lips are thick—does he have African blood? Likewise, one doesn't know exactly what nationality he claims: British? French? Malagasy? Perhaps he claims the three at once. For some he came from Bordeaux, for others from Saint-Malo (curiously, always seafaring towns). Some say he is American, others say he is Catalan. Maxime is like that. He mixes up all the signs of "civilization." He is colored and colorful: with him you never know with which ghost you are dancing. He is endlessly various, a spectrum of color. He is a color chart. One day this will be held against him, as might be expected.

Administratively, he has a "foreign visitor" visa that he has to pay for and renew every year. When independence comes, the stamp changes—a pretty, ruffled palm tree will replace the august republican statue, and that is that. Ironically, this card carries the statement "Definitive identity card," even though he has to take it back every year. No state, neither the colonizing nor the decolonized, will afford him any form of existence other than this paradoxical, transitory and renewable, eternally minority, definitively temporary definition.

CREOLE JAZZ BAND

Exploring the margins, the silences, such has always been one of the secrets of the act of writing. In the official history of France, memoirs are like bombs—perfectly ingenious devices, cluster bombs or time bombs. They alone reveal the complexity of the times, their animated torment, their secret turbulences. Clandestine. They do not monumentalize, they are, literally, *off the mark*, but unlike established genealogy, they detect original kinships, unforeseen affiliations, the proliferation of moments in time that work against the calendar's official passage of time.

La Fronde? It was not a historian but a memorialist, the Cardinal of Retz, who described it best. The century of Louis XIV, the courtly society? Norbert Elias, without any doubt, but certainly also Saint-Simon. A journey behind the scenes—differentiation of sources, the extension of interactions, the power of insurrection and resurrection. Memoirs crash into time, lift it up, and turn it over. The real memorialists are like acrobats: they know how to escape the chains of normal life, look for a poise that breaks the daily cycle of places and positions in space, slide into the interstices of time to bring out the truth of the body and of human practices.

It is an off-piste kind of work, a way of cutting across life. Listening to the old jeweler, I learn a few things about this . . . "the reverse of contemporary history," as the other one said.

*

By a sort of paradox that is quite typical of him, Maxime's bad reputation grows at the same time as his place in society rises. A certain odd personal quirk attracts the hilarity of some and the bile of others. Maxime has, in fact, a pronounced taste for symbols and signs. He is determined to inscribe his social ascension into the very figure of his name, with which he will play several times over the years.

One wonders in the first place what has come over him when he decides to call himself "Maxime de la Ferrière": the word is that this noble particule, the *de la*, relates him to the Girondin dynasty of the Ferrières, a celebrated family of maritime brokers. But this is only the beginning of his metamorphosis: soon he inserts into his name a new insignia and calls himself "Maxime le Roy de la Ferrière." The word then spreads that he is the descendant of a Saint-Malo privateer. Finally, a few months later, he transforms himself again: increasingly steeped in the Bible, he becomes "Maxime Saint Jean le Roi de la Ferrière," a signature he will use on various administrative documents.

If we try to represent on paper the successive lineaments of this baroque patronymic expansion, we get this strange figure, which is like the foliage of a palm tree:

Maxime Février . . .

Maxime Ferrier . . .

Maxime de la Ferrière . . .

Maxime le Roy de la Ferrière . . .

Maxime Saint Jean le Roi de la Ferrière . . .

The civil register at Mahajanga records with some reticence and a touch of irritation the history of these changes. But in the end Maxime has money, he pays, and with each change it is a little money that goes into the coffers, not counting the backhanders, commissions, tips, and bribes. Moreover, all this is done with a good dose of humor: every name change is the pretext for enormous feasts, which begin as he comes out of the city hall, when Uncle Pierre strikes up the "Vivat Bacchus" and the "Abduction from the Seraglio." The festivities continue late into the night, a good half of the town pours onto the terraces of the Nouvel Hôtel.

Many people mock Maxime's name-changing habit, some seeing in it an exuberant eccentricity born out of a misplaced sense of pride or, at best, a slightly childish caprice. However, there is more to this series of variations than a simple ornamentation of his name. Pauline is no doubt right when she tracks jubilantly this dizzying glissando by comparing it to the seven positions of the slide trombone and stating that it is his own way of being musical.

This play on his name, which began upon his arrival on the island (when he changed his family name from *Février* to *Ferrier*), continues almost to the end of his life and is one of the most constant traits in his character. It is like the very signature of his taste for liberty. Subtraction, recovery, and permanent articulations: it is the grand art of mutation. In this arrangement of dropped initials and words, in his combinatory insistence, in the vagaries of this turbulent signature, one can read the constantly renewed gesture whereby he affirms his existence, to the point of incandescence. Thus, the name becomes a weapon, charged with several triggers and equipped in each letter with an infinite reservoir of extra barrels: you never know what can come out from behind the scenes.

*

Wait until you hear what I have heard, about the grandfather . . .

His family situation also incites the worst gossip: in fact, Maxime never married Pauline. They will have seven children together—all of whom he will recognize—but he will never feel obliged to "regularize his situation," as they say. When they interrogate him on marriage, he responds with a pirouette—always the acrobat! A quotation from Saint Paul, whose First Epistle to the Corinthians he knows by heart: "So then he who marries his betrothed does well, and he who refrains from marriage will do even better."

But it gets even worse: even as she is bringing into the world her first child, Pauline learns that Maxime is having an affair with another woman, called Carmen. Not only an affair but also . . . children. Here Maxime has confused the issue to the extent that even years later and after numerous testimonies, it is impossible to pinpoint the chronology of these tumultuous affairs. Scornful looks, moralizing mockery, haughty reprobation, nothing made a difference to him: over several years he will live with many women and have children with two of them, lawfully, deliberately, and, one would almost dare write, faithfully. Go forth and multiply . . . When he is questioned on this subject—which is rare, as Maxime is not a man who leaves himself open to questioning—he replies once more with a quotation from Saint Paul: "But this I say, brethren, time is short, so from now on those who have wives should be as though they had none."

And he adds, always adapting, always smiling: "Chapter 7, verse 29."

Thus will be born in succession (and sometimes in the same year): Maxime, Ketty, Gladys, Daisy, Dolly, Cléto, Willy, Jacky, Johnny, Marilou, and Nico. Nature (or Providence) keeps watch over this double lineage by distributing equally roles and sexes: all the male children go to Pauline, all the girls to Carmen. When this strange law of harmony is broken, death falls like a guillotine blade: on Carmen's side little Maxime dies very young, around six months old; on Pauline's side little Marilou dies in 1949, at the age of four. It was said that from Pauline's womb it would be the boys who would survive and from Carmen's womb the girls, as if reality itself ratified a strange division of the sexes that must not be altered.

Maxime's attitude will appear surprising and perhaps even incomprehensible to many readers today: he will never think of getting married, and for a long time he will not envisage leaving either woman. It is because Maxime does not invest in the sexual act all the weight and the gravity that it has taken on today. His sexuality is not functional; it is ludic. *Meglio vivere un giorno da leone che mille da capra!* . . . Also, it is not impossible that there were other liaisons, more fleeting (but certainly not any other children, as Maxime made it a point of honor to recognize his children, all of them). Easygoing regarding sex, irreproachable on paternity, that was Maxime. And with absolute discretion in all his affairs.

However, in a certain way, Maxime is modern, absolutely modern. In the way he recomposes the family, he sets out a certain idea of genealogy and transforms it into a play of lateral alliances and filiations. The family is not for him Daddy–Mommy–and the kids, it is not reduced to a kernel or a base, it merges, splits, adds to itself, there are numerous ramifications, improbable couplings, unforeseen crossings and meetings. He conceives of existence as a succession of short notes, venules, arterioles, a real capillary happiness. He is as carefree as a piece of algae, or coral, which he knew so well from his diving: the multiple excrescences, transmission by the fibers, life is a fern with very fine stalks, a *cheveu-de-Vénus*. The birth of a child is like a new branch being added, love grows like a tree. Joy is always found at the intersection.

*

But Pauline's reaction to Maxime's infidelities is even more stupefying. Were there tears, shouts, teeth grinding? The most wonderful thing is that nothing points to any of that having occurred. After the initial difficult moments, Pauline understands that the situation is finally *logical*, that one cannot love Maxime for this taste of liberty that he can give so fully to life and at the same time condemn him for it. There is therefore no hysteria; there are no complaints and no reproaches. This is not to say that she did not feel completely humiliated. At that time it is music that, in the proper sense of the word, *saves her life*: music stops her from sinking into sadness and resentment or into condemnation and vociferation.

How can this be, were there no dramas, no wild threats, no rancor? No. Jealousy, then? Some bitterness? No. None, she lifts all those feelings from you.

After some hesitation, in fact, Pauline concentrates all of her attacks on the other, this Carmen with the destructive forename. Her decision was to fight with all her strength. Not to let go and, above all, not to give up. Her principal weapon was music. He will end up choosing between this booming comic opera and the new explosions of jazz that I will serve up to him on my piano. It is jazz against the operetta, the tousled spirals of the sax against the coquetries of the cigar maker, the twentieth century triumphing over the dying Second Empire. She cannot fail to win.

The irony is that Pauline is a great admirer of Bizet's opera, of which she would sing regularly the celebrated arias at the piano of the Nouvel Hôtel before she met Maxime. "Love is a wild bird . . . that nothing can tame." She could not have put it better! . . . But this time has come around again: she starts the war of sounds. Her aim is to push herself as far as possible in the dexterity and verve of her playing, while the other, this Carmen, is an expert in warbling and bragging. To replace the grand, languid arias of the repertoire with small, lively, mixed rhythms. She will see what I am made of, this dramatic soprano. She gives it to him with a wink; I will give it to him with my quick fingers. She wants to play it in parallel? I will flow over the whole thing, playing obliquely . . .

So, her hands take flight over the keyboard. She takes the whole town by surprise—she is a tornado. No one has heard anyone play like that on the island; the soirees at the Nouvel Hôtel are transformed into a musical rally, the dancers are unleashed, the hall, which is already full every Saturday night, also fills up during the week, they turn people away, people dance on the terrace, and soon enough on the sidewalks too.

Pauline is highly skilled in percussion and singing. Variations, onomatopoeias, changes in tone and rhythm, she knows all of that. She has practiced the piano since her childhood, she sings, she is always singing, with the family or solo, in her bedroom or on the boulevard. She has organized the soirees at the Nouvel Hôtel since her adolescence and lived all her childhood in an ocean of sounds and music. But now, stung by the rivalry with Carmen, she goes into top gear. Carmen is "olé-olé," as they say locally; does she seduce Maxime with her free morals, with her deliciously dissipated life? Pauline will show her just what a Catholic can do with regard to the sublime and exhilaration. The daughter of Goa will be a loose woman herself, in her own musical way.

A quick look at the program is enough to become aware of this. The rumba and the paso doble fade away, the tango and the waltz disappear, Aunt Émilia and her languorous violin are temporarily laid off, all of that seeming now weakened, lifeless, and neurasthenic. The soirees at the hotel will be based from now around the Hot Fives and Hot Sevens, the two groups founded by Louis Armstrong, and their pulsating tracks. Added to that is the repertoire of King Oliver's Creole Jazz Band. It is Pauline who introduces all this. From now on she will end each evening with "Heebie Jeebies," her favorite track, carrying the orchestra in her wake, in a sort of graduated great storm of all the instruments that she punctuates impetuously with her piano.

There is no longer even a second's respite: with her rhythmic playing, Pauline chases away the town's nervous depression; she turns anxiety into a great burning fire. Her attacks on the ivories become more audacious and complex, mixed with subtle, melodic touches. She displaces the accents, brusquely attacks the weak beats, climbs back up the scale, lights up the sounds. Every evening it is a different musical raid: she darts, cuts to the quick, stirs things up. Her voice also changes, in its intonations: from her head voice to the bass register, she now sings right on the consonants, in a constant timbral and tonal improvisation, all done impromptu, a scenic and sonic war carried out by an open, evolving vocal play. It is ragtime: she devours space, rips up time.

On certain evenings, when Maxime's infidelities leave her in a state of dark despair, she goes back to the blues standards of Bertha "Chippie" Hill, her voice heats up, becomes more gravelly and drawling: "Lonesome, All Alone and Blue," "Trouble in Mind" . . . Her heartbeat drops, the melody glides, the volume rises, the rhythms slow down . . . And when it is all going really badly: "Low Land Blues" and "Deep Water Blues" . . . Distress here becomes almost beautiful, appeased by the delicacy of her solos.

At this time what does she think of? Perhaps of this passage from the Song of Songs, which she copies in a letter to her cousin Maria: "I opened the door to my beloved, but my beloved had turned and gone. My soul failed me when he spoke, I sought him, but found him not; I called him, but he gave no answer." Perhaps she thinks about that first kiss that she had taken from him—"his lips are lilies, dripping liquid myrrh"—about that tender mouth that she could not hold on to . . .

Uncle Pierre has sensed the danger and taken up the baton. He breaks loose on the clarinet. His inspiration: Johnny Dodds. On his death they will find in his home the transcription of several pieces, for clarinet, for piano, and for banjo. "Clarinet Wobble," "Bucktown Stomp," "Shanghai Shuffle" . . . He listens to them once, and then he transcribes them, from memory. "Keep a Song in Your Soul" . . . When evening comes, he plays them over, with a few of his own variations but without ever missing a note. From time to time he sings also, with a slightly husky voice, it seems, but that doesn't matter. When the trumpet goes to his lips, the walls move, sparks fly and spread across the night. "I touch your lips, and all at once the sparks go flying, those devil lips."

At that point it starts up again: Pauline joins in with some Armstrong hits. Reading their titles, you can see that she is playing some of them for Maxime: "Alligator Crawl," "You've Got to Get Home on Time," "What Kind o' Man Is That?" . . . Coded messages in her sleepless nights. It is her own way of bringing the fight, subtle, indirect—enchanted.

She does some surprising things; she reinvents her body according to the music . . . "Weather Bird Rag" . . . Scat, the vowels open, the consonants crack. During this time, right hand, left hand, she spatters everything with her quavers, her mordents, her gruppetti, and her appoggiaturas. You would think that she has six voices, a hundred fingers. She shortens the sound, she repeats it and manipulates it, takes it apart, remakes it, seizes it, and unfurls it. She pushes herself along the length of a joyful, adventurous, and experimental range: she takes risks but never loses herself. She is on the same line in several times, she hums as she passes from one to the other.

Piano, voice, rebounds and returns that throw you, unexpected ellipses. All is done with dexterity and sensitivity . . . Then she smiles; her unhappiness is wiped away by her wonderful white teeth.

The battle lasts for seven years. The day in February 1939 when Maxime finally leaves Carmen for good, taking the girls with him, Pauline sits down at the piano and strikes up "Come Back, Sweet Papa" by Louis Armstrong in a rage of joy.

And when evening comes, to please him, she coats her breasts in honey.

PRESENCES OF THE PLAGUE

The interviews with the old Indian jeweler have taught me many things . . . I also saw Carreidas, another jeweler but younger, around fifty. It has not yet come for him, the time to look back and remember, and neither for Dodo, an Indian storekeeper working in the tailors' district, just two steps from the market. They have not yet entered into that stage of looking back and recollecting: their bodies are firmer, they are in the world in a different way; they are still expecting something from it. It is not they who interest me just now, as they do not yet have that knowledge of time that I am looking for, that way of standing there, at the bow or the stern, the last rampart, the forecastle.

When I meet older people, I see clearly that they have come into possession of a secret that transforms life definitively into destiny and makes them shift into another dimension. Their very body is not the same; they float in the atmosphere as if they have been extracted from the rock of time and yet are completely caught in its flow: they are lookouts, at the edge of another world that is not death but the renewed power of life, its permanent passage.

*

It is on the day after a great storm that Arthur makes his return to the town of Mahajanga. Early in the morning, he turns up in the lobby of the Nouvel Hôtel, puts his bags into a corner of the courtyard that has been spared by the storm waters, and goes to embrace the stunned Pauline. The day has hardly begun, but you hear already some hammering on metal and the eternal noise of the broom on the terraces. The hotel's roof has suffered, and everyone is working to repair the damage caused by the cyclone.

Arthur goes straightaway to lend a hand. He climbs up the big coconut tree that adjoins the western wall and jumps onto the roof... A man is already at work on the red tiles, mallet in hand: he turns around; it is Maxime. The two men fall into each other's arms, on the hotel roof: all around them the town is devastated by the passing rains, and several remember today this strange spectacle, the two acrobats together again in the splendid sky of the town, the sky a pure, intense blue, wiped clean by the typhoon. Their laughter echoes right to the boulevard.

Arthur has arrived directly from Antananarivo. He has just spent two days in a coach crossing the Big Island, and like everyone who returns, he has a thousand stories to tell. Then they call the family around, hail friends, and gather the neighbors together. The hotel musicians also rush around, and the old receptionist, the cleaning ladies, the maids, the *ramatoas* . . . everyone gathers around the acrobat. It is more than ten years since Arthur left for the capital: the children, who have heard talk of this Chinaman many times and seen the photos and newspaper articles, are particularly excited. They will long remember this morning; they will talk about it to their children, who will tell their own children. Arthur's face is barely aged by those ten years, a few crow's-feet at the corner of his eyes—when they point them out to him, he replies in good spirit, "They are laugh lines." And he quotes Du Fu, the "saintly Chinese poet": "Autumn on the border brings to one's ears the bird's cry." Everyone laughs.

From then on he appears calmer, more poised. A kind of yellow patina has settled onto his skin, which gives him the look of fine vellum paper. The questions come from all angles: what is happening? Why has Arthur shut the School of the Five Styles? What has pushed him to leave the house at Isoraka, so beautiful with its big windows and its wood flooring? The reply comes and plunges the audience into a sinister silence: the plague. Pauline tells the children that it is "the worst of all illnesses," as *pestis* comes from *pessimum*, even if Émile Littré in his dictionary says that the word comes, instead, from *perditis*, which is etymologically related to *perdre* and its connotations of loss. Arthur sighs: "Wherever it comes from, this word means one thing: certain ruin."

He continues: it is not the yellow plague of the banana plantations, mosquitoes, or monkeys; it is the murine plague, the worst, the one carried by rats. The rats' fleas spread the virus; it proliferates in the dust of the shacks. It passes from rats to humans in less time than it takes to say its name. In the capital the rats are everywhere, under the roofs, in the cellars, or underneath the rubble. You hear the noise of their scratching in the walls of houses, you smell their sickly odor that rises out of the pipes, you see them going around freely in the garbage dumps. People are affected everywhere, fevers are proliferating, faces are covered in pustules: the town is like a great candy box of red spots on the skin. Internally, it is even worse: buboes swell up all along the nymph nodes, bacilli spread through the liver and the spleen. Death takes hold of the lungs.

Vaccination is obligatory, but it is ineffective, and every year it starts up again: *screening programs, controls*, and *disease prevention* become the buzzwords. Terrible words have taken control of the city. People clean, clear away the dust, and disinfect. The medical organizations reign, though they are terribly impotent.

People, merchandise, goods, furniture, temples, huts, and animals are reduced to ashes. Houses are burned by the hundreds of thousands. As soon as a plague victim dies, they quickly set fire to the shacks, the thatches, the roofs, and the straw. They also burn the dogs, cockerels, and chicks. If they could, they would just as quickly burn the victims' wife and neighbors.

The contaminated houses are immediately surrounded by a barbed wire cordon: it is the "devil's cordon," say the terrified inhabitants. The relations, friends, and companions of the sick person are placed in isolation, in observation camps. Mistrust is found in even the closest families. The entire country is in quarantine: people look out for symptoms, listen closely to coughs, look out for phlegm, and anyone with the slightest sniffle is a potential victim. It is a time for looking askew at others, a great saga of glances and mistrust. Everyone observes, checks out, eyes up, and looks up and down at one another, the eyes slanted, the eyelids suspicious and shifty . . .

To fight against the spread of the disease, they have found a remedy that is almost as repugnant as the sickness itself: a chemical cataplasm derived from coal, repellent and disinfectant, which goes by the name of cresylic acid. A herbicide, larvicide, and fungicide, it is the Attila of the countryside and the defoliant of the towns. In a few moments mold disappears, and all that rests all over the ground is a vaguely blue color. Stones, walls, squares, and gardens are covered in a bitter, biting chemical smell, the fields are full of the rotten stink. Gripped by nausea, those who live in the richer parts fill their homes with incense, mango extracts, and cedar powder: together it makes a disgusting smell inside the ring of twelve hills that surround the city.

But on the first rat's tail that passes by, the plague comes back.

*

As soon as a death occurs, the body is wrapped in a shroud soaked in a cresyl solution, then put into a coffin between two layers of quick lime. When the quick lime runs out, they use straw, soil, sand, sometimes even just simple pieces of matting. The wrapped cadaver is placed at the back of a lorry that speeds to a special cemetery out of town . . . People cross themselves as it passes and then turn away as if they have seen death in person. The sanitary workers, equipped with masks and glasses, strapped in carefully sealed white canvas gowns (with elastomer on the wrists, heels, and at the base of the neck) spray both themselves and the dead person's house and its perimeter in cresyl. Then they close off the building as tightly as they can and, after two days, they restart the operation. The disinfection and rat extermination are carried out with a very toxic chloride solution: the nurses cry and suffocate as they spray it.

The doctors are also involved. Everywhere they are examining, studying, scrutinizing, and dissecting. People belch and clear their throats. In desperation they have to examine people's phlegm, as at other times they studied the intestines. It is not, as at Dodona, by the sound of the wind in the leaves of the oak trees that they hope to pierce the secrets of the symptoms nor in the entrails of animals or the flight of the vultures. In China, Arthur explains, they inscribed questions on sheep's shoulder blades and tortoise shells, which they then exposed to the flames of an oven. The seers then read in the shape of the cracks the response from the heavens: these divinatory practices are at the origin of the first Chinese writing. To get to the mysteries of life, one needed to know how to read and write, then to deploy the secrets of the shadows in thousands of magnificent inscriptions, on animal skeletons, on stoneware and clay ceramics, and on bronze slabs.

But today's doctors are haggard and defeated. Their cheeks are hollow, their skin pale, their features gaunt, and they scribble on plain paper their illusory prognoses. They ruin their eyes poring over spleen and lung tests and speculate on the various kinds of cough, on the color of the pupils . . . They scrutinize reddish guts and earthy gizzards, these oracles of a new kind. The liver in particular captures their attention—the stomach of the Malagasy has replaced the tortoise shells; it is a funereal dismemberment that no one understands anymore. Incapable of containing the epidemic, the doctors are knocked off their pedestal; they are compared to vultures that puncture the organs to get to their ineffective studies. All across the town there is trafficking of dead rats, people sell hens' blood and cow entrails. Little by little the horror takes grip: people realize that the plague has taken control of both bodies and minds.

So, the dead are no longer the dead, they become simple cadavers that are used and instrumentalized. They are turned over and again opened up, contemplated. The doctor's eye probes them; his scalpel digs into them. They are touched, moved, no longer respected, and are not left to rest in peace. The dead no longer die, they expire and perish, they are like curiosities in the hands of the practitioners. In the capital, without consulting the city's inhabitants, funeral wakes have been banned. It is no longer possible to inter a body at the family grave: the *famadihana*, the famous turning of the bones in Malagasy tradition, which after several years brings back together the mourners around the grave to exhume the body and recover it in a new shroud, is also banned. People are sickened: to die of the plague or any other cause, what did it matter! The important thing is to maintain contact with the dead! But the French doctors will not listen; it is a long time since they lost contact with their dead. People praise their courage but curse them: while the whole world falls apart around their laboratories, they continue the slow work of autopsy.

Every year there is talk of a new vaccine: Girard and Robic—two doctors crowned with a terrible glory and whose name is pronounced only with a shudder—were to have found a remedy, according to the newspaper, "based on weakened bacteria." But in a cruel paradox, just as they reach their goal, no one believes them anymore. The countryside and the towns are infested, people now trust only in old wives' cures, such as the leaves of a pear tree crushed up in a strong rum: an excellent remedy against parasites that could also have some effect against the plague.

Arthur carries a newspaper, which will be found much later, at the time of his death, among his papers. Taking up the whole first page is a black-and-white photo showing some shacks, and one wonders whether it is harboring people or waste. You can see leaves, branches, rusted corrugated iron, and tires in the mud. The people and their animals are hidden away in a corner. The caption reads: "The waste that is piling up everywhere, and the dirty state of the town, are also, for many, part of the epidemic of fevers that is gripping the nation. Rats and mosquitoes, which carry the virus, are found there, and with the rainy season and the high temperatures of these past few days, it is a very favorable environment for the spread of the virus. For the moment the epidemic is at a stable stage, according to the medical authorities, which fear a fresh outbreak of the worst and admit also that there is a lack of qualified personnel, especially when a part of that personnel is also afflicted."

And indeed, if the caregivers themselves are sick, what cure is there? In the tepid nature of his prose, the journalist found a terrible phrase, which explodes in the middle of his sentence and summarizes the situation: the "fresh outbreak of the worst."

The rest of the newspaper speaks only of this worst thing. In Europe they can use different names for viruses, acronyms, germs with precise names, and a whole range of scientific terms. Here, in Madagascar, they use the old repetitive, slightly vague words, the only ones capable, it seems, of evoking these illnesses from the depths of time. Plague, cholera, malaria: everything is called "fevers." In the written word everything is referred to as *fever*, used in the singular and plural. It is finally the only word that returns endlessly, it has neither synonym nor equivalent, it wraps everything in its dark shadow, it hovers like a ghost over every page.

Little by little Arthur has seen the numbers in his boxing classes fall away. The most passionate of his disciples have deserted the School of the Five Styles, for, as he says, "Boxing can't do much against fleas and buboes!" However, Arthur hesitated for a good while before returning to Mahajanga. There are periods of relative calm, temporary remissions that are like precarious victories, where life seems to take up its previous course again. In June and July, most notably, the fevers abate. But every year, from October, with the return of the rains, the fleas proliferate again, carried by the rivers and stored up in the rice fields . . . When the storms strike, the fields are drowned, the plantations flooded: the rats move to the higher parts spared by the floods, spreading the plague like wildfire.

The cycle of the plague has led the doctors to draw up a special calendar. From now on there will be a "plague year," which doubles and contests the official year. For some the plague year begins on 1 May of the calendar year and ends on 30 April the following year. For others it runs from July to July. It is a new division of time; people call it the "plague calendar." It inspires in Arthur a strange phrase, in a letter to Maxime dated 1931. "Time itself is determined by the plague!" he exclaims, his teeth clenched in a grimace, and no one quite knows if it is caused by terror or jubilation.

*

In the art of war you also have to know how to beat the retreat. A few years later, then, Arthur is back in Mahajanga. He gets out of an old bus laden with fish traps and rattraps, antiseptic and disinfectant products . . . The doctors say that the fleas are more sensitive to the higher temperature on the coasts and prefer the high plateaus. In the colder climate of the center of the island, the illness resides directly in the chest, and the bacteria propagate from lung to lung. Here, under the sun of the Boina, death will perhaps be more pleasant.

Arthur no longer has a penny to his name. The ticket for the journey, which was left folded between the pages of a newspaper, cost him 144 francs and 70 centimes. However, he does not appear to be completely beaten by the turn of events. To amuse the children, he even improvises one of his famous boxing dances (the "Fish Boxing" for Ketty, the "Wild Goose" for Dolly). That evening, as he shares his first meal back with Maxime and Pauline, his misfortune gives him the idea for a book that would contain the principles of a completely new combat technique, founded on the strategy used by the fleas. He even hopes, he says, to add a chapter to *The Art of War*: indeed, as in the greatest combats of Sun Tzu, he was beaten without fighting! He, the intrepid combatant, the floating boxer, fled from a flea, from the typhoon of typhus.

THE MADAGASCAR PROJECT

There came, in the middle of January, a storm so strong that with its northeasterly winds, you would have said it wanted to lift up the whole island and that all its inhabitants were thrown into the air.

First, there was a black swarm of muscular clouds formed on the right. On the left two great curtains of rain headed for each other and would soon join together. Then, farther away, a gathering up of gauzes, foams; white, orange, and yellow bands. The rain always comes in the evening; you would say that it preempts the night with its coating of clouds. Its noise is like the feet of an innumerable crowd—the terrible murmuring of storms. The sky is loaded with compact vapors, the winds howl, and the sea swells: on the waves the men are worried about a worrying sea.

It is the dictatorship of the shadow: something dark unfurls, and everything is erased under the advance of that great dark hand. Before you can even move, all you see around you is the presence of the rains. Suddenly, they have invaded the world, and at that precise moment, it is difficult to imagine that there is any place on earth where it is not raining.

Then there is a great commotion of lightning over the world. All of the laws of time and space are abolished, waves join up with clouds, tornadoes climb to the skies and descend to the abysses; the key to the winds has been lost. The sky passes in black and white, and you hear great rumbles of thunder so loud they could tear the earth apart . . . You hear murders and throats being slit, cries, cracks and groans, great waterfalls crash and rush into the catacombs—monstrous parturitions: you no longer know if these are childbirths or disembowelments. Ivory and gold streaks split the sky.

Sometimes the lightning is so violent that the light seems to be searching for a way into the very bedroom, in successive layers. The odor of the wet earth reveals the multitude of cadavers. In the cemetery crabs slide under the clay and devour the latest bodies. Nuns cross themselves in the little church, in the nearby mosque an imam mumbles his sutras, his hands folded like a book on his face. All of a sudden, the whole town is held in a great white halo. At the same time the candles are blown out, electricity stops, and you don't know if the world is still there.

Now there is no shadow anywhere. The world is now a great revelator; it is a gigantic white orgasm. Underneath, there is the uninterrupted spluttering of water like an orchestra pit. From time to time roars cut through the air, blazing planes take off in every direction, crossing diagonals of sound and light, the folly of the mad night, the demented sound of the ages, dislocation of the air, sky, and time.

It is the time of beasts and clamor, guerrilla warfare of lusts that are set alight and fears that run wild. Humans become again like any other animal. In my bedroom, at night, I listen, I prick up my ears . . . "It is the time to make love to a Negress, the time to rape a white woman! It is a time for races and dogs!" At the Nouvel Hôtel a client makes this terrifying remark. But maybe that was a dream.

Outside, the air is hot and the rain icy. The slightest drop on your shoulder turns you into an ice statue. The streets are transformed into torrents; the roads become lakes. In the hotel lobby there is water up to your calves. Distressed cars with all their lights on wander through the night, this night that is no longer night and is whiter than the day itself. A white man in a white shirt passes by outside under the white rain, but he no longer has a shirt, his shirt has become his skin itself, it is translucent, he will soon become a phantom. A black man, on the contrary, is more and more black, he falls back into his race, he is the knotty trunk of the tree, the shadow of the stone pillar.

And the unrelenting night lets loose its thunder, a night that is no longer night. And the great battle in the skies and the sound of the seas, as the sky is no longer the sky and the sea has left its boundaries. Man is no longer man, and fear has gripped him. Where does this rain come from? It must have crossed a world of ice, entire worlds devastated to join up with this one—ours—and to bring to us its icy message. Soon the electrical companies' generators will dare not rumble, and people themselves will fall silent. The storm holds the whole city in a bowl that lets nothing drip out. Filaments of light and the thunder's arrows mysteriously connect all the inhabitants, without their knowing it.

*

— Did you sleep well?
— You are joking! Did you hear that rain?
— Yes. Strangely, it has given me an idea.
— What idea?
— That I might talk about the Madagascar Project?
— Oh! No, please don't!
— Why not?
— Because it is past. It is not even history; it is prehistory. It goes back to the Stone Age, the days of the cavemen! Your grandfather was a contemporary of the mammoth and the lakeside villages.
— Yes, it's a bit old . . . and yet maybe it is we who have aged and not this particular bit of history.

Li-An stretches out, smiles at me. She wants me to give her a massage now. The storm makes her nervous, makes her stiffen up. That is no good for fencing: your body needs to be relaxed, supple, and free.

I see myself more as an acupuncturist: I insert a few needles at specific points . . . the wrong way around . . . Yes, we need to talk about it as nobody speaks about it anymore, go directly to the nerve, touch the most sensitive spot: Taoist energetics . . . a critical antidote . . . close examination of the knots and tangles.

*

As the plague runs riot over Madagascar, another plague is being prepared.

For the majority of historians it begins officially on 3 September 1939, when France and the United Kingdom declare war on Germany following the invasion of Poland. It is the Second World War. Few people concern themselves with the fate of Madagascar in the gigantic tornado engulfing the world; no one really sees how that will help in comprehending anything, right? And yet.

From 1940 the British forces impose a terrible blockade. Madagascar is a site of primary strategic importance in the Indian Ocean: the island is at the confluence of all the maritime flows, it opens or closes the routes to India, Pakistan, Sri Lanka, Bangladesh, and Burma (all territories of the British Raj) as well as to the Suez Canal and the oilfields of the Middle East. In a few weeks most communications are interrupted, and goods and supplies only trickle through to the territory. The Malagasy people suffer especially from this situation, notably in the countryside. Products, which arrive in lower quantities because of the blockade, no longer leave the big towns. It is strangulation: they try to diversify the points of distribution, but the country is living in slow motion.

There is no more gasoline; there are no more imports and no more textiles. Pauline stops working completely: the tailors are penniless and out of work. In any case nobody thinks any more about dressing well. In the great shortage of everything that is coming to be, people forget about their clothes. The Nuñes workshop closes its doors near the end of 1940, never to open again.

With it disappears the special way of cutting cloth and marrying it with the thread, a certain science of fabric and folding. The old Indian, Malagasy, and Portuguese tailors, who fill the workshop with their diligent humming, are the bearers of a millenarian know-how: Renaissance, Richelieu, Colbert, Venetian, Madeiran . . . they know the secrets of embossing, the detours of the raised satin stitch, they are experts of hemstitched fiction in all its varieties. With a choice of multiple materials—sometimes surprising and practically inexhaustible: wool, silk, sisal, paper, cotton, linen . . . they deploy an assortment of practices originating in India, Europe, and Africa. You find in their catalog a shimmering array of embroidery and stylish techniques: "painting with the needle," "old-time embroidery," "golden embroidery" . . . The beginning of the conflict marks the end of their reign: no more damask, gone the mantillas, seams, collars, lace . . . We will no longer see emerge from under their fingers the splendid flowery tablecloths adorned with a multitude of little colorful characters. With them disappears a certain idea of elegance, a sense of chic, a fragile and smart form, almost incomprehensible today, of beauty: when they take down the sign one morning in September 1940, it is a whole art of living that sinks into oblivion.

There is a shortage of rice; stocks of flour and corn drop. The colonists help themselves to the harvest; the natives are even more dispossessed than normal. Taxes rise inexorably, levies flourish: byway taxes, slaughter taxes, cattle taxes, spade taxes . . . To pay them—not to is equivalent to an act of high treason—people are obliged to sell their rice uncut. Mahajanga, the "City of Flowers," becomes tax city. As if that were not enough, the governors Cayla and Annet use the pretext of the blockade to increase forced-work punishments and reinforce the practice of "services": these compulsory work punishments included in the native code double between 1939 and 1941. It is the time of the corvées and burdens, tithes, taxes. When the Vichy regime is established, it gets even worse: except for certain very specific products (notably graphite, mica, and raffia, which are of interest to the Reich and are sometimes directly exported to Germany), shortages and scarcities are everywhere. It is a cold and dark time across the land.

In the country the testimonies are terrible. People fling themselves on a piece of biscuit the size of two chestnuts, on a piece of cheese the size of a thumbnail. They eat plant roots, burnt bones, dried lupines, and land crabs with furry flesh and a bitter taste.

Little by little Pauline also stops her English classes—speaking English attracts right away the suspicion of the authorities—but continues to give French classes. In 1940, by bravado or perhaps by rancor, she includes on the syllabus "Delfica" by Gérard de Nerval:

> They will come back, those Gods that you constantly mourn!
> Time will bring back the old ways . . .

A veil passes over her black eyes. She knows well that it is not true, that time never takes a step backward, that the days and night carry it along, like all of us, toward its demise.

The following year she puts on the syllabus "Épître à Marie d'Orléans" by Villon. In times of combat you need restless pupils who know "the sharper and his snare" . . . Pauline insists especially on the expression "the stemming of the false and the miserly." Encoded messages always circulate.

But if she buys a newspaper to learn the latest or if she leaves the Nouvel Hôtel for a walk, she sees around her only swaggering signs of abjection, decked out in the sinister assurance of triumphant discourses. In the streets and big towns of the island, it is quite simple: Pétain is everywhere!

After the debacle of 1940, the colonial empire is more or less the only thing that remains to save the honor of "Eternal France": all over they append to that phrase images of the Marshal. In Toamasina, the large island of the east, the Boulevard de la République is renamed Boulevard Pétain. In Antananarivo, in the Mahamasina stadium, members of the legion of French Volunteers swear allegiance before a huge portrait of Pétain, framed right and left by the battle-ax of the "victor of Verdun." An athlete of the Gymnastics Society lights the flame in the urn of remembrance. "The smoke that rises like incense into the sky symbolizes the rise of hope in the resurrection of the country," reports the *Bulletin of Information and Documentation* of the general government of Madagascar of 15 January 1942. At this point, in Europe, other flames are being lit—those of the crematoriums.

In Mahajanga, all over the avenue de Mahabibo, photos and drawings of the new master pile up in the houses along the craggy streets. In all the shacks you find the same punctilious, pale icon: handlebar mustache, oak leaf kepi, and khaki coat.

So that the Marshal's domination is complete, in space and time, they mix up the Malagasy traditions with the rituals of the new order. Philippe Pétain is thus to be compared to Andrianampoinimerina, the prestigious sovereign who unified the country in the nineteenth century and completed the work on the ten rice fields of Alasora. As the nickname of "Savior of Verdun" is a bit exotic, they find a circumlocution in the local language to describe the new guide of the nation: "Vovonana iadian' ny lohany," that is to say: "The apex on which sit the roof's rafters" . . . According to the newspapers, Pétain is referred to in turns as "the father and the mother," "our *Ray aman-dreny*," or again, in a nice lyrical and patriotic flight, as "the great *Ray aman-dreny* of all the *Ray aman-dreny*!" Finally, he is also given the title of "Mpanjaka," the supreme administrator . . . In its absurd spiral the nationalist fervor transforms the leader of the French into a Merina king, a Malagasy god!

The press, under orders, hangs on to the slightest movement of the new head of state, analyzes his actions and words, and drinks the juice of his words . . . Two stamps are issued in his image, and he is found even on the calendars of the PTT, the post and telecommunications authority. "Pétain is like the plague," Arthur exclaims. "He reigns over Time!" But you can't speak too loudly . . . The police are omnipresent; there are spies everywhere . . . the "rumor police" functions . . . attentive ears listen out on the café terraces. Everything you say could be held against you: conversations are monitored, people happily inform on others.

*

It is a British filmmaker who, in strange circumstances little known even today, conveyed better than anyone that atmosphere of subterfuge and generalized corruption. The film is called *Aventure malgache*, Malagasy Adventure: it was filmed in less than four weeks with a very small budget, and its director is . . . Alfred Hitchcock.

The least one can say is that you would not expect to find the name of the "master of suspense" on the credits of this short film commissioned by the British Ministry of Information. Completed in 1944, the film was to be shown in France after the Allied victory, to assert the heroism of Free France persecuted in the colonies by the Vichy authorities. In fact, it will be refused several times and not be shown publicly at all until . . . 1993. It is an invisible, undetectable film that has disappeared and been kept from cinemas to spare, according to a British report from the 1970s, "French sensitivities" . . . It is true: when it is rediscovered, after this purgatory of almost fifty years, written on its sleeve is the instruction: "to be burned."

This is because the scene presented by Hitchcock is far from the propaganda he was hired to do: on the contrary, in just over thirty minutes, he takes apart all the shrewd mechanisms of disinformation. The film begins with a great idea: a setting in a London stage dressing room, where one of the actors no longer knows how to play his gangster role and asks for advice from his colleague, a former lawyer who worked in Madagascar at the time the Pétainist regime was being set up. There follows a scene full of subtleties, convolutions, and intricacies—you can tell Hitchcock was educated in a Jesuit school—that denounces the Vichy regime but criticizes in passing the French colonial regime.

The spectator gradually sees that everyone plays a double or triple role in this film: books may contain coded messages, telegrams have double meanings, and secret messages are hidden in alarm clocks . . . An amorous woman is revealed, not unexpectedly, as the worst of traitors, while Pétain himself saves the skin of a resistance fighter. Everything has a false bottom, a triple drawer in this multi-triggered script: the acting becomes confused and disorientated, certainties fade, and the apparently good mood is undone. The hero has a chance in a thousand to get away: as always with Hitchcock, he manages to escape!

In the battle Hitchcock has chosen his side: he is evidently against the wretched Vichy regime, but don't rely on him to sing the praises of the French colonists. With all the irony he has of a big cat, he reserves for them a few swipes of his claws: from the opening images he describes them as "dangerous people who have transformed Madagascar into a fiefdom of exploitation." To whom can one then turn in the upheaval? The response is simple: to Molière—the troupe of actors is called the "Molière Players"—and to La Fontaine: it is La Fontaine's *Fables* (that mysterious unidentified people have distributed across the island to children and natives) that spread the secret messages of the Resistance.

Hitchcock is a laser: he goes through with a fine-toothed comb the ambiguous discourse of the forces who, in order to subjugate the people, claim to liberate them. From the first scene of the film, he gives us the key to this savage charade. The film, in fact, begins with these extraordinarily provocative words: "The story that we are about to show you will not teach you anything. We know that. If we are telling it to you, it is because it is true. And that it shows that in the most distant possessions of the French empire, across the seas people breathe the same air."

On first sight that could be read as a simple piece of propaganda glorifying the French Resistance. But what "breath" and what "air" is he talking about? Those of the national resistance or, more broadly, of the call for liberty? After a breathtaking half-hour diving into the shadows and half-light, you cannot but reread this introductory declaration as ironic praise in favor of all forms of liberty.

In any case the film would have pleased Pauline, who in 1939, while the war was just beginning, had just included in her evening class syllabus "The Two Pigeons" by La Fontaine and Molière's *Tartuffe* . . .

*

But while it waits for Hitchcock and his sarcastic camera, the island enters into a festival of fabricated images and verbosity. *Authority! Discipline! Allegiance, hierarchy, tradition* . . . all these trumpeted words reappear, throwing the country into an almighty babble.

New slogans appear, and words change their meanings. Every-where the words "Liberty, Equality, Fraternity" are replaced with "Work, Family, Fatherland." There reigns a perceptible sense of revenge: finally, one can openly denounce "the lie of universal suf-frage," the "electoral swamp." The Popular Front is transformed into a historical misstep and is no longer part of the History of France; the important thing is to close quickly once again this historical dead end. Jews and Republicans are castigated; Gaullists, Communists, and socialists are denounced . . . Voices become high-pitched and sink into the deepest tones.

Haven't you noticed that these Malagasy have long been quite insolent? The native no longer salutes! To neither his black chiefs nor his white leaders! There are also the freemasons and that old bitch Marianne whom the Jews love. And that whole clique of the laics, the antireligious, and not to forget the Voltarian dogs. Also held responsible for the nation's ills are the libertines, those with free morals, Sybarites, good-for-nothings, perverts, pleasure-seekers, Epicureans . . .

With that comes the great switch in people's ideas and coats being turned. Those who were socialists from the time of Augagneur and radicals from the time of Cayla become Vichyists under Vichy . . . You see all sorts of turncoats! Many key political men carry out spectacular complete turnarounds, draped in the elegance of the grand ideals and the excuse of being in service to the motherland. Their great speeches on liberty are transformed into long petitions in favor of dictatorship. It is the "opening"! They are welcomed, congratulated, praised for their sincerity, compensated with a minor role of some sort or a mission: it is a bonus for sycophancy.

It is, above all, *work* that becomes the general watchword, the great organizer of people's lives and thoughts, the universal door opener. Pétain is not only the "savior of France" but also the "father of the workers." Great labored tirades appear in all the newspapers, against a background of the Eiffel Tower and factories.

"Work has pride of place," as they say. The island's schools are transformed into vast workshops for manual labor. Arts and crafts are particularly prized. There is a turn to the rural, to sources and tradition. Old words that praise the hardworking village communities make their reappearance at the instigation of the colonists: *asa, fanompoana, fokolonona* . . . The Malagasy themselves witness with curiosity the resurgence of all these customs, some of which had fallen out of use and had been described to them before as the final remains of a savage culture.

Right away, let's get to work! Ah, we're going to put them back to work, all this rabble! The unruly, the walkers and strollers, had better watch out . . . On 24 April 1941 the first of May (Saint Philip's Day) becomes the "Day of Work and Social Harmony": great jubilant events are organized on the island. Suddenly, politics is mixed up with patriotism and the epic: they excoriate social leveling and egalitarianism, which have replaced the taste for work and the culture of results. Work is not sufficiently compensated, valorized, or respected, and they want to put it at the heart of society. The France of the lazy and fractious, the work shy and the shirker, is stigmatized. It is the great requisition of the lazy, the open hunt for the indifferent. As for the well-known indolence of the overseas populations, it will finally find in all this its antidote.

Faithful to his habits, a caustic Maxime quotes the Bible: "They made their lives bitter with harsh labor in brick and mortar and with all kinds of work in the fields" (Exodus 1.14), which immediately earns him some funny looks.

Finally, all across the town, in the form of large posters or little signs you see: "The Marshal has spoken."

You find them at the post office, the bakery, the rice seller's and the tobacco vendor's. Absurd and even shameful questions are on everyone's lips, without anyone taking offense: "Do you know better than him the problems of the moment?" or "Are you more French than him?" . . . All that is talked about is cleansing the country, getting it back on its feet, lifting it up, revitalizing it. Have faith in us: in regenerating France, we are years ahead . . . "All French people to be proud of France, and France proud of every French person, such is the order we seek to establish."

Suddenly, the language of Montaigne and Voltaire is freighted only with puffed-up slogans. The politicians' mouths are filled with the words *immigrant* and *national identity*: they are at once the problem and the solution to every problem. There is a certain tone that is synonymous with this discourse: waxy voices, syrupy like a balm, that gutturalize their vowels and rise at the end of sentences, aggressive syllables, and saddening metaphors . . . all of that makes itself heard, in every speech. They speak of "attributing to the naturalization decree a properly sacramental quality!" They go mad for economic comparisons: "The illusion that imagines that you can make one more Frenchman with a decree inserted into a register of laws is related to that which imagines one can become rich by handling the banknote plate . . . Let us guard against inflation of nationality! Let us not make any paper Frenchmen!"

There is also a certain distrustful and entangled relationship with time. They proclaim: "We should grant only *temporary* and *revocable* naturalization status." They forewarn and threaten: "We are going to dissolve the clusters of foreigners!" Many years later here they are, then, sons and grandsons of immigrants, dissolved under threats, torn to shreds, pulverized. Yes, *paper Frenchmen*, the term suits me. A Frenchman with little weight, a Frenchman of the borders and margins, an alluvium, branch, or outgrowth of Frenchness. And it is one of those who is writing these words. For the honor and glory of France, obviously.

*

In this context of disintegration outrageously dressed up as a national renaissance, people reveal themselves, as in all of history's puppet shows. A remarkable store of hatred rises up, and in a few months the island falls into a complete slump.

As soon as a country goes wrong, you see it in its way of treating foreigners. On this island that has for centuries blended cultures and colors, strangers are now like the plague itself. Arthur is one of the first to pay the price. One morning he is taken aside on the boulevard: he is accused of coming to fish for sea cucumbers by boat for six months of the year and leaving again without appearing on any official register! Arthur does not like fish and has never owned a boat, but that doesn't matter. He is in any case a Chinaman, with his lemon face and grapefruit head—a Barbary ape. Jeers and taunts gush out easily for these rice-eating monkeys. Everywhere their stranglehold—and that of the Indians—on the small businesses of the island is criticized: they are always on the make, use underhand methods, and commit dreadful acts of usury! Arthur escapes with a few punches and two or three acrobatic kicks that throw off his assailants, but he is emotionally affected by the incident. In the evening he is found in low spirits at a table of the terrace of the Nouvel Hôtel: "The plague is over the town," he says, "the plague is over the town."

The blacks and the Indians are not spared. Black people are called 'leather scrapers' and 'rubber chewers.'" There are some *rotakas*—the word crackles like a beating—disturbances in which some Karanes, the town-dwelling Indians, are singled out. For too long there have been massive arrivals of foreigners in the islands' big ports, people talk about an invasion and how it is time to have the purity of the race respected. Parasites! Vagabonds! Ethnic progress is coming; you just have to stay in line.

Even music is affected by this triumphant blight. In 1940 the Vichy government decrees 14 July as a day of national mourning. No more balls, no more jazzy sounds . . . At the Nouvel Hôtel, with the Nuñes family, people protest. Give us back our 14 July! No, no more parties, just gatherings. It is the new politics: moving from the streets to the stadium. At 13 rue Henri-Palu there is no more swing.

The secretary of state for the Colonies is called Charles-René Platon (Plato in French). "Plato! No surprise that he wants to chase all the artists from the town!" Pauline mutters, in a really sarcastic tone. It is true that the concerts at the Nouvel Hôtel don't exactly have the *color* of the musical shows advocated by the unbridled folklorist patriots of the new regime. Armstrong, Fats Waller, the Creole Jazz Band . . . brass, drums, dulcimers, all these guys with their tortuous tom-toms! For the propagandists and musicologists who strive to draw up a racialized theory of music, jazz is a black man's music. "Darkies and Jews—it's the same thing." As if to prove the point, little pictures appear, representing jazz in the figure of a black saxophonist wearing the Star of David.

In any case all that leaps and sparkles is now classed as a seditious element. The new masters want only predictable and ordered movements: the oral contortions of Uncle Pierre on his trumpet and the spinning vocals of Pauline on the piano are dangerous and unseemly. They point to a body state that is not normal, integrated, or regulated. In an *Information Bulletin* of 15 February 1942, the government of Madagascar gives notice of the principles of the new dance and sporting pedagogy: lots of sport for the boys, ballet and sewing lessons for the girls. It is a matter of "preparing the young girl for her feminine role by encouraging the normal development and functioning of her organs." In a few lines everything is said: distribution of roles and rules, physical torpor, the body broken down into its organs.

To top it all off, they learn that Johnny Dodds has just died in Chicago . . . That evening Pauline hums discreetly at the piano: "What did I do to be so (black and blue)?"

*

On 15 March 1941 the Jewish Law of 3 October 1940 is applied in the colonies. As in the metropole, a certain number of activities are forbidden to Jewish people in public administration, business, and industry. In concrete terms it means that there are no more Jewish officers, journalists, directors, teachers . . . More or less spontaneously, the island's administration receives numerous letters certifying one belongs to "the French race and the Catholic religion." Administrators, colonists, businessmen . . . all are French and Catholic! Stamped on letterhead, certified to be in conformity.

Conversely, for the first time in her life, Pauline no longer sets foot in church. During this entire period the Nuñes family goes into a form of silent resistance: no more music on a Saturday night, no more Mass on a Sunday morning, a real sacrifice. The churches, however, are full—of people who have never been seen there before! Those who had been strictly nonreligious under the socialist governors Augagneur and Coppet become holy Joes under Cayla and Annet. This new religiosity has to do with power, Pauline says.

Among the letters there are many instances of people informing on others. People write in order to hand others over to the law, to accuse them, to sell them out. In Antananarivo a man named Alexander Dreyfus—whose name attracts attention right away, of course—is denounced by a letter indicating that he is continuing to sell rice a few feet from the Saint-François Xavier Church . . . the profession of grain merchant is no longer one of those open to "Judeans": he will therefore be arrested and thrown in prison. One can from now be a crook and a good citizen. You can be an everyday racist, so to speak, spontaneously, happily, and conscientiously. There is an ordinary form of racism; you even get well-meaning racists. Guilty jealousies, re-baked hatreds, the dishonest and legalistic pens of the salaried scribes of everyday mediocrity: all the low-level personnel of the vast culture of viciousness.

*

The following summer the tone rises again: the Malagasy newspapers announce that all Jewish persons must declare themselves to the authorities for the census set out in the recent law of 2 June 1941. As in the "real France," they must declare not only their place of residence but also their profession and the value of their possessions.

The only thing is: what is a Jew? The count produces results that are, to say the least, speculative: there are altogether twenty-six Jews on the island (half of whom are French nationals). There are only twenty-six of them? No matter, they will be persecuted like the others.

I wonder a bit why, while there is barely a Jew to be found anywhere, the racial obsessions of the Vichy regime and the Nazis resonated and were applied with such zeal on the Red Island. It seems evident that the specific structures of the colony created the conditions for it: from the beginning of the conquest, Gallieni had put in place a "racial policy" based on the most recent techniques (cartography, anthropological photography), and racial separation certainly existed in the colonies: in the schools, in the markets . . . Could colonization have an insidious link to the persecution of Jews, even if it cannot be reduced or is even homologous to anti-Semitism? Underneath their radically different outward appearances (one charges itself with a civilizing mission, the other seeks to eradicate), there are certain troubling similarities, and colonization often creates a space for anti-Semitism, as is shown in the extraordinary saga of the "Madagascar Project."

*

The Nazi project to deport European Jews to Madagascar, little known and sometimes treated in an offhand manner even by historians, is called the Madagascar Project. It is the expression of this imaginary, or more precisely chimerical, configuration that has for a long time made Africa in general, and Madagascar in this particular case, a site of relegation, a dumping ground in the mapping of the world.

The first to have expressed this idea is apparently a German Orientalist of the nineteenth century, Paul de Lagarde. Lagarde was violently anti-Semitic. According to him, "You don't negotiate with bacteria and parasites, you exterminate them." Or which amounts to the same thing, you send them to Madagascar . . . In anti-Semitic circles the idea will gain ground. For his part Stalin was to try something similar, in sending Soviet Jews to an icy, desolate territory (which apparently still exists): Birobidjan. Argentina, Uganda, and even the Peul territory of Guinea also provide "solutions" to what was to become a real obsession: to expel the Jews from Europe. Jewish people sometimes let themselves, through enthusiasm or lassitude, be seduced by this idea.

In 1937 it is the Poles' turn to become interested in Madagascar: a delegation is sent to the island, discussions open with the France of the Popular Front. Sixty thousand, forty thousand, or twenty thousand? It is a big island, as big as France, Belgium, and Holland put together: how many people can it take? Between 1938 and 1941 the Nazis lean seriously toward this option. Hjalmar Schacht, president of the Reich Bank, looks for a financial arrangement, the German navy casts a covetous eye on the islands of the Indian Ocean (the Bay of Antsiranana is the second largest in the world, after Rio), the company IG Farben envisages setting up markets there: feasibility studies—strange vocabulary, still very close to our own—are carried out, and Hitler himself brings the subject up several times, on 20 June 1940, for example, during a speech with the leading admiral Raeder and then, a few days later, in front of Mussolini. In this affair there is constant manipulation: the point is also to divert the Duce's attention while not informing him of the attack against the USSR and to sow uncertainty around the intentions of the Nazis. To the east or the west? Africa or Russia? Make others believe in this or that, sow confusion in the various administrations in order to control them better, strategically avoid the doubts of some and reinforce the hopes of others . . . External manipulations, internal scheming: it is a good example of how the Nazi machine worked.

Soon the Madagascar Project will see the light of day. It is drafted by Franz Rademacher, the advisor on Jewish affairs at the Ministry of Foreign Affairs, and will pass successively through the hands of the advisor Luther, the minister Ribbentrop, and the Führer himself. In his journal Eichmann—who will himself draw up in August 1940 a dossier titled "Madagaskar Projekt"—presents this plan as a "humanist" solution to the Jewish problem. More recently, the same argument has been used by Robert Faurisson, who claims that the "Final Solution" was in truth a "territorial final solution," that is, not an attempt to exterminate but a plan (of almost Zionist inspiration) to finally give a country to the Jews.

A close reading of the proposal signed by Rademacher on 3 July 1940 shows that it is nothing of the kind. Indeed, the final sentence says the opposite, indicating, with the usual modesty of the men of the Reich, that the Germanic sense of responsibility prevents the Germans from giving the Jews a sovereign state. According to this plan, the Jews were to have a part of the territory under their control, notably administration of roads and communications, but the island was to be placed under German mandate, crisscrossed with German naval and air bases, under the control of a German military governor (the *Polizeigouverneur*). A European bank was to be created to ensure the financing of the population movements, funded by Jewish money and, if that did not cover it, by loans. The aim is clear: to make the Jewish indebted to a Europe of which they would no longer be citizens and to make them a stateless people under mandate. A reservation, in effect: the word is apt, a site for animals.

As for the Malagasy people, they are not even mentioned: all that is stated is the fate of the twenty-five thousand French people and the compensation that will need to be paid to them. Jews and natives, in the same bag. "Disposable people," you could say: people who can be transported, hawked around, and deported. And also detained, ordered, *lined up*. People you can get rid of.

The man who applies for the role of governor of the island is far from unknown: it is Philipp Bouhler, the head of the Chancellery and the man responsible for the program to eliminate handicapped people, Aktion T-4. So, the Madagascar Project was an alternative to extermination? It would be very naive to think so. A temporary hypothesis in the presumption of a rapid victory against the British? No doubt. It is revealing nonetheless, in its very urgency: in its absurd, crazy way, it played a role in normalizing the idea of Jewish deportation, in disseminating the possibility of their physical disappearance, of their *dismemberment* (Hans Frank, governor-general of occupied Poland, spoke of "sending them by ship, bit by bit, one by one, man and woman at a time, *every little girl*"), thereby habituating people's minds to the unnameable, getting them accustomed to the unacceptable.

THE WAR OF THE AIRWAVES

There are many ways to resist ignominy. You can frolic around with laughter or insolence, take up an active struggle or carry out symbolic attacks, find a vanishing point to redraw the horizon . . . According to what I could find out, Maxime practiced alternately each one of these methods.

First of all, he does not follow the great tide of planters, factory owners, and mine owners, who more or less all rally quickly to the regime. Nor does he follow some of his Malagasy friends, who reactivate the old ethnic classifications of the nineteenth-century monarchical regime: the "coastal folk" are simple and straightforward, the Betsileos of the countryside are honest and hardworking, the Merinas of the highlands are shifty and unreliable . . . No, in these troubled times Maxime reacts as an *ultramarine*. (I call "ultramarine" everyone who likes finesse and variety and does not accept the injustices of the world: his aim is to savor knowledge, to soften suffering—and to achieve that, he uses a few simple weapons: pencil, paper, colors.)

He could easily go with the flow and join up with the Pétainists.

Work, family, the fatherland? He works hard, as everyone knows.

The frenzy of sport, as peddled by the new regime? He is an acrobat, as everyone knows.

And family . . . he has two! As everyone knows!

But the deep racism of all these people disturbs him, their obsession with morality and the land—he who is so at ease by the seaside or in the air on his trapeze. He no doubt recalls at this precise moment his circus companions, the Siamese sisters and the Rat-Child, the dwarf Groseille and the two Venus girls. He will also recall Madame Bartolini and her laid-back ways: all this *tabataba*, this agitation, is unbearable, isn't it?

So, his body becomes once again that of a strange athlete, his face a passport of indeterminate color. During these years he describes himself successively as Malagasy, British, French, and Mauritian. To those who delight in heritage, filiation, and national identity, he offers in opposition this partial, precarious, mobile, and fluid response.

At the café he imitates the great personalities of the hour: he does Hitler; he does de Gaulle, down to the intonations, the hand movements, the slightest inflection of the voice. Right in the middle of the national consensus imposed by the visual image, he mocks the picture of Pétain's mustache, which has pride of place on the walls of the town. Stalin, Franco, Hitler, Pétain: "Mustaches are for bigmouths!" he says. Always there is humor and impertinence. The whole world is angry; he responds with lightheartedness. It is the acrobat's mode of warfare.

*

It is also at this time that he undertakes the construction of a strange edifice, which will be called the "Wall of the Mad." Not far from the large beach at Amborovy is a little unknown beach that has never had a name. It is called simply "Petite Plage," little beach.

It is there that Maxime throws out onto the sea a sort of parapet: every Sunday he is seen taking his trowel, knives, and spatulas, heading for Petite Plage. In a few months, with a few stones and some cement, he builds out into the sea a sort of small, narrow, low, shaped wall, which seems to cut the horizon with a perpendicular line. Arthur is by his side, and he nicknames this promontory "our Great Wall." The wall, however, has nothing of the fortification or the rampart about it: it is just a stone walkway built on the sea. At the time of its longest extension, the wall is thirty meters long. For a considerable time children use it for walking into the middle of the sea and fishermen for mooring their pirogues. After the war it will be progressively plundered by opportunist thieves and demolished by storms. In 2004 the two hurricanes Elita and Gafilo failed to carry it away completely. Today you can still see a little bit of it, licked by the waves and dotted with birds.

You have to wonder what spurred the two friends and what exactly their objective was in building the wall. Some say it was a building project, a house or hotel, others say it was a saltwater swimming pool, but none of these hypotheses is convincing: what good would it have been to either project to have a thirty-meter wall jutting out like an arrow into the ocean? None whatsoever. In fact, the wall will remain there, in its stone bareness, crossing the sea, a refuge for walkers who have lost their way, a promontory of the useless.

By an unlucky coincidence, the Wall of the Mad is the exact contemporary of the Nazis' Atlantic Wall. On the Atlantic coasts there were kilometers of barbed wire, machine gun boxes and gun turrets, concrete fortifications, and steel bells. It was a fixed defense system, an impenetrable line, as if the sea were a space never to be crossed. On the other side of the world, conversely, some granules, some bits of gravels, and a few yards of stone that serve as a refuge for birds.

*

The Wall of the Mad attracts the protests of the authorities right away. There is no construction permit, no announcement of the work, Maxime and Arthur don't pay the taxes, and, of course, there is no portrait of the Marshal on the horizon. According to Jean Pivoine, the old Indian jeweler, this wall, which is actually quite long, was built simply to welcome the landing of the British forces. No historian has ever engaged with this hypothesis, nor does any work on these questions today.

But at the same time Maxime makes things worse for himself: indeed, it is at this time that the rumor spreads of his *faty-dra*, an old Malagasy custom, a "blood oath" according to which two men promise reciprocal aid and protection for all of their lives. Maxime has just undergone the ceremony with a Malagasy called Ando. There is no need to underline the symbolic charge of this act. At the very moment when all across Europe people's facial features and skulls are being calibrated, when one's merit is calculated according to the size of one's nose (the Negroes' lime kiln noses, the Yids' hooked noses), the two men have just been playing with a dangerous taboo.

People suddenly remember that Maxime is originally from Mauritius and therefore has British nationality, which at the time was enough to arouse suspicion: was he a secret agent? What secret pact had he just sealed with the Malagasy? People were calling on the spirits of dead sailors in the British attack against the French navy at Mers el-Kébir. "It is Fachoda all over again!" You hear phrases like "The British stole Mauritius from us, they wanted to take Quebec from us . . . now it is Madagascar's turn." People have not yet forgotten that it was the Franco-British archipelago of the New Hebrides that was the first to rally to de Gaulle, on 23 July 1940. This time it is certain: this Englishman is a traitor, who is plotting with the Malagasy.

Enough is enough. New letters denouncing Maxime arrive at the administration: Maxime was heard to declare—according to one letter—that it was a strange historical juncture where, to be worthy of France, you had to go through England. Another letter attacks his family, with the smooth genealogical fastidiousness that people are capable of in times of decay and rot: Pauline's aunt, Émilia Jane Nuñes (called Tatamiya), is living with Nicolas Pagoulatos, a Greek, who works in a bakery owned by his brother-in-law Zapandis. And the Greeks, as we know, are rabid Gaullists. Another letter asks: what does he get up to all these days he is at sea? His business is virtually dead, like everyone's. For the Vichyists there is no doubt: people are aware that Maxime knows "the science of the currents," so he must be helping the British set their floating mines. Finally, a missive affirms that the Wall of the Mad could be used to help the British troops land on the island (which is also the opinion of the old Indian jeweler). Presented with this avalanche of "proof," the authorities move quickly: a few days later Maxime is thrown in prison.

As for the Malagasy with whom Maxime made his blood pact, no one knows much about him. I had long thought his name was Zamy, before learning that this name signifies *uncle* and that it is the Malagasy term for "blood brother." I learned later that his name was Ando, which means "dew": he was a descendant of slaves who became a farmer, was known for his plant grafting skills, and was a seller of flowers and fruits. But that is it: Ando disappeared from all records, all books, and virtually all memories. Maxime was imprisoned for the first time in August 1941. It is also at this precise time that we lose track of Ando.

*

As soon as you are imprisoned, you find people who want to complete your incarceration. Bars are not enough, you need trapdoors, cages, dungeons, isolation cells, dark deep pits from which you will never get out. You have disappeared physically, but they will do all they can to eliminate you completely from people's memories. You are thrown into the oubliettes, with their connotations of forgetting and oblivion.

However, Maxime's first prison stay lasts only a few days. People say he must have pulled a few strings or greased the palm of his guards. Perhaps through bravado or recklessness, he doesn't change his behavior much. On the contrary, he is hardly out when he launches into selling radio sets illegally with Arthur. At this point their tracks become hard to follow, a fine game of hide-and-seek begins. At this time, to buy radio parts is a crime: you gamble your life for an antenna wire, you could lose it for a few grams of galena, for a bit of crystal, an ounce of lead sulfide.

Hiding, making contacts, vanishing, moving around—Arthur is in his element in this world of secret agents. The acrobat from Wuqiao proceeds with such discretion in running the operation that it is difficult, even today, to work out how it ran. He is always working behind the scenes, in secret, clandestinely. Prudence in the planning, precision in the execution. It is also quite possible that the two men worked together to cover their tracks: Maxime attracts attention to himself by provoking, firing up, and prodding—during this time Arthur works in the shadow cast by his partner, furtively, in parallel. A police report drafted in Antananarivo in May 1941 even suggests the strange idea that they could be the same person. During this time ideas spread in waves, and spare parts circulate.

The enemy is omnipresent and all-powerful. The Vichy regime broadcasts its programs across the whole of Madagascar from a little village called Allouis, in the Cher region of France, using a formidable radio transmitter: four aerial masts in a radiating system, using 150,000 watts of broadcasting power, the largest station in Europe. In Madagascar people resist as they can. It is the battle of the airwaves: they try to tune in to Radio-Brazzaville or Radio-Algiers, instead of Radio-Paris and Radio-Vichy. It is not said often enough: the capital of Free France is not London or even Algiers; it was first of all Brazzaville, with its crew of European and American scientists and Congolese technicians.

The crystal radio set is the least expensive, with no need for batteries or electric current. But there are also cathedral-style radios, with the speaker in the upper part of the arc. *Radia . . . Radio Sigma . . .*

Radiola . . . Sonora: they have the names of Greek divinities with open final vowels that enchant Arthur and Maxime. They dream of making a set with the materials they have. Everything can be used in battle. A few meters of copper wire, a cardboard cylinder, and a metal cigar box can be transformed into a condenser. A bicycle rim, three leaves of tin, a spring and two ball joints: you have an excellent inverter, which will allow you to amplify the frequency and increase diffusion.

The two friends are known as experts in odd jobs, they are helped in this field by three Malagasy about whom I have been able to find only their names—Rakoto, Ramanarivo, and Ratoandro: they were known as the "three Rs," they were masters of recycling. Rakoto, Ramanarivo, and Ratoandro are geniuses in recovering and reusing things: they understand quickly, adapt perfectly, rediscover, spruce up, and renovate. All three venerate the cathedral in the town of Ambanja, which was built at the beginning of the century from the former metal railway station in Strasbourg, taken down, and put back together bit by bit. They say that if you can transform a railway station into a cathedral, anything is possible. And there you go—they'll transform for you an old iron pot into a radiator.

On the Pétainist side the strategy is different: faced with this out-break of technical inventiveness, they try to scramble the airwaves and confiscate radio sets . . . Above all—in a tactic that would be used extensively—they mix propaganda and entertainment: messages designed to mollify are wrapped up in a few popular hit songs. In the battle even jazz is used, that music of black people! A contemporary music critic called André Cœuroy has just shown that "at its origins" jazz is a French musical form . . . In this case the recuperation of memory is at its peak. "Lady Be Good" becomes "Les Bigoudis," or "The Hair Curlers"! And "Some of These Days," even this tune, this magnificent jazz track that Michel Leiris, set sail at the same time on a cargo ship bound for Greece, describes wonderfully as "those great blasts of horns that carve cliff sides into your heart," the same one that is sung by the black woman in Sartre's *Nausea*, finally saving Roquentin from his existential depression—the radiant "Some of These Days" is passed through the saccharine propaganda mill: it is renamed "Bébé d'amour," or "Love Baby." And that is how a ragtime composed by a black man, Shelton Brooks, and popularized by a little Jewish woman of Ukrainian origin who performs in blackface, Sophie Tucker, becomes a sugary nursery rhyme, with insipid rhythms. Playacting, mushiness, generalized deafness. Jazz under the jackboot of Propaganda-Staffel, it is all too much: Pauline flies into a rage, and Uncle Pierre turns off the radio, a sad look on his face.

*

But when evening comes, they switch the radio back on.

The Voice of France is on every evening from 6:00 p.m. to 6:45 p.m. GMT. The show begins; a green glow fills the room . . . The sound is sometimes very feeble, almost inaudible. You need to learn how to use the radio-weapon: you listen, you concentrate, you don't touch the antenna. You turn the buttons gently, looking for all possible sources. The needle shifts across the dial, but you have to have great dexterity in your fingers.

In this regard Pauline works wonders. The old radio set crackles, first emits a terrible background noise, but soon the whistles and interference are transformed into clear, measured words, with barely discernible crackling sounds, like stitches of clarinet playing woven into the sound. The rectangular dial becomes a musical scale on which Pauline's deft fingers move in small anticipations and unexpected rhythmic substitutions. She advances, goes back, one more two-bar coda, and that's it, no more movement, she has found the exact place: it is the science of the lateral movement.

From there they can listen to New York, Berlin, Washington, London, Stockholm, Ankara . . . it is a question of technique. Maxime has a soft spot for Radio Mauritius, which retransmitted General de Gaulle's call, and especially for the BBC and its show *Les Français parlent aux Français*, the French speak to the French. The language of this show pleases him, the easy blend of spoken and written expression, the maritime metaphors ("the lighthouse of Free France"), the tone of voice also, extraordinary voices rising from who knows where, charged with gum and resin. And more than anything, he likes the supernatural poetry of the coded messages: "Here in London, Marguerite will not come this evening, and yesterday the torrent overflowed." Or else, "Five friends will visit tonight Xenophon's wig." Or again, this one, which has lost none of its relevance: "The humming is overwhelming (the telegraph needs to be suppressed)."

Evidently—a sign of the times—all we retain today are the violins of Verlaine's "sanglots longs" that served to announce the landing, but behind these amusing, incongruous, surprising phrases are often hidden serious decisions: calculations about places and sites, raids from the sky, reception of materials and parachuted agents, financial transactions, resistance operations . . .

Listen.

Listen. "Andromaque wears lavender scent."

Let your inner auricle open up, in a great auditory ecstasy. "Athalie has remained in ecstasy. We say it again: Athalie has remained in ecstasy."

There is an extraordinary logic, which is implicit and immediately perceptible to the trained ear. There is a simultaneous translation from the mouth to the ear, a passage from the throat to the physical act; the word is transmitted by hand . . . You need to know, of course, all the workings of this clandestine poetry. The atmosphere is electric; the calls are extremely subtle; it is a poker game.

"Gentlemen, place your bets"—and it is a sabotage.

"The cock will crow at midnight"—the agents have entered into enemy territory.

"From Marie-Thérèse to Marie-Louise: a friend will come this evening—we say it four times": that is a parachute landing (four airplanes).

And what do you do when you hear the following phrase: "He has a falsetto voice?" Of course, straightaway, it is the triggering of guerrilla warfare! No question of submitting to the falseness of the voice.

Then fruits and vegetables come into play. "The carrots are cooked," "The die are on the table," and "The strawberries are in their juice": "It is time to cook the tomatoes"! In this loaded radiophonic poetry, anything can be used as a weapon in the struggle. Climate and geography are also used: "It is hot in Suez," "It always rains in England." But there is also political and religious history: "The death of Turenne is irreparable," "Saint Liguori founded Naples"; proverbs: "Fortune comes in sleep"; and songs: "There is no more tobacco in the snuffbox."

From time to time there are a few excursions to the Far East, to Japan: "The sun rises to the east on Sundays."

I repeat: "The sun rises to the east on Sundays."

Do you understand?

The battle is a great sonic treasure hunt, a game of clarifying misunderstandings. There is also created a whole fantastic, amazing bestiary: "The elephant has broken a tusk," "The Angora has long hair" . . . Suddenly, tastes and colors are discussed ("I like Siamese cats," "I do not like crêpes Suzette"), mixed up and debated, with all due respect to the old consensual compulsion: "I do not like veal blanquette." It is the time to throw a smutty stone into the water, to mess with the narrow-minded: "Yvette likes big carrots" (immediate action: to dynamite the fire station!).

All is possible in this parallel world of free sounds and actions that lead to very concrete results: "The invalid wants to run" (sabotage of a railway line), "Giraffes do not wear false collars" (taking down an electricity line), and "The cow jumps over the moon" (we thank agent Charlie Parker for this courageous act).

Of course, all of French literature is evoked: Du Bellay, "Happy is he who, like Ulysses, has made a long journey" (transfer of banned books); La Fontaine, "The two pigeons walk along the balcony" (contact made with a comrade); and Pascal, "He cried with joy" (parachuting of weapons and agents, wrecking of railway points, bombardment of all the branches in the system) . . . "Joy, tears of joy!"

At all hours of the day Maxime plays in this way on the nerves of the authorities, muttering terrible phrases and words that soon no one will know if they are allowed or banned, charged as they were with gunpowder or inoffensive and meaningless. Under the noses of the informers installed on the terrace of the Nouvel Hôtel, he lays false trails and spreads real information. Let him read the news while sipping on an orange and cinnamon drink, and he will intone, slowly: "The Benedictine is a sweet liquor." He is also heard, many times, reciting in a very distinct way: "The wine is in the library."

People say that this phrase maddens the chief of security in Mahajanga, who desperately seeks to decipher its meaning. During this time Maxime sets himself up on the chaise longue, a little smile lighting up his lips, his head leaning back toward the sun, as if to say: "Make of it what you will."

*

At the end of 1941 there are a growing number of acts of sabotage in the Mahajanga region: fires in hay warehouses, thefts of government supplies, destruction of signal equipment . . . A member of the Vichyist French Legion of Combatants and Volunteers of the National Revolution is thrown into the sea close to the Garden of Love. More seriously, two bridges are blown up round the Betsiboka River. To what extent are Maxime and Arthur involved in these diverse operations? It is precisely because they were efficient and discreet that we will never know for sure. It is also true that with one or two exceptions, no serious historian has ever looked into this subject, as if this overseas Resistance movement had never existed.

One thing is sure: the police keep a close eye on the pair, especially Maxime. At the beginning of 1942 the situation is very tense: combat rages in the Indian Ocean, right up to the Gulf of Bengal. Japanese forces, led by Admiral Nagumo, win several battles and plan to set up a submarine base in Madagascar. Terrible-sounding names circulate across the whole region—*Akagi, Hiryū, Ryujo, Shōkaku, Sōryū, Zuikaku*—and spread fear of submarines and aircraft carriers.

It is at this point that Maxime decides to lighten the tense atmosphere, in his own way. From now he will not go out without two bamboo poles, green and bendy, one on each shoulder. He says he is using them to pick mangoes or to drive the zebus. The authorities don't quite get this clever allusion to the general "deux gaules," a synonym for two poles . . . At this time new legislation permits the imprisonment of any individual for carrying a non-approved symbol. This law is directed principally to the Cross of Lorraine, but it will be invoked to demand Maxime Ferrier's second incarceration: the police report indicates that the defendant went into his cell "humming a tune, and still accompanied by his two bamboos."

Even under a Ubuesque regime, it is rare that anyone is condemned for walking with two bamboos. With the absurdity of the situation, with a bit of money and using the last of his contacts, Maxime leaves prison again. His house is searched, all his electronics material is confiscated, and they put a spy beneath each one of his windows. You might think that he would finally stay on the straight and narrow. Not at all: one week to the day after his second prison release, Maxime is incarcerated again; he was caught trying to light a fire on the beach. No doubt a signal for the British planes.

From that point Maxime finds himself in a perilous situation. He is taken to be, in turn, a professional diver in the pay of the

British, a relay radiotelegraph operator from Free France, or simply a madman. They hesitate between his multiple, knowingly arranged misdemeanors; no one quite knows anymore with what to charge him. As for his Chinese friend, where has he gone? Whatever the case may be, he is an "intransigent who should be locked up in the interests of public safety," according to a new police report. He is a civilian, but in these senseless times he risks a court-martial for his bridge of stone, for his fire on the beach, and for his two bamboos.

Confused by the atypical prisoner who mutters between his four walls some enigmatic sayings—"The nuts are dry and the fir tree is green, I repeat, the fir tree is green," "The sofa is in the middle of the living room"—the administration makes a serious tactical mistake: they let him out for half a day, under military surveillance, to get some toiletries. An hour later Maxime has disappeared, as if it was as easy for him to escape as it is for a bird to take flight. The two police officers charged with guarding him would be discovered the following day, bound and gagged in the church at Mahabibo.

This time Maxime has to flee; he has no time to lose. He thinks first, of course, of the Red Circus, of his numerous little hideouts. He could hide there for a few days, but the place is too close to the town, and he will swiftly be recaptured. He thinks also of joining up again with his old friends among the Bara people, those seminomadic herdsmen of the southern plateaus, who steal zebus and weapons and live all year surrounded by music and dance. It is an attractive prospect, but it is far away, and what would he do with Pauline and his children? Pauline, moreover, a fine strategist, makes the most of it: it is time to leave the town, to also leave the other women, to shelter all the children . . .

The decision is made in one night: they will go to Nosy Be, where there is not only the big house at Anfelana but also Maxime's soap factory, which is supplied with coconut oil from the

Seychelles. Even if he is in hiding, she could work at the factory. How can they do it? All his boats have been requisitioned, and in any case the island is too far away for one man to sail there, encumbered by a woman and several children. Thanks to a few secret arrangements that no one can unknot today, they travel by night, in a cargo ship called *L'Île Bourbon*. The journey is long and made in silence: they sail with all the lights out, in fear of the Japanese submarines that patrol the area. Maxime goes up to the deck a few times, the children sleep down below, among the cashew nuts and the vanilla pods.

As for Arthur, he is also threatened and leaves to hide out in the caves at Anjohibe. Eighty kilometers north of Mahajanga, it is a desert region and difficult to access. It harbors a network of tunnels formed by innumerable limestone corridors, full of vertiginous chasms, and crossed by an underground river: no problem, no one will find him there. He will live there right to the end of the war, in the passageways, braiding creepers and fishing for eels, suddenly returned to a quasi-prehistoric life, a clear and calm existence amid the surrounding chaos—whatever the circumstances, there is always a strange, muted poetry in the life of these men, they have no precise plan, but they let themselves be carried by the very movement of life, they are capable of existing in the way trees, fruits, and flowers do: a poetry of the chase, of the hunter and the hunted.

All that night, during the long crossing, to calm the children's anxiety or perhaps quite simply to celebrate the new twist his life has just taken, Maxime hums these wonderful phrases that he will be fond of for the rest of his days: "The beautiful Helen's eyes are not cold," "The blue horse walks along the horizon" . . . He knows hundreds of them, with their specific intonation, their own color, and the fire of their meanings. But he particularly likes this one and its sublime simplicity: "Veronese was a painter."

What does it mean, exactly? While everything around him is sinking into obscurity and noise, women and children on the run, his property seized, the world listless, boats and bamboos confiscated, he continues to hum this simple melodic line, this little background music, this art of the fugue in the layering of tones, the celestial glory of colors . . . On the ship's deck, in the terrible sweetness of his escape, he speaks to the sea in a half-voice: "Veronese was a painter."

I repeat: *Veronese was a painter* . . .

WALKWAY OF LONELY DEATH

"Brothers, I don't want you to be unaware that our fathers all came out of the clouds and mists, that they all journeyed over the seas . . ."

These are, according to her children, the first words that the pious Pauline pronounces on arriving in Nosy Be, her Bible under her arm, on the morning of 5 May 1942. It is at the same time a message for her children, together with her in the ship's hold, and a prayer whispered to the heavens. There she is, alone now with her seven children: Maxime has just left the boat to swim to the coast. He dived, she will recall later, "into the sea and into the night . . ." Pauline is afraid, the crossing has been difficult, she fears for Maxime, as the island's waters are infested by sharks. As for her, the police might be waiting for her at the quay: she constantly fears being jailed for having absconded and for complicity.

But the exotic Vichy regime has for now other fish to fry. Pauline hears the news as soon as she sets foot on the quayside: the whole island is boiling over; the British forces have just launched a large offensive on the north of Madagascar. It is Operation Ironclad, the most important British amphibious campaign since the Dardanelles. At stake is the control of the Mozambique Canal and the route to the Cape, within the line of fire the Trans-Iranian Railway and the oilfields in the Gulf. The Royal Navy 121 fleet lands in the immense bay at Antsiranana (Diego Suarez), of which a French sailor once said it could hold "all the squadrons of the world" but which has never seen so many corvettes, destroyers, and minesweepers.

On land, on sea, and in the skies, the battle rages . . . An uninterrupted air and sea ballet streaks the sky with curls of smoke and trails of powder. In the middle of the white clouds, the Swordfish and the Albacore do battle with the Moranes and the Potez bombers of the Vichy regime, which have flown up in great haste from Antananarivo. Their cockpits closed, the biplanes swarm overhead: a machine gun in the shooting position on the right wing, two others at the back in the gun carriage, they dump over the whole northern coast a carpet of bombs and torpedoes, accompanied by leaflets that call for the immediate and unconditional surrender of the island. On the other side, Vichy sends to the front line three battalions of Malagasy infantrymen and a battalion of Senegalese infantrymen: by one of those paradoxes of which History holds the secret, it is black and colored soldiers who defend the racist regime of Pétain!

Four months later the British launch an attack on the rest of the island with two new landings, one at Mahajanga and the other at Toamasina, before taking control of the capital. During this whole period the battles are fierce, explosive, and fiery. There is firing on the lakes, the bays, and the forests; the rumble of the gunboats rolls over the island like a storm, the smell of gunpowder hangs for miles around, bridges are destroyed, rivers burn . . . In November, finally, after months of guerrilla warfare that is rarely mentioned in history books—even if it is a part of the History of France—an armistice is signed, Madagascar passes into the hands of the British, who will hand it back to "Free France" toward the end of the year.

*

If it gives back to Maxime a certain room to maneuver, we owe it to truth to say that the British victory, then the handing back of the island to Free France (the Gaullist representative, with the delicious name of Paul Legentilhomme, arrives on the island in 1942), does not change much in the situation in Madagascar. On the contrary, forced work continues unabated, and taxes are raised even higher, all in the name of the war effort.

At the end of the hostilities, Maxime is summoned twice to Mahajanga, once by the British authorities and the other time by the "Free French," who have heard talk of the "General Deux Gaules" and his bamboos. All of the proceedings against him are annulled, and he receives a decoration. But he is financially ruined, and in any case none of that interests him, and he returns quickly to Nosy Be.

In Madagascar the situation is tense, in the towns the people are irritated, in the country they are exhausted. In the bush cattle thefts rise, and they have lost count of the number of robberies and assegai attacks. The first newspapers in favor of independence are making an appearance—*Imongo Vaovao, Maresaka, Sahy*—and will soon replace *Le Combat de la Côte* and *Le Madécasse*, the colonists' newspapers. The French defeat of 1940 to the Germans, coupled with that to the British in 1942, has destroyed the myth of French invincibility, while all across the world nations rise up against the colonizers. In Indochina the war has already started.

During this time, deaf and blind as they rarely are in their history, the French speak to the French and only to the French, without, however, really knowing anymore what exactly is a Frenchman or woman. In September 1946 the Malagasy deputies return from the constituent Assembly without having been able to have Madagascar recognized as a free state at the heart of the French Union. All across the island the black market grows, poverty increases, and anger rumbles. The following year a great revolt breaks out on the eastern coast. In 1947 there is carnage and pillaging, massacres and peasant revolts, which accompany an insurrection that was to be the first stage toward independence, even if no one knew it at the time. The French administration uses every means of repression: torture, summary executions, deputies arrested despite their parliamentary immunity, villages burned, militants locked up in railway cars and shot by machine gun.

Accused of being the instigator of the Malagasy revolt of 1947, it is a poet, Jacques Rabemananjara, who will be condemned indefinitely to forced labor following a trial, the injustice of which will be denounced by François Mauriac, one of the few to do so. The poet will finally be granted amnesty in 1956, but it is a stain on the French flag, which rings out like an alarm: when a poet is sent to prison, France is not really France anymore.

*

Extract from the *Official Journal* of the French Republic, Annals of the National Assembly, 15 March 1950, p. 2078:

Aimé Césaire: (. . .) In truth, while, in our territories, poverty, oppression, ignorance, and racial discrimination are the norm, while, increasingly, without regard to the Constitution, you strive to make the French Union not a union, but a prison for diverse peoples . . . [*Exclamations on the left, the center, and the right. Applause on the extreme left.*]

Paul Caron: You are quite happy that the French Union exists!

Marcel Poimboeuf: What would you be without France?

Aimé Césaire: A man who would not have had his freedom threatened.

Paul Theetten: That's ridiculous!

Paul Caron: You are insulting the motherland! [*To the right.*] Such ingratitude!

Maurice Bayrou: You were quite happy for us to teach you to read!

Aimé Césaire: It was not you, Mr. Bayrou, who taught me to read. If I have learned to read, it is thanks to the sacrifices of thousands upon thousands of Martinicans who have given up everything so that their sons may be educated and so that they may defend them one day. [*Applause on the extreme left.*]

*

For many years you might have thought that Maxime was a force in continual expansion, the luminous equivalent of a black hole that might have, so to speak, achieved its escape velocity, the speed that an object reaches as it escapes the forces of gravity. Invisible, reduced to an infinite point of density somewhere on the coast of an almost inaccessible island, he pursues his undetectable rotation, magnificently indifferent to all that goes on beyond the horizon. He follows his own singular trajectory, in a sort of immense insular respiration.

The year 1960 sees a veritable festival of African independences: Cameroon on 1 January, Togo on 27 April, Mali on 20 June, and Madagascar six days later. The month of August heats things up: Dahomey, Upper Volta, Niger, Ivory Coast, Chad, Congo, Gabon, Central African Republic . . . In Mahajanga there are smells, colors, rhythms, the flowers bloom like never before.

*

The weather, however, prepares its revenge. On 21 December 1961 a violent hurricane named Ada batters the Mahajanga Cathedral. The wind tears off the red tile roofing, and the heavy rains damage the organ: the torrent continues for three days and three nights, and it takes its leave only on Christmas Eve. Nosy Be is also affected. A bad omen? Maxime's sweet-smelling still is seriously damaged.

Three weeks later a new typhoon ravages the Indian Ocean: this time it is named Daisy. Pauline is afraid, as that is the name of one of her daughters—or rather, the name of one of Carmen's daughters, but what is the difference to her? Possessive and generous, she has always considered them to be her own. Will the hurricane take her loves from her? Hidden away in the house, the children see the daylight extinguished through the slats in the blinds. The wind cuts like a knife under the doorways, the rain smashes against the walls and batters the windows. On the second floor the library that stood at the southwest corner of the house, the most exposed section, is completely devastated.

At the same time Arthur disappears at sea. He had gone out in the morning on a fishing trip, never to return. He is among the three people who are reported missing the following day, carried away by the tornado, swallowed up by the Indian Ocean, or, who knows, grabbed by a shark. In Anfelana, where the news arrives a few days later, people find it hard to believe. Sure, the storm was raging, but all the same . . . Arthur can swim, and he knows the sea. Or maybe then . . . was it a shark? Maxime roams across the terrace the whole day, brooding over his anger. When evening comes, they dine in a deep silence in the middle of the acacias: the lightning has struck, the wood burned, and the sun is definitively extinguished.

The following day Maxime and Pauline hurry to Mahajanga. They will take part for two days in the sea search, but they must accept the truth: Arthur is dead.

It is at this point that Maxime has built in the cemetery by the Corniche the first of the three graves. The ceremony is simple and sober. Before the open grave, Uncle Pierre and two or three musicians, who are all that is left of the heaving orchestra of the Nouvel Hôtel, play Mozart's "Tuba Mirum." Maxime places in the empty casket a stick of bamboo, a vestige of the Bartolini Circus, and a simple bowl of rice. It is a hybrid rice variety that is called "tsemaka," a mix of a Malagasy variety, the *Makalioka*, and a Chinese variety, the *Chehuan*.

Tuba mirum spargens sonum per sepulcra regionum . . .

The trumpet's sonorous tones call out across the graves: the casket is sealed, and Arthur's invisible corpse descends into the shadows to the sound of the tubas.

Maxime senses it: a dark period has just begun. Death now is weaving its dark velvet into the jade foliage of the frangipanis. A few weeks later it strikes again, right at the heart of the home this time: in February, Pauline is hit by a virulent cancer, which takes her in a matter of weeks.

*

Now the night descends. I am entering into the darkest part of Maxime's story.

When evening falls, the wind rises. It picks up newspapers, makes the curtains tremble, and rattles the doors. The banana leaves seem to huddle together, trembling. In town you hear the sounds of engines, car doors shutting, cars throbbing: it is the end of the working day, and dinnertime approaches.

It is the time for shadows, the time when the sky dims on the horizon and the hills fade into the night. It is the last procession of clouds before the day ends and the passersby return home, their heads sunk into their shoulders, rushing slightly.

The hills resist for a long time the night that overtakes them. In the country, near the mountaintops, men, women, and birds slowly climb back up.

So, in this night that swallows everything, slowly, progressively, enormously, all you can see are the colorful parts of the buckets on the heads of the women.

*

Death at this point turns in the lock. An empty background imposes itself. The night falls, the birds pass by in the sky.

Pauline will die tonight; he knows it. The previous evening she could still get up. The doctor came, and in the way he moved his head, the way he repeated a thousand times the same gestures (take the pulse, touch the forehead, move the curls in her hair a bit farther back, behind the ears), he understood: Pauline is going to die.

Even yesterday she could get up.

Toward six o'clock in the evening she left her bed and walked to the sea, alone, barefooted. From his bedroom window Maxime watches her cross the sand and touch the water with her toes. In her white dressing gown she looks like a ghost. She must have made an almighty effort to make this final caress of the waves. Out of breath, close to falling over, she stops. Then, turning back, she sees the superb house, its tile-peaked roofs and its wood balconies, its little shutters opening onto immense ravines, its verandas.

Then it is the bedroom.

When she understood the gravity of her situation, Pauline did not want to stay in her bedroom; she wanted her bed to be set up near to the piano, on the west side of the house. She wanted to stay there, between the white rattan chairs, right beside the black piano. There are not many people around, but all those who saw her die remember it, close to eight o'clock in the evening, she suddenly utters this strange phrase:

— Ah! That is it beginning . . . she mutters.

— What are you saying?

Maxime is worried. She is unwell. Her breathing is halting, uneven; her cheeks are on fire. Now and then long shivers pass across her shoulders.

But she looks at him: her head rolls to the side in a very soft movement; then she opens her mouth . . . Her teeth are whiter than ever in the half-light of death. She pushes her lips out softly as if she were carrying something very light on the end of her tongue. Then she begins to hum a tune, her long slender fingers stretch out and tap on the bedsheet. She laughs. She says that her pulse, which beats very irregularly, is like a melodic line, that she hears, in the beating of her arteries, the echo of a music whose sounds she does not know.

She is thirsty. The doctor approaches, hands her a glass of water. She drinks from it and turns toward the balcony.

— Open the window, if you could . . .

The sea breeze blows into the room. It is beginning to rain. Pauline's chest rises, and it is almost like death has made her joyful, attentive as she is to the last swirls of life, to the backwash of blood in her uncertain veins. To every question she replies in a weak but clear voice . . . She smiles many times.

— I would really have liked to play a tune on the piano, she says, resting on an elbow.

But she is now too weak to get up. Soon the symptoms grip her again. She seems more agitated, her lips close tightly, her chest rises more uncontrollably. Lying on her back, her mouth closed, she feels her limbs tighten. The doctor rushes over. Her pulse slides under his fingers like a taut wire, like a harp string ready to break. He puts his finger under his nose and repeats:

— It is not a good sign, not a good sign . . .

But Pauline does not want to leave in this way, in solemnity and sorrow. She asks calmly that the doctor leave the room. Then slowly, in a superhuman effort, her hands slide beneath the sheets, and she starts to sing once again, in a soft and clear voice, the song of a she-wolf, a strange wordless monotonous chant . . . The lights of the house shine far into the fog, and the musical notes go to lose themselves there, among the branches of the trees.

A domestic went to find a priest. He is an old graying Malagasy who has taken a long time to arrive, as the roads are devastated by the two hurricanes that have shaken the island these past few months.

Pauline knows him well. She turns her face slowly toward him and seems happy to see the purple stole.

— Good evening, Pauline. Forgive me, I have kept you waiting.

— Good evening, father. Don't worry, I am in no rush.

Unfortunately, in his haste the old priest (whose name no one can remember today) has forgotten his bag. There is no holy oil, no Host, no consecrated wine. Not to worry: he asks Maxime to go find in his store a bottle of rum. "This one time your still will serve as the blood of Christ," he says to him.

Then he recites several prayers, soaks his thumb in the rum, and begins his anointing: the eyes, Pauline's big dark eyes, her nose that understands the secret of perfumes, her singing mouth, her piano-playing hands, and finally the soles of her feet. Pauline laughs at this incongruous caress:

— The Good Lord is tickling me . . . Is this, then, how we should abandon ourselves to the divine mercy?

— The ways of the Lord are impenetrable, Pauline. He can enter into you by the roots of your hair as by the tips of your toes.

The old priest's eyes are misty. He knows Pauline's sense of humor, but he did not think that today she would be at once so weak and so strong, like a high-wire dancer above the precipice.

A smell of old rum floats across the whole room. Pauline hears the ticking of the clock, the sound of the waves that comes in through the open window, and Maxime, standing near the bed, breathing. Outside, the rain shower opens up some wildflowers.

Pauline leans her head on her left shoulder. The corner of her mouth is now shut, her eyes move uncontrollably. Her breasts, her knees, her eyebrows, everything shakes under the stretched sheet; it seems like she has suddenly become as light as a feather. She is suffering.

Maxime watches over her, hums to her . . . He sees her head move, her mouth, as she sinks into that secret country into which he cannot enter. He sings for her all the songs she sang, lovers, happy lovers, would you like to travel, he mixes them with all that he knows of her, her prayers, her poems, do not go too far away my love, my Bengali bird, with all that might keep her close to him for a moment longer, always be kind and loving to one another, stay close to me my weaver child . . . He repeats many times, while standing closest to her in the shadows: "Make use of everything, think nothing of the rest . . ." She sweats, her hair is stuck to her forehead, he holds her tight to him, the slightest thing rocks her; every beat of her heart is like a detonation.

The lamplight is low and makes her face look like a house of shadows and highlights the outline of her undone nightshirt. She is still beautiful; she is desirable, even in death. Completely weak at this point, her gaze comes through a thin glazing on her black pupils. The pain is too strong, and she can no longer speak. But she whispers and continues to sing . . . Maxime . . . All those years that she has loved him, she will not leave him in the time she has left on earth.

She no longer sees him. She runs her hand through his hair. She caresses his neck, his cheeks, his forehead, her hands walk across the front of his face, she no longer speaks at all, she is far too weak, but she says that she loves him through the magic of her fingers. A gust of wind blows into the room and carries her away. It is the end. She carries him along with the wind, she holds him, keeps him, in a breath she takes him away, she holds him inside her, right to the very end. It is on his face that her long fingers unravel for the last time. In the death that is coming, it is she who passes her fingers across his temple; she gives him once again her hands, her mouth, her song, so that he may be saved.

*

What do you do when death carries away a life? Nothing. Who can abolish or suspend time? No one. Maxime spends the whole day doing nothing, lost in a sort of stupor, caught in a cramp of time. Is he beginning to lose his mind?

He begins to live like a sleepwalker. He gets stuck in the sands of life. His internal compass goes awry. He babbles. He spends his time flicking through the Bible but without really reading it; when he opens it, the lines immediately begin to dance. He is stabbed by a strange pain, the ocean becomes cloudy, even the colors of the evening change, he no longer sees the ocean in the same way.

Fatigue, a mental block, torpor. Days without words, a black felt falls over the seasons.

Maybe he feels the great uselessness of everything; he is indifferent to colors, to smells, and sounds, more closed off than a stone. When the evening comes, he looks over the wake left behind by the passing day and the enormous chaos and havoc of his useless conquests. People recall having seen him passing by the port at nightfall: he was humming the Bible and fragments of Psalms . . . *Rex gloriae, libera animas omnium* . . . God of Glory, deliver the souls of all the departed faithful from the sufferings of hell . . . *ne cadant in obscurum* . . . and from the deep pit, deliver them from the mouth of the lion . . . *sed signifer sanctus Michael* . . . may they not be swallowed up by hell, may they not fall into darkness . . . Only the Bible seems able to contend with this gigantic abyss, the Bible, which pours silence onto events like the sand of the beach stops the murmur of the seas.

From time to time, always with the Holy Book in his hands, he falls into a kind of debauchery. Is the still working now in the gardens at Anfelana? He knows the temptation of Semele, the genie of springs and rivers; he follows the cortege of Dionysus and frequents the Satyrs. His children are worried: is he to become a grotesque old man, falling over the girls and almost always drunk? He replies, more enigmatic than ever: perhaps if I were opened up, inside you would see that I have within me the statue of a God.

*

Now it is almost finished. There is nothing to do, wait until it happens, and then that will be that.

Time has passed, as they say, to make them forget that it does not pass, that only the signs change and that desire is always there.

After the deaths of Arthur and Pauline, Maxime went back to Mahajanga. In an ironic twist of fate he went to live in a little house on the Quai aux Boutres, a few steps away from the place where, nearly half a century before, he had landed. It is one of the old Indo-Arab houses that make up what is now called "Old Mahajanga": there is nothing fancy about them, but they are known for their antique sculpted two-paneled doors. Sent from India in the previous century, these are doors divided into panels and decorated with floral motifs that run over the frames and rise up over the lintels. It is the only form of decoration in the house. Otherwise, there are two simple rooms, with bare walls. In the main room, on a little wooden table, there is a blue vase: every day, right to the end of his life, he will place in it a new rose.

What does he do all day? He walks. People call to him at the corner of the street or shout across to him from a café terrace:

— Do you have nothing else to do, other than walking all the livelong day?

— *All the livelong day.* Yes, that's exactly right.

And he laughs.

The house is about ten meters from the sea. Seated on the doorstep, he looks out: the patchwork of red colors on the land, the coves sheltering under the first hillside to the left, the deep silo of the channel. He observes the men working slowly, the loading and unloading operations: coconuts, bananas, oranges, cement, flour, salt jars . . . He admires the procession of dockers with their superb backs, their muscular thighs. He contemplates the play of flirting and heckling, of nets and plaice fish, the blue dance of the schooners.

He notices that the maritime traffic is decreasing: on the other side, on the rosewood coast, the port of Toamasina, more accessible and better equipped, has progressively gained more traffic from the pirogues and the splendid ballet of the dhows. Right to the end of his life, he will be fascinated by fish. Every morning he watches the lifting of the nets: sea bream, barracuda, moray eels, there are fish of all sorts and all colors, they are the multicolored stalks of the sea.

Yes, growing old while fishing, finding again just before dying the undulating, unpredictable trajectories.

He observes: the deals and the negotiating, the compromises and exchanges, the agreements, the transactions. When he arrived on the island, Madagascar didn't have its own currency. Today the whole country has entered the fiduciary era: they have moved in a few years from rubber to bronze, from bartering in piasters, then from piasters to coins, and from coins to notes. Money passes from hand to hand, in jingling fingers and rustling palms: he likes the beauty of this simple gesture that requires nonetheless speed and coordination. As for him, he has very little money, but that does not bother him.

During all those years new houses and buildings have sprung up all over Mahajanga. A new town house, a stadium, a high school . . . Maxime has lost count of all the new constructions. The town is expanding, the village of Mahabibo and the port district of Aux Boutres have joined together, the surrounding neighborhoods have been absorbed: the areas of Résidence, Douane, and Trésor have been transformed; all that exists is being carried away in a great, stormy movement that is called the past. Only the baobab remains intact, it is there to defy the centuries; it is time itself in its wooden patience. It is not for nothing that it is the town's symbol, an enigma for its longevity, a living historical monument, several centuries old but every year renewing its foliage and its fruits.

Maxime takes up drawing again, quietly, gently. He is an eye, a great solar translator. A fruit can catch his attention, a splash of color, a porch nearby, a letter out of place on the paint of a poster. At the end of his life he draws almost uniquely contours, silhouettes, black ink on white paper. Big drawings of women, sailboats with white sails, birds . . . You would say that he is divesting himself of all embellishments and that he is trying to touch a critical point, something that normally escapes us, a sense of grace, something external, a vibration.

*

But Maxime is not cut off from the world; on the contrary, he is permanently connected to it, through listening to it. He lives in orality: he is a man of the radio, not of the moving image. A listening man. Not yet gripped by the multiplication of screens that separate us from life, the all-consuming image, the narcissistic investment, the sacrosanct *public image*. He hears all the world's events through the radio: the radio at that time is not that endless buzzing punctuated by commercials with bits of speech inserted; it connects via its electric veins all the towns of the planet. Often in the evening he listens to jazz. But also (scrawled in a little notebook that accompanies his drawings): "the whistling of the wind in the riggings, the shivers of the foliage and the ropes, the soft murmuring of the masts eaten up by the sun." And all the sounds of the port, the fizzing sounds of all the various human activities: "rubbing, scraping, painting, sanding, stroking." He enters into the pure time of sensory experience.

He also dives into the written word, into the only book that he can read without losing interest: the Bible. He reads it every evening, he comments on it, sometimes with a certain critical keenness. He compares, for example, the story of Moses to that of Andriamandisoa-rivo: while looking for a place to build the capital of the Sakalava kingdom, the latter puts his granddaughter into a pirogue and leaves her to float at the mercy of the currents. The pirogue drifts to the actual site of the town, and it is thus that the city of Mahajanga was born. Other times he annotates the Bible with terrible slogans in large purple handwriting that is today almost indecipherable. For example: "The problem of the *outre-mer* is related to the problem of the afterlife: this is evident (he underlines the last word three times)." There is also this beautiful phrase: "The ocean is proof of the Divine light, from which it grabs still its brilliance."

He is particularly interested in the return of Christ: which forms could it take? Do you need to believe in the afterlife? In a certain way his has always been thus, a life of the future. In strange pages, which we can perhaps no longer understand at all, he furiously reproaches Christ but prepares himself for His glorious return. He believes firmly in eternal life. Maxime always read the Bible diligently, but this time one can say that he does so with great excitement and energy: he *throws* himself into the Bible, his head down, like a diver. He says often that Moses was eighty-four years old and Aaron ninety-three when they spoke to Pharaoh. It is never too late to open up to the kingdom of heaven. You will find in these cardboard boxes, mixed up with technical manuals for car motors (internal combustion engines, which he loves), *Les Évangiles en créole* (The Gospels in Creole) by Samuel Honeyman Anderson (1893), the *Catéchisme en créole pour les Zîles là-haut* (Catechism in Creole for the Chagos Islands, 1936), as well as the *Bible de Port-Royal* (Port-Royal Bible) by Lemaistre de Sacy and Hugo's *Les Misérables*. A sacred viaticum.

The rest of the time he is there, in his little final home, behind his Indian doors. He receives a few friends; young people especially come to see him, as they like his stories and his unusual way of telling them. From time to time he will do a pirouette on the metal bar above the entryway. Maxime is never first to raise the topic of the circus, but when someone talks to him about it, he launches straight into his stories. His stories do not flow from beginning to end, there are some sudden turns backward, quick accelerations, and slow, expansive parts. These are flexible stories that leap around and are retractable, as is his way.

And then he whistles, he starts to whistle again.

The young people love spending time with this old man who pulls some incredible sounds from the movement between his tongue and his mouth. Agile, supple, ductile, it's a whole operation of the lips and the uvula, the blowing of the cheeks and the harmonica of the teeth. He carries the conversation into a musical universe made of arrows of sound and branches of octaves and all the sounds of the forest.

There he is, unmoving, on the old stone bench that looks out to sea, across from the Quai aux Boutres. He is fish-lookout, fish-rock, he watches the ships passing; he counts the curves of the waves. He imagines all the routes of production, exchanges, and finances that cross over off the coast of this simple estuary. All those other cultures, all those other customs, those other values . . . He has in front of him an open door to the Orient and the other turned toward the African coast and the Islands of the Moon, the Mitsio archipelago, the Comoros Islands . . . If you could see farther, you could see French Polynesia, Wallis and Futuma, New Caledonia, the Affars and Issas territory, the New Hebrides, Saint-Pierre and Miquelon, the austral lands and the boreal lands, the whole silvery poetry of the *outre-mer*. And then, farther still, well beyond the people and the countries . . . He grasps now the ultimate lightness of time.

*

Little by little the core becomes more tangible, the pulsations slow down, and the star begins softly to burn out. A slow dispersion begins. Through the years the external envelope is carried away by the winds. The body is transformed, and the children leave, one by one. You don't change completely, but you feel in yourself something is changing and, you might say, refining itself.

As if he is aware that a new metamorphosis is under way, over all these years, Maxime changes again—but in the opposite direction this time—the shell of his name . . . The other end of the book is about to close over, the slide trombone of his name pulls back progressively in accordance with its internal melody:

Maxime Saint Jean le Roi de la Ferrière
Maxime Le Roy de la Ferrière
Maxime de la Ferrière

It is on Monday, 14 August 1967, at eleven o'clock in the morning, that the Mahajanga civil registrar records his last name change:

Maxime Ferrier

Like a hydrogen molecule that contracts and returns to its essential nakedness, Maxime thus brings to a close—provisionally, as I am relaunching them here—the adventures of his name. However, he will always refuse to take again the name of Février, as if to state that the game has not been played for nothing; that something has been gained.

*

One evening, an evening when the thunder rumbles—the rain is murky, the monkeys howl at the night—he tastes inside his mouth something more serious. He is cold; he is short of breath. In an instant it comes: he feels death catch his throat and grip his organs.

When night comes, he has a dream. He is surrounded by his Bara friends; he is walking on the land of the great plateaus of the South, and he begins to dance the Papango with them. It is an impressive ceremony, during which a man perched high up on a wooden post throws himself into the emptiness, mimicking the flight of a bird of prey. This man is him, Maxime. He dives, but it is not the sea that awaits him below; he falls heavily onto the ground. He feels his two calves swelling up, his ankles are broken; the dream turns into a nightmare. Now he is lying on the sands of the Anfelana beach, his head against the sand, he sees the crab of cancer that took Pauline away, then a net climbs out of the depths, the big eye of a coelacanth looks at him . . . He wakes up, soaked in sweat.

Daybreak finds him with his eyes and hands abnormally swollen: alone on his doorstep, he sits on the stone bench, slightly leaning to the side, like an abandoned sailboat.

It is an initial attack. The doctor diagnoses a uremia outbreak. It is the kidneys that are affected: toxic substances are no longer being cleared out; urea is passing into the blood. It is a serious case, and he is encouraged to stay in hospital. The nurse prescribes him a diet without salt; he is told to avoid avocados, nectarines, plantains, chocolate, broad beans, and nuts . . . In short, all that he loves. But Maxime is not the kind of man who wants to die in hospital. "Uremia-fa-so-la-ti-do!" he hums when he hears the news. He wants to shave, wash, comb his hair, he wants to go out into the street, drink some cool wine and walk in the sunny streets.

The same evening, against the doctor's advice, he returns to the little house on the Quai aux Boutres. On the doorstep he shakes the sand from his sandals. A little dust rises up. All of his life seems far in front of him: the memories of ash.

*

During the week he returns one last time to the Jardin d'Amour. He stays there the whole day, in a sort of happy lifelessness. Perhaps those trees remind him of the red flamboyant, the yellow acacias of Mauritius, the times spent with Pauline. There are places like that, which in a moment bring everything back to you. Here his past times are resuscitated and surround him like a band of phantoms. Out of the abyss come dreamlike figures that hang in the air, houris, chimeras, which take him by the hand and lead him back to the time of Pauline. Together they remain there for hours, among the conversation of the flowers.

Some very old names come back to him . . . Beau Bassin, Mauritius . . . It is from there that he set out. Perhaps he remembers Marie Adélia d'Albrède, his mother, who had also changed her name—how had she thought of swapping the beautiful name of Marie Adélia d'Albrède for the dry name of Clifford, her stepfather? Perhaps it was quite simply for that reason, something to do with the name, that Maxime left; he no longer knows why. Who can say what he thinks about during this last walk? About the circus, no doubt, about Carmen perhaps, the concerts at the Nouvel Hôtel: why not?

But everyone remembers as they want to. A river that is half-green and half-red, a palm tree and water in the background, the changing colors of memories . . . Recollections, or *souvenirs* in French, are related to lies: we fix them, embellish them, and enhance them. Memory is not recollections or *souvenirs*: memory is alive, it regenerates itself and changes, and brings out a very ancient truth that is also sparkling with newness. It rediscovers by inventing. That is why, counter to what people say, memory is made up of forgetting, that is why it is alive, it leaves a place for emptiness, for play.

Soon, he knows, he will be buried not far from there. No one knows when exactly he had the other two tombs built; he said nothing to anyone. Always his taste for secrecy, for the clandestine. But he has taken steps so that he may die by the seaside.

Now he barely remembers his existence, and sings in a low voice a song of the sea: he is going to die.

*

His skin has taken on its last color, a pretty yellow-gray shade, like parchment. He wears always, right to the last, his famous Venetian collar shirts. He is elegant to the very end.

He eats little; he barely drinks anymore. On the other hand, he sleeps and walks a lot. He visits his neighbors and a few friends. Everyone finds him to be strangely serene, some even complain about this detachment. He has not lost his taste for provocation and playfulness: to the doctor who tells him to take his medication regularly, he replies that he has no need for it as he is very proud to die from the same illness as Mozart! Some say that he wants to go out with a flourish. One last exploit, the acrobat's stunt. I don't believe that. On the contrary, he returns to the inexhaustible things: the birds, the flowers, the sand on the beach. Death, he sees it no more than he does this blue vase where a red rose fades. He often cites the Malagasy proverb: *Manaova fatin-tantely, maty mamela mamy* . . . "To die like a bee: in death it leaves behind only sweetness."

While he waits, he sleeps. That he is very good at.

He sleeps more and more; he sleeps better and better.

Toward the end of the month, the last Friday in June, his son Willy is with him. This evening it will be his wife, Éliane, who looks over him while, in the shadows, two little children play. Many times Maxime said to Éliane that he does not want to die before sunset. According to him, you must not die on a Saturday, as that is the Sabbath day. He is completely calm and serious, even if he also throws in a little humor, levity even, to this final resolution: there it is—it seems easy enough—he decides to not die in the period from Friday before sunset to Saturday "after the stars come out."

That night he has some difficulty breathing: he asks for a fan. He is thirsty. He takes some pieces of ice that he lets melt in his mouth. The night is long. But he is dreaming, he turns over. The following morning he tells of his night: he dreamed that he is the branch of a tree right at the top of a waterfall . . .

During the day that follows, he falls into a half-sleep, which turns into a deep coma. All of his vital functions seem to be suspended, but he is still breathing. His breathing slows down.

He enters a very slow, calm, immobile time.

A deep intake of breath, followed by a brief breath out. Then, nothing more.

Everything happened like he said it would. On Saturday, 1 July 1972, after sunset, at the moment the first stars are appearing in the sky, he makes his final escape.

EPILOGUE

A meeting with a journalist. The book will be published soon.

— So, your grandfather was called Maxime Ferrier, he was British . . .

— Mauritian.

— I'm sorry?

— Mauritian. It is not the same thing. The island of Mauritius was French from 1715 to 1810, British from 1810 to 1968, and has been independent since then. (1968: quite a few things went on that year, didn't they?) If you like, Maxime was born British, but he died Mauritian, even if he never knew it. In between, all his life was spent in Madagascar.

— Okay, a Mauritian grandfather. Your grandmother Pauline was Indian . . .

— No, not completely. Born in Madagascar, of an Indo-Portuguese family from Goa. The former capital of the Portuguese Indies, the "Goa Dourada," which Saint Francis Xavier called the wonder of wonders. He is still there by the way, in the big Jesuit basilica, except for his right arm, which was transported in a reliquary of the Church of the Gesù, in Rome. That's how it is: the dead also travel . . . Pauline was, moreover, Catholic. She held her faith dearly. That is to say, you know: universal.

— Okay, Mauritian, British, and Malagasy grandfather. Indian, Portuguese, and universal grandmother. Your father?

— Enlisted in the French army. Wounded in the Algerian War, he stood on a mine. He lost three-quarters of his lungs, had splinters in his thorax, arm, and even his fingers. Emergency operation. National Order of Merit, Military Medal, and Legion of Honor. Very rare to have the three at the same time. He will be buried with them, he earned it. Is that enough?

— And on your mother's side?

— Alsace forever. I will write about that one day too. Mother, grandmother, grandfather, all Alsatians, for a very long time.

— You mean to say—French?

— Or German, it depends on the time in history. One could also say: Europeans. Reread your history books . . .

— Yes, yes, I know . . . Okay, where were we: Mauritius, Madagascar, Goa, Indians, and Portuguese, merchants, tailors, adventurers, Alsace, Germany, Algeria . . . Your family is a bit complicated then, you might say! And what does all that add up to?

— You know the song.

— Excuse me?

— *D'excellents Français*, Excellent Frenchmen.

*

Every year, at the beginning of spring and at the end of summer, there appears in the sky, to the south of Mahajanga, between the Mahavavy River and the Kinkony Lake, a prodigious choreographed spectacle. Above a tangle of rivers, bays, and forests that form one of the most diverse biotopes on the planet, some tens of thousands of lesser-crested terns trace in the skies phrases as beautiful as they are unpredictable, alternating long swoops with brief stops and the capture of their prey. During this time, in the rivers and under the seas, far below the surface of the water, fish of all varieties sketch out their own knowing parables.

Birds, fish, these unstable particles, which constantly change their level of energy, cross space, and tear up time, into delectable hooks and brackets. They are sorts of punctual singularities that move from place to place. All along their arabesques, they deliver a certain theory of rhythm that belongs only to them, a consummate method of perturbation, which nevertheless enters in its own way onto the great sketch of the world.

Since I have begun this story, the beautiful Arabic, two-floor house that served as a landmark for boats entering the bay and that you find on some navigators' drawings no longer exists; it fell down during Hurricane Kamisy, in April 1984.

Of Maxime's last home, on the Quai aux Boutres, there remains nothing either. The house right next door to his is one of the last to have preserved the famous Indian doors made of sculpted wood that were long the pride of old Mahajanga: Maxime's house had more or less the same doors, they say, and it is all that you can hold onto, this next-door vestige, this more-or-less of the ruin, this displaced memory.

*

I am leaving soon, returning to Paris. Li-An has already left for China, to start back at training. I will go and see her in the springtime. For now I am going to see for a final time the three tombs in the cemetery . . . It is very early, nearly five o'clock, the day is dawning. The entrance, the monument to the war dead, the herbaceous border . . . I push the broken black iron gate; I enter . . . We have arrived at the end of the world; that is clear. We can go no farther, after this there is only the dead.

On the path I think of things . . . I think again of the last conversation I had with the old Indian jeweler, last night, when I went to say my farewell. Georges had told me: only he could tell me who was buried in the third grave. I was not convinced, however. In a way I did not dare pose the question to him.

Finally, I decided I would ask him.

— In your opinion what is in that third tomb? A well? A tunnel, an underground passage? A mine?

— In a way, yes . . . A mine of information.

— At this point I am ready to listen to anything.

His reply comes, simple and clear:

— There is no one in the third tomb.

— No one?

— No one.

So, that, that is the best one . . . It is his last lap, my grandfather's; his final piece of acrobatics.

Jean Pivoine smiles. He savors the effect of his revelation. Then he starts up again:

— As you know, Maxime had the first tomb made for Arthur, when he died at sea. Then the second tomb for himself, a few months later.

— But what about the third tomb?

— Empty. Some people thought it contained an illegitimate child; others thought it had another acrobat from the circus or Madame Bartolini herself, even an unknown mistress . . . Others even claim that it could be Ando, Maxime's Malagasy blood brother.

— Yes, I have heard that suggestion.

— But the truth is that it is empty. When Maxime had the third tomb built, everyone thought that it was for Pauline, obviously. But Pauline had for a long time wanted to be buried at Nosy Be, where lies her first daughter, who died at the age of four. So, Maxime left the tomb empty.

How do you know this?

— He told me so, young man. He quite liked the idea. You see, he was destroying the very meaning of the monument at the same time as he was building it: he didn't want a closed and completed memory, delivered like in a coffin. He wanted someone to come, move around, ask questions . . .

— And that epitaph?

— *So that it may be living and not destroyed?*

— Yes. What is the meaning of this inscription on the tomb?

— It is a very simple phrase. I am surprised that your erudition has not yet seen through it.

— My erudition is a lot less impressive than you think.

— *Ho velona fa tsy ho levona.* It is the motto of the town of Mahajanga.

— What? As simple as that! . . . Maxime lived such happy times in this town that he wanted to engrave its motto on his tomb?

— Yes, of course. But there is something else . . . Have you not guessed yet?

— No.

— It is not only an epitaph; it is an epigraph.

— An epigraph?

— That of the book you are going to write.

— . . .

— There are many means of communicating between the world of the living and the realm of the dead . . . These words are the only means by which your grandfather can still speak to you today. He wanted to believe that one day someone would come, that they would ask questions, that they would discover this whole story, the circus, the acrobats, and above all the Madagascar Project, the Jews, the Natives, all these people chased and hunted like rats. Memory is the only thing capable of fighting against death. *So that it may be living and not destroyed* . . . And against that second death that is to be forgotten. You see, you are here; he was not mistaken.

*

Between the weeds and the moss, there are three stones. These stones are no more exempt than the others from the ravages of time, from mold, sea spray, or bird droppings. They are not next to any path, and no one likes going that way as the grass is high and your feet get soaked right away. When there is a little sun, the lizards go there. There is, all around, a quivering of wild grasses. In the springtime a Eurasian curlew sings in the tree.

More so than the others, these stones are white, naked, miserable. You don't read any name on them, apart from the one on the left, which has Maxime Ferrier's name.

Except, already many years ago, a hand had written there in pen these simple words, which have become more and more illegible with the rain and the dust and which are probably today erased:

Ho velona fa tsy ho levona . . .

So that it may be living and not destroyed

It is late now. The day is beginning; the night is already over. It is time to leave the cemetery. A few steps along the main pathway, I turn back, I cross again the old iron doorway that looks out onto the central reservation on the Corniche: the ocean is everywhere. From wherever one looks in the light of daybreak, all you see is its unbroken surface, which offers neither beginning nor end, and the more you look at it, the bigger it gets.

Around the three tombs, and as if enlivened by them, nature unfolds in the incredible variety of its operations and the vast extent of its power, overgrowing the walls and grates that mark the cemetery. An impressive number of birds nest around the ditches and ponds: herons, ducks, sacred ibises, and ospreys. Life's own colors dance freely in the anarchy of the bushes all around, the emerald mass of the foliage that provides shade for them—palm trees and tamarind trees, tropical almond trees—and the deep blue of the Madagascar sky. The green arrows of the grass, treelike ferns, creeping vines . . . It is now no longer a cemetery, it is a garden peopled by a thousand life-forms that are waking up: fountain-trees, bottle-trees, and octopus-trees, multiplying plants sprinkled with flashes of color. You have never seen such a festive mausoleum nor better decorated vaults.

Here, there, the periwinkles grow bushy; the palm trees push their graciously arched leaves, offered to the salty winds of the seaside. In successive tufts the flowers launch their leaflets in all directions, on different levels, in various axes. All around are purple jacarandas, red bougainvillea, frangipani with red quills and their scent in the air. You would say that the dead themselves want to come out of the earth and leap to the other side of the sky, in processions and cascades, in floral spirals, in bouquets of feathers and birds.

Behind me the three tombs spin for one final time. They come out of the chasm now; they leave far away toward the beach . . . They take with them the entire town and the days and the people, different territories and times, far, farther still . . . It is dawn: ten fingers from the Great Bear, you can see them fly from one sky to the other across the squalls and vapor of the open sea, with full clouds of extravagant angels, they flood the aurora with their turbulence; it is the great rush of the skies. The horizon turns red, and the joy of the day rises through a great hole that they have made by bursting through the night to flee, a precarious victory, senseless, as if to prove to us that the joy of men is not made to die in the war of time.

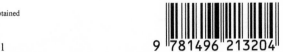